A Sea View Christmas

Books by Julie Klassen

FROM BETHANY HOUSE PUBLISHERS

Lady of Milkweed Manor
The Apothecary's Daughter
The Silent Governess
The Girl in the Gatehouse
The Maid of Fairbourne Hall
The Tutor's Daughter
The Dancing Master
The Secret of Pembrooke Park
The Painter's Daughter
The Bridge to Belle Island
A Castaway in Cornwall
Shadows of Swanford Abbey
Lady Maybe

TALES FROM IVY HILL

The Innkeeper of Ivy Hill
The Ladies of Ivy Cottage
The Bride of Ivy Green
An Ivy Hill Christmas: A TALES FROM IVY HILL Novella

ON DEVONSHIRE SHORES

The Sisters of Sea View
A Winter by the Sea
The Seaside Homecoming
A Sea View Christmas: An ON DEVONSHIRE SHORES Novella

AN ON DEVONSHIRE
SHORES NOVELLA

A Sea View Christmas

JULIE KLASSEN

BETHANYHOUSE

a division of Baker Publishing Group
Minneapolis, Minnesota

© 2025 by Julie Klassen

Published by Bethany House Publishers
Minneapolis, Minnesota
BethanyHouse.com

Bethany House Publishers is a division of
Baker Publishing Group, Grand Rapids, Michigan

Printed in the United States of America

Library of Congress Cataloging-in-Publication Data
Names: Klassen, Julie, author.
Title: A Sea View Christmas / Julie Klassen.
Description: Minneapolis, Minnesota : Bethany House, a division of Baker
    Publishing Group, 2025. | Series: On Devonshire Shores
Identifiers: LCCN 2025000966 | ISBN 9780764242441 (paperback) | ISBN
    9780764245640 (cloth) | ISBN 9780764246227 (large print) | ISBN 9781493451258
    (ebook)
Subjects: LCGFT: Christmas fiction. | Romance fiction. | Novellas.
Classification: LCC PS3611.L37 S38 2025 | DDC 813/.6—dc23/eng/20250205
LC record available at https://lccn.loc.gov/2025000966

This is a work of historical reconstruction; the appearances of certain historical figures are therefore inevitable. All other characters, however, are products of the author's imagination, and any resemblance to actual persons, living or dead, is coincidental.

Cover design by Jennifer Parker
Compilation of cover: Mike Habermann Photography; Abigail Miles / Arcangel; and Rachael Fraser / Trevillion Images

Published in association with Books & Such Literary Management, BooksAndSuch.com.

Baker Publishing Group publications use paper produced from sustainable forestry practices and postconsumer waste whenever possible.

25 26 27 28 29 30 31   7 6 5 4 3 2 1

To my dear sister-in-law, Kristn,
who always knows how many days
it is till Christmas.

❧ Old Sidmouth ❧

1 - Sea View
2 - Westmount
3 - Woolbrook
4 - Peak House
5 - Heffer's Row
6 - Old Fort
7 - Fortfield Terr.

8 - Wallis's Library
9 - Parish Church
10 - Old Ship Inn
11 - Baths
12 - York Hotel
13 - Poor House
14 - Water Mill

15 - Marsh Chapel
16 - London Inn
17 - Marketplace
18 - Beach
19 - Chit Rock
20 - Lime Kiln
21 - Western Beach

I sincerely hope your Christmas . . . may abound in the gaieties which the season generally brings.

—Jane Austen, *Pride and Prejudice*

She threw up the window . . . to pluck that beautiful half-blown Christmas rose that grew upon the little shrub without, just peeping from the snow. . . . And, having gently dashed the glittering powder from its leaves, approached it to her lips and said, "This rose is not so fragrant as a summer flower, but it has stood through hardships none of them could bear . . . it is still fresh and blooming as a flower can be, with the cold snow even now on its petals."

—Anne Brontë, *The Tenant of Wildfell Hall*

ONE

Often, the bride's sister or closest female friend
accompanied the couple [on their wedding trip].
—Maria Grace, *Courtship and Marriage
in Jane Austen's World*

OCTOBER 1820

Miss Sarah Summers sat on her neatly made bed, a treasure in each hand. In her left she held a letter from the man she'd been betrothed to before his death at sea more than three years before.

In her right palm lay a dried thistle—stalk, spiny bulb, and purple flower crown—the symbol of Scotland. It had been given to her by a Scotsman who, despite her efforts to forget him, still occupied a large part of her thoughts . . . and, if she were honest with herself, her heart.

Callum Henshall and his stepdaughter had been their very first guests at Sea View the previous year, and all the Summerses had liked them. Mr. Henshall had expressed interest in Sarah during his stay, but Sarah had discouraged him. Now she wondered if she had done the right thing.

She carefully tucked both the letter and the thistle into the chest at the foot of her bed. For the impending trip, she was taking only a small leather trunk, one bandbox, and her reticule.

Was she really about to leave Sidmouth for an extended absence?

Her pulse beat hard at the thought. Since moving to Sea View two years before, Sarah had never left for more than a few hours at a time. What was she doing? How could she just leave the guest house and Mamma? Leave their guests, their staff, and her responsibilities? Might there still be time to change her mind about traveling with Claire and her husband?

Sadly, no. Their plans were set.

A knock sounded on the bedchamber door and her youngest sister, Georgiana, entered. At seventeen, Georgie was the picture of blossoming womanhood, although Sarah still saw glimpses of the rough-and-tumble tomboy she had been.

"All packed?" Georgie asked.

"Nearly."

"I wish I were going with you."

"I thought you loved it here?"

"I do. Yet I long to see more of the world. I've only ever been to Sidmouth and May Hill."

"You're young. You shall have other opportunities. For now, I need you to help with things here while I'm gone."

"I know." Georgie sighed.

Sarah regarded her usually cheerful sister with concern. "Are you unwell, my dear? You seem . . . well, sad."

"No, not sad. Restless, more like. But I am glad you are going to Scotland. It's time you had an adventure. Besides, Mr. Henshall's not a bad fellow—you could do worse."

"Why, thank you," Sarah dryly replied. "Remember, we are primarily going to Scotland to look over the house Claire inherited. Seeing Mr. Henshall is only a secondary consideration."

"Right." Her sister snorted. "You will pass along my greetings to Effie, I trust?"

Sarah's heart warmed at the thought of Mr. Henshall's stepdaughter. "Certainly. If we manage to see them, that is."

"Why should you not? Mr. Henshall will probably convince you to remain in Scotland, and then there go our plans for a jolly Christmas here."

"That is unlikely to happen."

Georgiana studied her. "Still no reply?"

Sarah shook her head. This wasn't a topic she cared to revisit—best to change the subject. "Now, don't worry. I shan't forget my promise. I know the last few years have not been ideal, but we shall have a far more festive Christmastide this year. You'll see. William and Claire don't want to leave Mira for too long. We plan to return in time for Stir-Up Sunday."

"I'm counting on it."

"By the way," Sarah added, "Claire told me you have offered to spend time with Mira while she and William are away. That is kind of you."

Georgie shrugged off the praise. "Armaan and Sonali will be busy with the boarding house, and a girl Mira's age needs to play out-of-doors."

"You certainly did. Still do."

Her sister nodded. "I'll also visit the Sidmouth School as usual to play with the pupils there. When I am not needed here, of course."

"Excellent." Sarah rose and embraced her. "And keeping busy like that, you'll find the time will pass quickly."

She said it as much to reassure herself as Georgiana.

The family gathered to bid them farewell. Her sister Emily took Sarah's arm and led her out of the house. She leaned close and confided, "It's your turn, Sarah. I just know it. I hope Mr. Henshall kisses more than your hand this time!" She grinned and squeezed her arm. "Oh, and if you should happen to meet Sir Walter Scott, don't forget to tell him your sister is a great admirer of his work."

Their brother-in-law William stood at the open door of the yellow post chaise and handed Sarah inside to join their eldest sister, Claire. Several others encircled the waiting vehicle: sister Viola and her husband, Jack Hutton. Sonali and Armaan Sagar, little Mira in her uncle's arms. Mamma waved her handkerchief, and Georgie held the town stray by the scruff to keep him from nipping at the horses. And finally Mr. Gwilt, their diligent man-of-all-work, stepped to the open window. Being short in stature, he raised himself to his tiptoes and reassured her one last time, "Please don't worry, Miss Sarah. We shall take good care of Sea View while you're gone."

Would they?

After one last kiss to his daughter's cheek, William climbed in and closed the door. He took Claire's hand and leaned forward to address them both. "Ready, you two?"

"Ready," Claire agreed.

Sarah managed a wooden nod.

A few moments later, the hired post chaise rattled away from Sidmouth, beginning the long journey north. The snug interior held only one forward-facing bench, and she felt Claire's shoulder press into hers at every turning.

Sarah shifted on the padded seat, agitation gnawing at her, urging her to demand the vehicle stop and let her down. The cord that bound her to Sea View, to Mamma and her other sisters, stretched tighter and tighter, pulling at her ribs, until it seemed about to snap in two and tear out her heart as well.

She became aware of Claire's worried gaze on her profile and felt her sister squeeze her hand. Sarah had no wish to dampen Claire's pleasure on this, her wedding trip. She turned to her and mustered a smile.

Claire and William had remained in Sidmouth for a few weeks after their nuptials before departing on this trip. They had delayed because they'd wanted to witness the quiet wedding of Mira's uncle, Armaan, and Sonali Patel. And because they'd wanted to help the couple as they took over ownership of the boarding house until they had things well in hand. Armaan and Sonali had generously offered to care for Mira during their absence.

Did Mamma, Georgie, Emily, and Mr. Gwilt have things at Sea View well in hand? She hoped she'd remembered to show them everything that needed to be done: the menus, the orders and payments to butcher, greengrocer, coal merchant, et cetera. Had she left anything off her many lists? What if something went wrong? Would they be able to deal with any demanding guests?

Sarah reminded herself that she truly wanted to go to Scotland—or at least to see a certain handsome Scotsman—but perhaps she should have refused. Let her sister and new husband travel alone together.

Both Claire and William had assured Sarah she was welcome to accompany them. A bride's sister or close friend often traveled with a new-wed couple. Husband and wife would, of course, have their own room at inns along the way, but the sisters could help each other dress and enjoy each other's company and conversation during the long hours on the road.

On Claire's other side, William lifted his wife's hand and kissed her knuckles.

Sarah pretended not to notice.

Instead, she gazed at the passing countryside through the front window. She looked past the two postilions, who rode the left-hand horse of each pair pulling the chaise. The men's boots and coats were already splattered with mud, and they had not yet crossed the Devonshire border. Sarah felt sorry for whoever had to do their laundry. At the thought, her stomach twisted. Had she remembered to detail the laundry lists?

Sarah forced herself to breathe slowly and deeply and admonished herself not to worry.

The days passed quickly as they traveled, even though they had to pause every few hours to change horses, and often postilions as well. It would be a long journey to Scotland, and they broke it up with several stops along the way.

They visited Bath, the picturesque ruins of Tintern Abbey, and the spa town of Cheltenham. Now and again, Sarah witnessed a sweet caress or stolen kiss between her traveling companions and looked away, feigning interest in the view and feeling like a gooseberry.

As the distance between them and Sea View lengthened, Sarah slowly began to relax and enjoy herself. They'd come too far to turn back now.

Continuing north, they spent a few days admiring the scenery of the Lake District. Sarah sometimes joined William and Claire for meals, sightseeing, and shopping, but she insisted the two spend time alone together as well. She happily remained at the inn while they hired a boat for a romantic excursion on Windermere Lake. She recalled her own excursion in a small boat a year and a half ago, sailing along the coast with Callum Henshall, the sea breeze ruffling his hair, his warm gaze lingering on her face. . . . Would he look at her that way again? She certainly hoped so.

Every night, the new-wed couple retired to one room, and Sarah to another. Observing the tenderness between the two and Claire's glow of contentment, Sarah felt a pang. She was genuinely happy her eldest sister had found true love, yet she increasingly longed for a love of her own.

They did not stop in Carlisle—a place of bitter memories. A few years before, Claire had been abandoned there by a lord who'd convinced her to elope with him and then changed his mind before they'd even reached Gretna Green.

Instead, they continued on toward Edinburgh. Their aunt Mercer had stunned them all by leaving Claire her house as thanks for the time she had lived with and cared for her. Claire was eager to show it to both Sarah and William and gain their opinions on whether to keep the place or sell it. She had written to their aunt's solicitor to inform him of their upcoming visit. The man wrote back to assure them of a gracious welcome, explaining that Agnes Mercer's elderly butler had stayed on to oversee the property while it was unoccupied and would be there to open the house for them and provide a set of keys.

Once all was arranged, Claire had urged Sarah to write to Mr. Henshall, letting him know of the planned trip. Sarah had protested that it would be too forward to suggest they meet, but Claire had assured her there was nothing untoward about it. They were traveling a long way to look at the house. While they were there, it would be only polite to visit an acquaintance, especially one who'd performed such kind offices for their family. After all, Mr. Henshall had paid a call at Aunt Mercer's on their behalf to learn how Claire fared, and later redeemed Claire's necklace from a pawn dealer.

Sarah had relented and written to him yet had received no reply.

She had already been nervous about the prospect of seeing him again, and his silence only added to her unease.

Her sisters had tried to encourage her, saying Sarah's letter may have been lost in the post. Or his reply had been delayed for some reason. Of course he would be happy to see her again.

Sarah hoped they were right. Otherwise, how mortifying the reunion might be.

Reaching the outskirts of Edinburgh at last, Sarah craned her neck to take it all in. Upon entering the city, Claire pointed out the Palace of Holyroodhouse and the Edinburgh Castle high on its rocky hill.

As they wound through the Old Town and into the New, the tightly packed shops, sooty grey buildings, and smokestacks soon gave way to rows of elegant terraced houses of lighter sandstone, church spires, and tree-lined squares.

Finally they reached Aunt Mercer's home in just such a row of tall, connected houses, where they alighted with stiff limbs and eagerness. William helped unload their baggage and dismissed the postilions with an extra gratuity for delivering them safely. The men would take the chaise and horses to a local livery.

As they approached the imposing home, the door opened and an elderly man dressed in black appeared.

Claire beamed at him. "Mr. Campbell! How good to see you again. And how glad I was to learn you still live here. Allow me to introduce my sister Sarah and my husband, Mr. Hammond."

"Welcome, one and all. And pleased I was to learn who the new owner was to be! Your aunt did not breathe a word. A woman of surprises, was she not?"

"Indeed, she was."

The former cook, maids, and footman had acquired new situations elsewhere, but Campbell explained that he had engaged two new housemaids and a kitchen maid to serve them during their visit, despite Claire's offer to take their meals at a nearby inn.

Campbell's own sister, who like her brother had been in service for many years, had come out of retirement to serve as cook.

He said, "I hope you approve of the arrangements, Miss . . . er, Mrs. Hammond."

"Wholeheartedly. Thank you so much."

Claire insisted Sarah waste no time in sending a message to Mr. Henshall, who lived north of Edinburgh, near the town of Kirkcaldy.

"Just to let him know we've arrived safely and would be pleased to receive him here or to meet somewhere at his convenience."

Sarah wrote a brief note in a shaky hand, and Campbell dispatched a messenger to deliver it.

Then the three settled in to explore Edinburgh while they waited.

They set off for the Old Town to visit the Palace of Holyroodhouse and the castle. On the way, Claire pointed out the shop where she'd pawned the necklace Aunt Mercer had left her, to pay for the journey to Sidmouth.

The Edinburgh Castle had opened to visitors only that May. Before that it had been a military fortress and hospital and had also housed prisoners of war.

They purchased their tickets from the stationers on Bank Street for one shilling each and toured the Crown Room to see the Scottish regalia. The rest of the castle remained off limits.

Sarah wished Mr. Henshall were there to help explain the significance of the various items on display.

Over the next few days, the three strolled through the leafy squares of New Town, perused shops, and sampled Scottish cuisine.

And all the while Sarah was waiting and worrying. Why did Mr. Henshall not visit? Or at least send a reply? Had something happened to him or Effie?

Not long after reaching Edinburgh, William had written to an old friend, and soon they were invited to dinner at the home of Sir Robert and Henrietta Liston, who lived several miles west of Edinburgh. William, a former diplomat, had served with the Listons in Constantinople, where Sir Robert had been the ambassador.

Sarah and Claire dressed with care, both of them somewhat intimidated by the prospect of dining with an ambassador and his wife. But upon arrival, their hosts quickly made them comfortable with their warm, unaffected manners.

When Mrs. Liston learned they lived in Sidmouth, she gave them a sad little smile. "One of my brothers is buried there. Nathaniel Marchant. A physician who spent much of his life in Antigua before his health declined. I understand there is a memorial to him in the church there."

"I'm sorry for your loss," Sarah said. "And I shall look for it."

Over dinner, the couple entertained them with tales of the customs and mishaps they'd experienced in the Ottoman Empire and other far-flung places where they had resided during their long diplomatic career.

The evening passed quite pleasantly. And again, Sarah could not help thinking how much Mr. Henshall's company would have added to their enjoyment. Or at least to hers.

TWO

And who, indeed, that has once seen Edinburgh, but
must see it again in dreams, waking or sleeping.
—Charlotte Brontë, letter

All too soon the time they'd allotted to Edinburgh began
to draw to a close, and there was still no sign of Callum
Henshall.

"We can't return to Sidmouth without at least trying to see
him," Claire insisted. "You have his direction from his letters. Let
us pay a call. Then you will learn why he hasn't responded instead
of assuming the worst. And you need not fear you are being too
forward. I will say *I* insisted."

William grinned. "And I shall happily share the blame."

Sarah relented. "Oh, very well. Just to put my mind at ease."

Had Mr. Henshall given up on Sarah and begun courting someone else? Was that why he had not replied nor come to see them?
She hoped the truth would not prove to be worse than she imagined.

The next morning, Sarah dressed in a becoming frock and
Claire curled her dark hair with a hot iron.

"You look lovely, Sarah," Claire assured her.

Sarah thought the blue eyes staring back at her in the mirror looked weary as well as wary. She had not slept well, anxious as she was about the upcoming visit.

They set out for Kirkcaldy early that day, taking the new steam-powered *Broad Ferry* across the Firth of Forth to Dysart. From the harbor, they hired a driver with an old landau and even older horses to take them the rest of the way. Since the day was fine, they lowered the folding hood to enjoy the scenery. The wind spoiled the curls Claire had arranged so neatly on either side of Sarah's face, but the views were worth it.

About a mile from the harbor, the driver pointed out the ruins of rough-stone Ravenscraig Castle, and recognition flashed through Sarah. She recalled a long-ago meal around the Sea View dining table and Mr. Henshall's green eyes alight with nostalgia as he enthralled them with tales of his childhood, describing the abandoned castles near his home and a time he and a few other lads *"stormed Ravenscraig and laid siege to it with our wooden swords. . . ."* A land agent had set his dogs on them, and they'd had to hide in a shepherd's hut until the beasts gave up the chase, lured away by haggis.

Even now, Sarah smiled at the memory. His handsome face, good humor, and rich, accented voice were still clear in her mind.

The driver hailed a passing farm wagon and asked for directions to Whinstone Hall. Leaving the town of Kirkcaldy behind, they followed a wooded track until they reached a rambling two-story house of dark stone, its front door and windows framed in lighter sandstone. Sarah saw stables, a few other outbuildings, and fields dotted with grazing sheep beyond.

The front lawns were neatly trimmed, but the shrubs were in need of pruning and the flower gardens grew in weedy disarray.

After helping the ladies alight, William led the way to the front door and knocked.

As they waited, Sarah's heart beat painfully hard. She pushed a limp curl off her face and then twisted her gloved hands together. A friendly cat approached and rubbed against Sarah's ankles, seeking attention, but Sarah was too distracted to oblige. Would Mr. Henshall be there? How would he react to seeing her on his doorstep? With pleasure or discomfort?

A few moments later, a housemaid welcomed them inside and showed them into a nearby parlour. "The master is away," she said, "but the lady of the house will be with ye shortly."

The lady of the house?

Was the maid referring to Effie, or . . . ?

As they sat down to wait, Sarah's stomach sank. Had Mr. Henshall married someone else without telling them? Perhaps a Scottish woman who shared his homeland and way of life? If so, could she truly blame him?

The woman who entered a few minutes later was perhaps a year or two older than Sarah's seven and twenty. She had a thin, pretty face and light ginger hair, and she walked with the faintest of limps.

"Good day," she began. "I wasna expectin' callers. What may I do for ye?"

Definitely a Scottish woman, down to her accent and red hair. In fact, she looked a bit like Effie.

William had risen at her entrance, but she gestured for him to be seated, while she perched on the edge of the settee.

Sarah said, "I did write to Mr. Henshall to let him know we were coming."

"Did ye, now? I don't recall him mentioning it." She chuckled. "Then again, I tend to forget things or mislay them now and again. Are ye acquainted with Callum?"

Callum. The woman's familiar use of his given name stung.

"Em, yes," Sarah faltered. "I am Miss Sarah Summers. Mr. Henshall and Effie stayed with us in Devonshire the summer before last. We have corresponded several times since then."

"Ah, I do remember Effie describing the long journey and the boarding house they stayed in, somewhere in the south of England. So terribly far from here. Managed by a family of sisters, I believe."

"Y-yes." Sarah gestured to her companions. "And this is my sister Claire and her husband."

Sarah turned back to the woman, who had yet to give her name. Dare she hope she was only the housekeeper? The woman seemed too young and well-dressed for the role.

"Mr. Henshall has been very kind to our family," Sarah explained, "and we simply wished to call on him while we were in the area. To thank him."

"Miss Summers, ye say?" the woman repeated, testing the name on her tongue with no recognition evident in her expression. "I'm afraid it's not familiar."

Had Mr. Henshall truly not mentioned them? Hurt filled her at the thought. Apparently his time at Sea View had meant more to her than to him.

The woman went on. "Then again, he's mentioned several ladies in recent months, so it's difficult to recall details. Well. I shall be sure and pass along your gratitude."

Claire spoke up. "He is not here, then? Or Effie?"

The woman shook her head. "They have gone to visit her grandfather in Perth, many miles from here."

"Do you expect them back soon?"

"I really canna say. Could be hours. Could be days. Depends on how soon he recovers. He's fallen ill again."

"I am sorry to hear that."

The woman shrugged. "My father is often ill. Yet he has survived far worse and will no doubt rally again."

"Your father?" Sarah echoed. "Then you are Mr. Henshall's . . . sister?"

"His wife's sister, aye. Miss Isla Ross."

"Ah." Relief flooded through Sarah.

From the corner of her eye, she noticed William send Claire a confused look, which Sarah translated as, *The man Sarah admires has a wife?*

She hurried to correct that misapprehension. "So you must be Katrin's sister. Mr. Henshall pointed out her grave in the Sidmouth churchyard. I am sorry for your loss."

"Thank ye. Katrin was my only sister—God rest her. And Effie is her daughter. My one and only niece."

Sarah nodded her understanding, then asked gently, "If your father is ill, do you not wish to be there with them as well?"

Miss Ross nodded. "Aye, were I welcome. He and I had a

falling-out some time ago. It's why I live here now. That, and to be close to Effie. I oversee things here in the house for them."

"How kind."

"Happy to do it. Effie is precious to me. The mere thought of her moving far from here, far from Scotland . . . Nay! It canna be borne."

Sarah hesitated. "I am sure no one is suggesting such a thing."

"Are ye? I hope you're right. Thankfully, he has been spending time with one of our neighbors, Miss Sorley, who lives just down the road. Charming woman."

At the news, Sarah's heart banged like iron against her ribs, and she dared not meet her sister's gaze.

They left the house a short while later, with no offer of refreshment and little encouragement to remain.

Claire squeezed her hand. "I am so sorry, Sarah."

"Don't be," Sarah said, a dull ache in her chest. "Perhaps it's for the best."

"Nonsense."

"As I have said before, a relationship with someone who lives so far from Sea View, and Mamma, and the rest of you, would be impractical. Today's disappointing visit will make it easier to come to terms with that reality."

They climbed inside the waiting landau. Once they were all seated, Sarah glanced back at the charming stone house with its neglected garden and bid Whinstone Hall and Mr. Henshall farewell. As the vehicle lurched into motion and drove away, Sarah turned her eyes forward. She drew a long breath, squared her shoulders in resolve, and faced her companions.

"So there is no reason to factor my future into your decision about the Edinburgh house. You must choose what is best for the two of you alone."

"Well . . . there is no need to decide now. We have several factors to consider, including what is best for Mira."

"Of course. Family comes first."

They returned to the terraced house and packed up their things. Sarah donned a practical carriage dress and her most unaffected demeanor. She was not crushed. She was fine. Self-sufficient and capable. She glanced at the longcase clock and felt a kinship with it: tall, steady, and dependable.

She helped Claire pack, and then assisted Campbell and the house-maids in covering the upholstered furniture and Turkish carpets to help protect them from sunlight until Claire made her decision.

All the while, she was aware of Claire watching her, a worried expression pinching her pretty face, but her sister wisely chose not to say anything.

Sarah sent her what she hoped was a reassuring smile and kept busy.

Many times throughout the lengthy return trip, Sarah repeated to herself that this outcome was for the best. A closed door. A defi-nite sign. Mr. Henshall's silence coupled with hundreds of miles between his home and Sea View were impediments that seemed indisputable now. And even though the "lady of the house" had only been his sister-in-law, she had hinted that he was pursuing a woman who lived close by. Yes, that would be better for Effie. Bet-ter for them all. Sarah had been right to conclude that any future between them was impossible. Apparently, he had come to that conclusion as well. She resolved to remain single and content. Life would be less complicated that way.

Sarah shifted toward the side window and made a concerted effort to turn her thoughts away from Mr. Henshall and toward the Christmas season ahead. The effort felt like trying to turn a huge ship against the tide. But with determination and self-discipline, she managed to take her thoughts captive.

She recalled her conversation with a melancholy Georgiana before they'd set out on this trip. Recent Christmases had been dismal affairs, first with mourning and the move to Sidmouth after Papa's death, and then last year, with royalty come to stay next door, they'd been called on to host three of the Duke of Kent's staff. Amid all the busyness as well as straitened finances, their own celebrations had been minimal at best.

Georgie had been quite disappointed, and Sarah had promised her the next year—this year—would be better, and they would enjoy a far more festive Christmastide.

And as soon as she returned to Sea View, Sarah meant to make good on that promise.

THREE

Puddings gained status during the early eighteenth century
during the reign of George I, the "Pudding King."
—Jeri Quinzio, *Pudding: A Global History*

Miss Georgiana Summers stood in the center of Fort
Field, kite string in hand. Nearby, young Mira Hammond, her niece through marriage, held another such
string. Georgiana had helped the girl send the kite into the air and
then ran to launch a kite of her own. She had not flown a kite since
early summer, but the autumn day had dawned warm and sunny with
a steady wind—not too light, not too gusty—perfect for kite flying.

In the weeks since Claire and Mira's father had left on their
wedding trip, Georgiana had been collecting Mira from Broadbridge's a few times a week, a welcome respite for her uncle and
his new wife, who were busy overseeing the boarding house as well
as caring for Mira. And a welcome change for Mira, who spent
far too much time indoors, in Georgiana's opinion.

Armaan and Sonali knew and trusted her, and Mira liked her.
Georgiana liked the girl too and was enjoying the new experience
of acting the part of doting older sister, instead of the youngest,
as she was in her immediate family.

Together she and Mira had gone for walks along the beach,
collected seashells, and played games together. They also played

fetch with Chips, the local stray that followed Georgiana wherever she went. The dog was slowly coming to trust Mira as well, although the girl's happy shrieks during play still frightened him. Currently Chips sat hunched several yards away, sniffing a discarded wad of butcher's paper in hopes of a treat.

Mira was too young to join the boisterous outdoor games at the charity school, but Georgiana had begun to teach her a few games so she might one day join her there. In fact, a cricket bat and ball lay on the grass nearby, awaiting their turn.

Georgiana still went and played with the students as often as she could, although she had less free time with Sarah gone. During her absence, they all shared Sarah's usual duties. Thankfully, Mamma had recovered her strength and was able to act the part of gracious hostess to their guests. Emily helped in the office with guest correspondence and room assignments. Bibi Cordey, the fisherman's daughter who came over to clean and make beds, added a few more hours to her weekly schedule, and Georgiana assisted her and performed other tasks as well, even serving at table when needed—although she was not very good at it. Thankfully, between their maid, Jessie, and efficient Mr. Gwilt, her help was not often needed in the dining room.

Georgie truly did not mind helping but chafed at being confined indoors during glorious autumn afternoons. She'd much rather traipse around the countryside greeting other walkers or talk with their fishermen neighbors, admiring their catches and occasionally going out in their boats with them. Or even fly a kite, as she was now.

Suddenly the wind lulled. Georgiana managed to adjust the string tension and keep her kite aloft, but Mira's faltered and crashed to the ground.

"Oh no!" the girl exclaimed.

"That's all right," Georgie assured her. "You kept it up a good long while."

A young man came strolling across the field, taking the back way from the eastern town to the west. It was Colin Hutton, carrying a shiny leather valise. He was fashionably dressed in a long greatcoat, brushed beaver hat, and polished black-and-red shoes.

He walked with the confident swagger of a strutting peacock, but Georgiana could not deny the man drew the eye.

Her sister Viola was married to his brother, Jack. Major Hutton's younger brother might be a dandy, but he was sweet and funny and wouldn't hurt a fly.

"Colin!" she called and raised her hand. Mira joined her in waving.

He waved back and diverted his course to join them, a sincere, boyish smile on his handsome face.

"Ah! Miss Georgiana and Miss Mira. What a pleasure." Reaching them, he removed his hat, exposing wavy golden hair, and gave them a formal bow.

Mira giggled.

"How fortunate I am that yours should be the first familiar faces I see in Sidmouth. I've just arrived by coach."

"What are you doing here?"

"Come for the Christmas season, of course. Thought I'd come early."

"And your father?"

"He'll join us in a few weeks, closer to Christmas Eve." He tilted his head, gazing up at the single kite still aloft. "Kites, ey? Haven't flown one in ages."

Georgie pointed to the one on the ground. "Want to see if you remember how it's done?"

"Why not?" He set down his valise and picked up the kite. He tossed the silk diamond into the air, but it quickly fell to the grass.

"Keep your back to the wind," Georgie advised.

He did so, but still the thing would not fly.

"Try a running start."

He ran, holding the line, and the kite rose with a jerk behind him. "There we go!"

It turned a few frantic circles above his head and then dove to the ground.

He picked it up and returned it. "Ah well. More of a cricket man, myself."

"I remember that. And you're just in time. I was about to show Mira how to bat." She pointed to the cricket things on the ground.

"Now that's more like it."

Reeling in her kite, Georgiana exchanged it for bat and ball.

Holding the cricket bat in one hand, she tossed up the ball with the other, quickly shifted the bat into both hands, and gave the ball a whack that sent it a dozen yards.

Chips tore himself away from the wad of butcher's paper to chase after it, returning the ball to Georgiana in a matter of seconds.

"Good boy."

Then it was Colin's turn. He did the same, tossing up the ball and smartly smacking it across the field. It sailed over the fence, past the esplanade, and onto the shingle beach beyond.

Mira cheered, but Colin sent Georgiana an apologetic frown.

"Sorry. I have a few new balls in my bag and will replace it."

"No need."

Chips bounded through the gate and across the esplanade, then disappeared down the rise to shore.

"He'll never find it among all those rocks and pebbles," Colin said.

"Don't underestimate him. He has an excellent nose."

Sure enough, a minute later the scraggly terrier ran back through the gate and trotted up to Colin, depositing the ball at his finely shod feet.

"I say, that's quite a fielder you have there. Ought to recruit him for the next fishermen-versus-visitors match." Colin leaned down and patted the dog's head, then wiped his glove with a handkerchief.

Georgie said, "Unfortunately, he would field balls for both teams, indiscriminately."

"Perhaps we could train him."

"He is not highly trainable, I've found."

"Ah well. Neither am I." Colin winked. "Now, shall I bowl? It's Mira's turn to bat."

He tugged off his greatcoat and hung it neatly over the fence. Then he stood several yards in front of Mira while Georgie showed her how to stand. From behind, Georgie put her arms around the girl and helped her position the bat, resting its lower end on the ground, and prepared to help her swing.

"Gently now," she told Colin.

Colin obliged with an easy lob of the ball. Georgie guided Mira's hold on the bat and struck the ball with a satisfying thwack.

"Well done!" he praised.

They practiced until Mira managed to hit the ball once unaided, then Colin straightened, looked at his pocket watch, and said, "This has been pleasant, but I had better continue on to Westmount. I'll need an hour to wash and change before dinner."

Georgie wrinkled her nose. "Good heavens. That's twice as long as I take."

He pulled on his coat and straightened his cravat. "Well, you are not the swell I am. People have certain expectations."

Georgiana rolled her eyes, then said, "That's all right. It's time I took Mira home anyway. Her father and Claire are still away on their wedding trip but should return any day now, and Sarah with them."

He nodded. "I shall look forward to seeing them all again, and spending Christmastide with you."

Sarah, Claire, and William returned to Sidmouth the third week of November, in time to prepare for the first item on Sarah's Christmastide task list: Stir-Up Sunday.

She informed her family in calm, resigned tones that they had not seen Mr. Henshall or Effie. Unfortunate, but understandable, considering their ailing relative. She deflected their sympathy and avoided probing questions. Of course it was a disappointment, but she was not bereft. Of course not.

On the last Sunday before Advent, Sarah, with help from their cook, Martha Besley, compiled the necessary tools and ingredients to make a plum or "figgy" pudding, although the recipe called for neither plums nor figs, but rather other dried fruits like raisins, currants, and candied orange peel.

29

In the workroom off the kitchen, which Sarah had long ago claimed as her own, she laid out all in readiness for that afternoon's project. While Sarah cut the cheesecloth, their elderly manservant, Lowen, grated the suet and sugar, and Mr. Gwilt filled a large pot with water, ready to set to boil later.

Then the family set out for church together. Claire, William, and Mira, as well as Viola and Jack, along with Jack's brother, Colin, met them there.

During the service, Sarah felt distracted, her mind wandering to the many things she had to do. Christmas Day was less than a month away.

With effort, she returned her focus to the service long enough to hear the part of the liturgy that had given the day its colloquial name. The vicar read the familiar words from the Book of Common Prayer, "Stir up, we beseech thee, O Lord, the wills of thy faithful people; that they, plenteously bringing forth the fruit of good works, may of Thee be plenteously rewarded, through Jesus Christ our Lord."

Sarah knew the prayer was not really about stirring up pudding but was meant to "stir up" the congregation for Advent and remind them to do good works for others, especially at this time of year.

Sarah was determined to do just that.

They had invited the extended family, including Jack's younger brother, to join them at Sea View after the service. William and Claire decided to spend a quiet day with Mira, Armaan, and Sonali after being gone so long, but the others came over to enjoy the food prepared by Mrs. Besley and arranged on the mahogany buffet: cold ham, bread, butter, and cheeses. Potted shrimps, meat pie, and bottled fruit. Sarah herself retrieved hot coffee and tea from the kitchen to complete the meal.

After they had eaten, they all trooped down to the workroom at Sarah's behest. Once the dried fruit, suet, eggs, breadcrumbs, milk, sugar, brandy, and spices were in the bowl, they each took turns stirring, starting with the youngest, Georgiana, and moving up in age.

"Remember to stir from east to west," Sarah reminded them. "The direction the wise men traveled to visit the infant Jesus."

Georgie was followed by the twins, Viola and Emily, and then Colin, James, Sarah, Jack, and Mamma. Jessie and Bibi were spending the afternoon with the Cordeys, but Mr. Gwilt, Mrs. Besley, and Lowen took turns as well.

Some families mixed coins and other charms into the batter. A sixpence in your serving foretold you would be rich, a thimble indicated you would always be a spinster or bachelor, while a ring meant you would soon marry, et cetera.

Sarah had meant to add only a single coin, but Colin Hutton had other ideas. During his turn at stirring, he'd pulled a few charms from a folded handkerchief and slipped them into the batter.

"What did you put in there?" Georgiana demanded.

Sarah wished to know as well.

"You shall have to wait and find out on Christmas Day." He winked and tweaked Georgie's nose.

Sarah hoped no one would break their teeth or choke on whatever he'd added.

She looked from the handsome young man to her youngest sister, who was grinning up at him. Had Georgie taken a liking to a "boy" at last? Colin must be six or seven years older than Georgiana's seventeen, but he was quite boyish for his age, and Georgie, for all her rough-and-tumble ways, was wise beyond her years.

Sarah told herself she was probably only imagining it. Colin was, after all, known to flirt and tease. Even so, the irony struck her. It would not surprise her if her youngest sister—ten years her junior—married before she did. She felt a prickle of sadness at the thought.

After the mixture was thoroughly stirred, Sarah and Mrs. Belsey tied up the round mass in fine gauze cloth. They would boil it for several hours, then let it age in a cool place until Christmas Day.

⌒⌒⌒

The following afternoon, a letter arrived for Sarah from Scotland. Emily handed it to her, eyebrows high, her expression a mix of curiosity and concern. "I will leave you so you can read in private."

Sarah waved a dismissive hand, hoping her sister did not notice it tremble. "No need. Probably just the explanation we have already heard."

Sarah unfolded the letter with unsteady fingers and began to read.

Dear Miss Summers,

You cannot imagine how surprised and disappointed Effie and I were to return home and learn we had missed your visit. We had gone to Perth to visit Effie's grandfather—Katrin's father—who had been ill. But he was improving by then, and we could have and would have returned sooner had we known.

I at first assumed you must not have sent word before you left Sidmouth, perhaps not knowing if you would have time to see us during your trip. Then I found the recent message you sent from Edinburgh—it was there waiting for me in my study—letting me know you had arrived. In it, you mentioned having written previously, but that first letter had not reached me and was not with the correspondence that had come during our absence. I concluded it must have been lost in the post.

Then Effie, who spends a lot of time with her aunt, found your original letter under a ladies' magazine in her room. Isla said she must have picked it up with the periodical and not realized it was there. She insists it was an unintentional oversight. She does tend to misplace things and, between us, is not very organized. Yet I admit it crossed my mind that she might have had other motives. She is fond of Effie and was not happy with our previous trip to Devonshire. It is possible she sought to discourage another such trip, but I have decided to give her the benefit of the doubt. Although my disappointment over not seeing you made that difficult, if I'm honest.

I would have welcomed the opportunity not only to show you around our house and grounds, but also to join you in seeing more of our beloved homeland. I hope what you saw met with your approval. I also hope you had a safe and pleasant journey.

Again, so sorry to have missed you.

Yours sincerely,
Callum Henshall

Conflicting emotions washed over her. Firstly, relief. His letter—with his explanation and sincere regret—was a balm to her sore heart. Yet secondly, doubts still plagued her and left her dispirited. He had not said anything about staying in contact or finding a way to see each other again. As polite as his letter was, had he lost interest in her? That would certainly make things easier, considering her recent resolve to remain contentedly single.

Should she reply? What would she say? Mr. Henshall had once told her his house was old and in need of repair. What she had seen of it, she had thought utterly charming. And the grounds? Also lovely, though in need of some care. Yet what would be the point of writing back and saying as much?

No point at all.

She became aware of Emily's scrutiny and glanced up at her. Sarah had all but forgotten she was there.

"So? What does he say?" she asked.

"Much as I guessed. He and Effie were sorry to miss us, and he hopes we enjoyed our visit to Scotland."

"Which you did not. How could you?"

"Nonsense. I still found much to enjoy."

"Does he say nothing else?"

Sarah shrugged. "Nothing much. He did say the letter I sent from here letting them know of our upcoming trip had been mislaid by his sister-in-law."

"Sister-in-law?"

Sarah nodded. "Apparently she came to live with them after a falling-out with her father. She serves as a housekeeper of sorts. I believe I mentioned that's who received us when we reached Whinstone Hall."

Emily's eyes narrowed. "Hmm . . . What was she like?"

"Difficult to say after such a brief meeting. She was not terribly friendly, but we were uninvited guests as well as strangers to her. She reminded me of Effie in looks. Evidently, the two are quite close. I am glad Effie has an older woman in her life to help guide her."

"Are you?" Emily did not look convinced. "I can think of someone better."

Sarah chose to ignore the suggestion and changed the subject. "And how goes the writing? Any reply from the publisher about your Gothic novel? Or Mr. Gwilt's?"

"Not yet. I may send it to another publisher Mr. Wallis knows. . . ."

As Emily chatted on, Sarah realized she had succeeded in diverting the conversation away from Mr. Henshall's letter, yet her thoughts remained there.

FOUR

The giver of every good and perfect gift has
called upon us to mimic God's giving, by grace,
through faith, and this is not of ourselves.
—Attributed to St. Nicholas of Myra

In preparation for St. Nicholas Day, Georgiana and her sisters banded together to buy or make small gifts for the children at the Sidmouth charity school: knitted scarves, mittens, needle cases, pincushions, carved rulers, bound paper notebooks with pretty covers, and more. Mr. Gwilt had even fashioned a decent cricket bat from wood he'd found in the old work shed behind the house.

Colin Hutton came to call while they were organizing the gifts. Finding them clustered around the mounded dining room table, counting and sorting, he said, "My goodness. How industrious you all are. I grow exhausted simply watching you. What's all this for?"

Georgiana replied, "St. Nicholas Day gifts for the children at the charity school." She looked up at him and challenged, "Perhaps you might contribute something as well?"

His brows lifted. "Me? I don't know what I could give. Though I do have two new Duke six-seam cricket balls, if one of them would be of any interest."

Georgie's mouth fell open. "Of course it would! I would like one myself."

"Then you may have it."

Georgie hesitated, then with a deep exhale resolved, "No. It's Christmastime, and I have so much more than they do. And sadly, most of what my sisters and I have gathered will be more appreciated by girls. Better to give one of your cricket balls to the boys."

"You impress me, Georgiana Summers."

"I should hope so, Colin Hutton."

He grinned, then asked, "What else might the boys like?"

"Goodness, most have so little. Anything, really. Gloves, toys, games . . ."

"I am at your service, miss." He gave her a bow and another lopsided grin. "Give me one hour."

He returned nearly two hours later, arms laden with the promised cricket ball, games of spillikins, dominoes, and cards, a new leather foot-ball, and a pair of gloves.

"Any of these of use, do you think?"

"Good heavens, yes."

"The gloves are an older pair of mine. If you think they're too shabby, just tell me and I will take them back."

"Not at all. Still lots of wear left."

"I suppose the lads are too young for cravats or cologne?" Innocence rounded his fair eyes, but Georgie knew he was jesting.

"I think so, yes."

"Ah well."

"Your offering is most generous as it is. Thank you."

"You are very welcome, Miss Georgiana. You seem to bring out a generous side of my character I did not know existed."

She studied him in astonishment, slowly shaking her head. "Who are you, and what have you done with my friend Colin Hutton?"

The following day, Georgiana and Colin, along with Emily and her husband, James, set out for the Sidmouth School. Sarah remained at home reviewing the books with Mr. Gwilt, who had taken over the bookkeeping tasks during Sarah's absence.

Mamma remained as well, engrossed in the novel *Sense and Sensibility*.

The early December day was sunny and mild, so they might have walked were they not burdened down with their offerings.

The hooded cabriolet James used to travel to and from Killerton seated only two and had insufficient room for all the gifts, so they borrowed the Huttons' larger carriage. Taggart, the Huttons' footman and sometimes coachman, sat at the reins, ready to drive them. They filled its interior with their bundles and barely managed to squeeze in themselves.

They traveled up Fore Street, through the eastern town, and toward the mill until they reached the school, located near the River Sid and next to the poor house. The simple two-story building and yard were enclosed by a brick wall.

When they arrived, Colin helped the ladies alight, while James handed around the bundles. He then sent Taggart home, saying they would walk back after their gifts had been delivered. He opened the gate for them and together they crossed the yard, Colin skirting the muddy patches to spare his polished shoes.

The front of the school held two doors, one with a stone plaque marked *Girls*, the other *Boys*. James held open the girls' door for them, but looking at the plaques, Colin made a comical face, wagged a finger, and entered through the boys' door.

Georgie shook her head. Boyish indeed.

Inside, Mr. Ward welcomed them into the large schoolroom, where his pupils were assembled.

The children were sitting on low benches, looking up at the visitors expectantly. A few grinned shyly at them. The children knew Georgie well, and Emily and James had come to play with or read to them several times before. Some of the boys, however, looked askance at newcomer Colin in his fine clothes and stylish D'Orsay top hat with upturned brim, while a few girls stared at him with barely concealed admiration.

The children politely waited their turns yet were clearly eager and appreciative as the visitors distributed the gifts under the benevolent eye of Mr. Ward. Colin's gloves, which proved too large for any of the pupils, were gratefully received by the humble schoolmaster.

The boys—along with sport-loving Cora—oohed and aahed over the games Colin had brought, as well as the bat, cricket ball, and new foot-ball, stroking each almost reverently.

Colin appeared overwhelmed and even sheepish at their effusive gratitude.

He leaned near Georgiana and whispered, "Next time I'll bring more."

"This is your first visit here, is it not?"

"Yes. Though not my last."

Georgie nodded. "Glad to hear it. You shall no doubt fall in love with these youngsters, as I have."

"Are you not a youngster yourself?"

She sniffed and lifted her chin. "I am not. I will have you know I am now seventeen."

"Goodness. As ancient as that?" He winked.

When the gift giving was over, Mr. Ward released the children for a short recess to enjoy the gifts. The girls and a few boys elected to remain indoors to play spillikins or dominoes. James and Emily remained inside with them.

Meanwhile, the other boys and Cora headed outside.

Georgiana turned to Colin. "Come on," she urged, and he followed her without complaint.

A game began in the yard, and Georgie was quick to enter the fray.

Many feet had worn the yard's patchy grass to dirt in places. It had not yet snowed, but they'd had mizzle in recent days, so the yard was a bit muddy. Soon the ball was muddy as well. Georgie hoped Colin would not refuse to play for fear of spoiling his fine clothes.

She kicked the ball to him. "Join us. I'll be on one side, you the other."

Colin gingerly picked up the muddy ball, then instantly dropped it. He pulled a handkerchief from his pocket and began wiping off his gloves.

"Come on!" Cora shouted her encouragement.

Georgie sighed in disappointment, and one of the mouthier boys grumbled under his breath, "What a coxcomb."

"One moment." Colin returned the handkerchief, then pulled off his gloves and frock coat, laying them over the gate. He placed his hat atop the wall.

Still wearing shirt, waistcoat, cravat, and trousers, he turned back to her and stretched out his arms in white shirtsleeves. "Many apologies for my state of undress, Miss Georgiana."

She rolled her eyes, and he smirked and kicked the ball back to her—smartly and on target.

Georgie stopped the ball with her foot and grinned. "Now, that's more like it!"

He jogged to the center of the yard to join them, maneuvered the ball away from her with fast feet, dodged his would-be defenders, and with the side of one polished shoe, sent the ball into the makeshift goal, earning the cheers of his teammates.

The informal game continued for nearly half an hour. Colin seemed to thoroughly enjoy himself, laughing at his own mistakes, encouraging the less-skilled players, and good-naturedly teasing others as he darted around the yard, often passing the ball to smaller lads.

As the game—and Colin's antics—continued, Georgie's cheeks began to ache from smiling.

At one point, she leapt for the ball and slipped, falling and landing on the ground in an unladylike heap. Muddy shoes appeared in her peripheral vision, and she looked up to find Colin gazing down at her, mild concern on his handsome face. "Are you all right?"

"Of course."

He reached down a hand and helped her up, saying, "I admire your dedication to the game." His words and warm smile melted away her embarrassment.

Later, Cora outmaneuvered Colin and scored a goal against him. Hands on his slim hips, he looked at the cunning player with interest, perhaps only then noticing the muddy skirt hem peeking out from under the girl's long coat. "What's your name?"

"Cora." And without pause, she stole the ball from him and once again kicked it through the goal.

At that moment, Mr. Ward stepped outside to call the children back into the schoolroom, his announcement met with good-natured groans.

Colin retrieved the ball and handed it to Cora, resting his hand atop the knitted cap that poorly concealed her dark curls. He glanced at Georgiana and said, "I like this wily rascal. Reminds me of you."

Georgie laughed thoughtfully. "Yes, she reminds me of me too."

Emily and James came out and joined them, and they walked home two by two. As they crossed Fort Field, the married couple moved ahead, while Georgie and Colin walked more slowly, pausing at intervals to toss a stick for Chips to fetch.

Colin took a turn throwing the stick, then said, "Thank you for including me today. I enjoyed it. Though my poor shoes will never be the same. Almost as bad as your dress."

Georgie looked down at the dirt stains on her skirt and gave them a half-hearted swipe.

"Is that a boarding school or a day school?" he asked.

"It's a day school for local poor children."

"Lucky kids. Wasn't fond of boarding school myself. Only going home a few times a year. Shudder."

She nodded. "These children go home every day after their lessons. I believe they all have at least one parent living, except for Cora."

"Oh? What's her story?"

"I don't know all the details, but my understanding is that Cora lives with her grandmother, who moved here hoping the sea air would improve her health. She is not a wealthy woman, so the governors accepted Cora into the school here."

"She certainly seems to enjoy it."

Georgie nodded. "She has friends at the school, and Mr. Ward is kind to her. Kind to them all."

"I am glad she has her grandmother. Even so, to have lost both father and mother at her age? Seems hard."

She looked at him with interest. "I suppose you can sympathize. I've met your father on several occasions, but I think Viola mentioned Jack's mother—your mother—died?"

40

Colin's usually happy countenance turned pensive, even mournful. "Yes, many years ago when I was quite young. I don't really remember her. Does it make me namby-pamby to say I still miss having a mother in my life?"

"Not at all. You're namby-pamby because you dress like a fop." She winked, and he laughed, the serious mood broken, to her relief—and no doubt his as well.

FIVE

You know full well as I do the value of sisters' affections:
There is nothing like it in this world.
—Charlotte Brontë, *The Professor*

A fortnight had passed since Sarah's return, and she quickly adjusted to being home and fell back into her former routines. After going through the house, guest register, and accounts, she was pleased to find everything in good order. They had only two guests at present, but for the time of year, that was not surprising.

Sarah found herself missing Claire. She had seen little of her since their return to Sidmouth. After spending so much time with her treasured older sister during the trip, she longed for her company. Deciding she could spare an hour before dinner, she rose from the desk to retrieve cloak, bonnet, and gloves.

Georgiana came down the stairs, looking bored. "Where are you off to?"

"I thought I'd go to Broadbridge's to see Claire."

"May I go along?"

"Certainly. I would enjoy your company."

Together the two sisters set off for the boarding house near the marketplace.

When they reached Broadbridge's and knocked, the front door

was opened by Armaan Sagar, Major Hutton's good friend and Mira's uncle. He and his wife, Sonali, had encouraged William and Claire to remain in residence while they were still growing accustomed to their new role as boarding-house keepers.

Armaan gave them a broad smile, which showed off his perfect white teeth to great advantage.

"Good day, Miss Sarah. Miss Georgiana. Please come in."

"Thank you, Armaan. How are things going here?"

"Fairly well, I believe. There is much to learn, but we are blessed to have assistance and advice when we need it. The Hammonds and even your old friend Mrs. Farrant have been most helpful."

"I'm not surprised. Fran was helpful to us when we opened our guest house as well. Always knows 'just the right person' for any task that needs doing."

Another smile. "Indeed she does. Well, I imagine you are here to see your sister, yes?"

Sarah nodded. "If she is available."

"William has gone out to climb one of his hills, but I think Claire is upstairs with Mira in the apartment. I would be happy to escort you, although I believe you know the way quite well by now."

"Indeed we do. I am sure you are busy, so we will show ourselves up, if that's all right."

"Of course. You are always welcome."

She and Georgie went upstairs and through a nondescript doorway that led from the main house to an apartment over the former stable block.

Finding the apartment's outer door open, Sarah knocked on its frame to announce their presence. They waited on a small landing that led to two inner doors—the bedroom door was closed, but the other stood open.

Mira bounded out through the open door. Seeing them, her big brown eyes brightened with delight. "Georgie!" She launched herself at Sarah's youngest sister, who bent and scooped the girl into her arms.

Sarah felt an odd pinch of guilt. She was always so busy that she had not made much of an effort with Mira. She had certainly always been kind to the girl but had not taken the time to play with her. Playing together seemed to create a bond of affection like little else. Perhaps Sarah ought to take the trouble of learning—or relearning—how to do so.

Claire came out after Mira, a warm smile of welcome on her pretty face.

"What a lovely surprise! Do come in."

What had once been a spacious office for William alone now served as informal parlour as well, with two armchairs, a table, and a small bed for Mira. William's desk had been pushed against one wall to make space. The couple had decided Mira's former bedchamber in the attic of the main house was too far away, especially now that her former nursery-governess, Sonali, had moved into a larger room with Armaan.

The sisters sat down to chat, Claire turning the desk chair to face the two armchairs. Mira climbed onto Georgie's lap.

"Thanks again for playing with Mira while we were away," Claire said. "Ever since our return it's been 'Georgiana this, Georgiana that.'"

Claire turned to her. "I am glad to see you as well, Sarah. I thoroughly enjoyed spending so much time with you during the trip. Now that we're home, it feels strange when a few days pass without seeing each other."

"I quite agree."

The rattle of cups and careful footsteps announced someone's approach.

The housemaid, Mary, came in, a tray of tea things in her hands. Georgiana's eyes grew large as she surveyed the young woman's rounded abdomen, no longer concealed by snug dress and apron. "Goodness!" she blurted. "You look ready to—"

Sarah quickly laid a hand atop hers. "Georgie . . ." she admonished under her breath.

"That is, you look, em . . . really well. The picture of robust health."

"Thank ye, miss." Mary grinned. "And you're right. I feel ready to burst."

"You needn't have brought us tea," Claire said. "You ought to be taking things easy now."

"I don't mind. Mr. Sagar mentioned you had guests, and I like to be useful."

Mary bent with effort, set the tray on the low table, and straightened again, pressing a hand to the small of her back.

Sarah had already overcome her shock at learning the housemaid who had traveled with Claire from Edinburgh was expecting a child and not yet married. Her intended was a surgeon's mate on a ship undertaking a voyage for the East India Company. They had planned to marry as soon as he returned, but he had sailed off before either he or Mary knew there was a child on the way. William had used his connections to have the young man sent back on the next available ship and kindly kept the young woman in their employ, despite her condition. The Sagars kept her on as well, although for Mary's comfort and that of their guests, she remained primarily in the background these days, tidying the apartment over the stables, lending a hand in the kitchen, and helping with Mira.

"How are you feeling?" Sarah gently asked her.

"A bit uncomfortable, I can't deny. Back aches somethin' awful. Still, it's nothin' to how sick I was early on. It feels like this wee one may appear any time. As eager as I am, can't help wishing my Liam would arrive first."

"It is a long journey," Claire cautioned her. "Remember, Mr. Hammond said it is unlikely Mr. MacBain will reach England before the child is born. If all goes well, hopefully soon after."

"I know. And as long as they both arrive safely, that's what's most important. Well." Mary bobbed a shallow curtsy. "I shall return later for the tray."

Once the maid left, Sarah asked, "Is there anything Mary needs for the baby?"

"She has gathered a few things. We found some of Mira's baby clothes in one of the trunks, which Mary will be welcome to use. And she has made a few nightdresses and cloths. I have been teaching her to sew and knit. She has not got the knack of knitting, but her sewing is coming along rather well."

"Then I shall make a point of knitting something for her."

"How generous. I have been knitting a baby blanket for her, but perhaps a cap or booties?"

"Good idea. I can manage those."

"That makes one of us," Georgie said, not at all skilled or interested in needlework of any kind.

They chatted over tea for several minutes, but then Mira rose and tugged on Georgiana's hand. "Will you come and see my dollhouse? It is up in the nursery. There is no room for it here."

"Mira, let Georgiana finish her tea."

"That's all right." Georgie gulped down the remainder and stood. "I'd love to see it. Lead on."

When they had gone, the eldest sisters shared amused grins.

"Those two make quite a pair," Sarah observed.

"I agree."

During the years Claire had been separated from the family, Sarah had missed her older sister a great deal. Growing up, Claire had been her confidante—someone she could be honest with, safely be herself. And now that it was just the two of them, Sarah leaned forward, grateful for this private opportunity to share her news.

She told Claire about the letter from Mr. Henshall. His explanation of what had happened and his disappointment over having missed them.

"Sarah, that is excellent news! It is, of course, unfortunate about the misplaced letter and the timing, but now you know his absence was unintentional, that his interest in you has not wavered."

"Do I? He said nothing about staying in contact or seeing each other again. Nor did he explain away the 'charming neighbor' his sister-in-law mentioned."

"Even so, it is something—something far better than you imagined. Is it not?"

"I suppose. It's reassuring to know we remain on amicable terms, although I am unlikely to see him again."

"Don't say that. Winter may not be ideal for traveling, but perhaps in the spring he and his stepdaughter might visit again?"

"Effie detested the long journey the last time."

"Then maybe he shall come alone."

"I doubt it."

"Sarah . . ." Claire tucked her chin and gently chided her. "Why must you always think the worst?"

Sarah looked away from her sister's knowing gaze. "I suppose to protect myself from disappointment."

With Sarah home, Georgie had more free time. So a few days later, she made another visit to the school to play with the students and chat with Cora, her favorite. On her way home, Georgiana stopped at the window of Kingwill's Repository, looking at the local fossils and Devonshire marble displayed there, and now a variety of seashells as well. The shop door opened and Eliza Marriott exited, her ever-present seashell basket over her arm, now unusually empty.

"Good day, Miss Marriott."

"Georgiana, a pleasure to see you." The young woman glanced down. "Good heavens. What's happened to your petticoat?"

Georgie followed her gaze and saw the muddy petticoat showing from beneath her dress. "Just playing ball with the school-children."

Eliza said, "I admit I sometimes misjudge an incoming wave and my half boots get wet, but how my stepmother would rail if I came home like that."

Georgiana was about to say her mamma was more understanding, but didn't want to remind Eliza that her own mother had died. And in truth, Mamma often complained over the state of Georgie's clothes and boots.

Instead she changed the subject. "Are those your shells in the window?"

"They are—or rather, they were. I can't usually bear to part with any, but Christmas is coming, and I wanted the means to buy gifts for Papa and . . . Mamma."

Georgie noticed the young woman often hesitated before referring to her stepmother by that maternal title, even though her widowed father had remarried many years ago now. Georgiana supposed she might find it difficult to call another woman Mamma as well.

She and Eliza were not close but shared a friendly acquaintance, frequently seeing each other, since both of them spent a lot of time out-of-doors. While Georgie loved to take long rambles and play sports, however, Eliza's outings were centered on her tireless pursuit of finding interesting seashells on area beaches.

Whenever the two happened to meet, Georgie stopped to admire Eliza's latest discoveries. Since her basket was currently empty, Georgie looked again to the offerings in the shop window.

Displayed there were shells of various sizes and colors: chalky white, shiny pearl, golden yellow, pale pink. Some were solid, while others were striped. By now, Georgie recognized many of the shapes: cockle shells, scallops, augers, and limpets.

"I think I like the striped snail shells best."

Eliza nodded sagely. "Ah yes. *Cassis strigata.*"

Georgie pointed to a few brightly colored whorled shells. "What are those?"

"Flat periwinkles, or *Littorina obtusata.*"

"Well, they're all very interesting. Pretty too."

"Thank you. Mr. Kingwill thinks he will have no trouble selling them and paid me a good price. So now to decide what gifts to buy. What are you giving your mother?"

Georgie blinked and shifted uneasily. "I don't know. We don't go in for big gifts. Usually just something handmade."

"Oh." Eliza appeared disappointed by her answer.

The truth was, Georgiana had not yet given any thought to gifts.

Footsteps and a jovial, if tuneless, whistle caught her ear. She looked over and saw Colin Hutton striding up the street, impressively dressed as always, small parcel in one hand.

"Ah, Miss Georgiana." He doffed his beaver hat. "And pray, who is your lovely friend?"

Georgie inwardly sighed. "Miss Eliza Marriott, allow me introduce Mr. Colin Hutton."

"Enchanted." He bowed, and Eliza curtsied.

"I believe I have seen you before," Eliza said. "At church and such."

"Quite possibly. My brother, Major Hutton, lives at Westmount, and I often visit him and his wife. And her lovely sisters, of course." He nodded to Georgiana.

Eliza looked at her. "Ah, so he is your brother-in-law."

"I . . . well. He is Viola's brother-in-law to be certain but not mine . . . exactly."

Eliza turned back to Colin. "I have met Major Hutton. He served with my uncle, Major Charles Marriott, in India. You appear to be much younger than your brother. Though perhaps it is his scars, if that is not rude to say."

"Not at all. Yes, I am the youngest. We had another brother between us, but—" Colin abruptly broke off and turned his head, as if his attention was seized by something in the window.

"And what has caught your fancy here, ladies? The seashells?"

"Miss Marriott found those," Georgie explained. "She is quite the avid collector."

"Ah!" He looked up, apparently impressed. "A conchologist."

"That's right," Eliza said. "I have many more at home. I've invited Georgiana more than once to come to Temple Cottage and see my entire collection, but she has not yet done so. You would be welcome to join her."

"I should enjoy that."

For a lingering moment the two smiled at each other.

Georgie interjected, "And you, Colin. What have you been shopping for?" She gestured to the parcel in his hand.

He grinned. "You tell me."

"How should I know?"

"What do you smell?" He leaned closer.

"I don't know, but whatever it is, is rather strong."

"It's a new cologne—Albany. Named after one of London's most exclusive addresses for fashionable bachelors. A blend of lavender and citrus."

Georgie leaned away. "Ah. Thought I smelled a fruit seller."

"Well, I think it smells quite nice," Eliza said.

Of course she did.

"Is it a gift for Jack?" Georgiana asked.

"For me. Got Jack one called Spanish Leather. Sounded more his style. And traditional Bay Rum for our father."

Guilt pinched. Even self-absorbed Colin Hutton had bought presents for his family. What did that say about her?

Colin turned back to Eliza. "And you live here in Sidmouth, Miss Marriott?"

"I do. For many years now, though I lived in India as a child. My father is a lawyer—King's Counsel—but my uncles are still there."

"How interesting."

"Thank you. I think so. Well, if you will excuse me, I had better get on with my shopping. Good day, Mr. Hutton. Georgiana." She curtsied and started down the street.

Watching her depart, Colin murmured, "I say. What a beauty."

As the elegant woman of two or three and twenty walked away, Georgie stood there feeling inelegant, immature, and rather awkward in her muddy hems and unkempt hair.

Why did she care? She had never cared before.

SIX

Early, bright, transient, chaste as morning dew,
She sparkled, was exhaled, and went to heaven.
—Memorial, Sidmouth Church

After the following week's divine service, Sarah stayed to talk with the ladies of the Poor's Friend Society, discussing agenda items for the next day's committee meeting. The monthly meetings were attended by the committee secretary, treasurer, and superintendents—all men—as well as the local magistrates and other leading gentlemen of the parish. Several of them contributed their ideas and resources toward the charity's efforts, but it was the women who did the majority of the work, and they liked to be prepared.

When the other ladies left, Sarah paused to collect petals that had fallen from an arrangement of chrysanthemums and winter viburnum before the pulpit, and then picked up a dropped glove to place in the lost property box.

The Reverend William Jenkins nodded to her on his way to the vestry. "Ah, Miss Summers. What would we do without you?"

When he had gone, Sarah looked around the nave once again to see if there was anything else that needed tidying. An unexpected wave of weariness washed over her, and finding herself alone, she sat heavily in one of the pews.

After a few minutes of staring at nothing, her gaze was drawn to the many monuments in the church, there to commemorate the virtues of the dead, or to extend admonitions to the living. The inscriptions lamented the losses of daughters, sons, wives, and husbands. Many of them had come to the seaside hoping for a cure but instead died there.

Remembering her promise to Henrietta Liston, Sarah searched until she found her brother's memorial. The square marble slab read

Near this place lie the remains of
Nathaniel Marchant, Esq.
. . . He died in the 49th year of his age,
and his disconsolate widow,
after receiving uninterrupted proofs
of his affection for 18 years,
caused this stone to be erected to his memory.

How lovely. How sad, Sarah thought. What would it be like to be so deeply loved and cherished by one's spouse? His poor wife! His poor sister too.

She looked next at a sarcophagus near the Communion table that held the remains of Maria Elizabeth Bucknall, who came to Sidmouth for the benefit of her health, and

. . . after a long illness,
borne with pious resignation . . .
departed this life,
to the inexpressible grief of her family, aged 25.

So much loss. How uncertain and brief life could be, Sarah realized. At the thought, her mind, as it often did, traveled back to Callum Henshall, who had been heartsick over his inability to save his wife. When he first came to Sea View as a guest and began leaving the house by stealth early in the mornings, she suspected him of something nefarious: meeting with smugglers or a clandestine rendezvous with a woman.

One morning, she had trailed after him through thick fog, following his flapping greatcoat and the flash of fair hair beneath his black hat. How surprised she'd been when he'd slipped through the churchyard gate. There, she'd spied him standing before a grave, bare head bowed, hands clasped over his hat brim. She had turned and crept away, not wishing to interrupt his private grief, feeling guilty and embarrassed over her baseless suspicions.

Some time later, she had gone to see the grave alone and realized he'd been standing at his wife's headstone, topped by a Celtic cross.

Eventually, he had told her about his wife's deep depression of spirits, made worse by her first marriage to a cruel man. Mr. Henshall had married Katrin, a young widow with a daughter, sure he could make her happy. When he failed, he had brought her to Devonshire, hoping the south coast—renowned for physical health benefits—would be good for her mind and spirit as well. Instead she had died. And while it was possible she had fallen from the cliff into the sea, he believed she had probably taken her own life. Since then, he had done his best to be a caring stepfather to Katrin's daughter, Effie.

During their stay at Sea View, Effie had often been tetchy, as any adolescent could be. Despite that, Sarah had liked the girl and wondered how she was doing now. Was she fifteen yet? Georgie had befriended her, even though Effie was a few years younger, and the two had corresponded since the Henshalls' stay at Sea View. Yet in recent months Effie's letters had trickled off. Apparently she had lost interest in them as her father had.

Stop feeling sorry for yourself, Sarah inwardly chastised. She should hope for Effie's sake that Mr. Henshall would marry a kind, affectionate woman who would love Effie and treat her as her own daughter. Mr. Henshall had confided that Effie's real mother had been unable to care for her. When Katrin looked at her, she saw her cruel husband and could not fully love her. He'd said he hoped Effie did not realize this, but Sarah guessed the poor girl had been all too aware.

With thoughts of the two heavy on her heart, Sarah exited the church by the south porch only to find the outside air thick with mist, which transported her once again to the foggy day she had followed Callum Henshall there to the churchyard.

Now as Sarah started down the path, her gaze naturally drifted to that familiar Celtic cross beside the bendy elm tree.

She stopped midstride, shoes scuffing the path. A man stood before the grave, fair head bowed, hat in his hands. Her pulse accelerated. Surely it was a trick of the fog. . . .

The man looked up.

Her feet moved of their own volition. She was determined to get closer, to make sure.

Her heart thumped in recognition. "M-Mr. Henshall. I . . . am sorry to intrude, but—"

His fair eyebrows rose. "Miss Summers. Not at all. I am happy to see ye. I planned to stop by Sea View next but thought I ought to pay my respects first."

Sarah swallowed, her throat suddenly tight, and murmured, "Of course."

He was well dressed in buff trousers, light waistcoat, dark blue coat, and simply tied cravat. With his hat in his hands, his coppery blond hair fell over his brow, ruffled by the breeze. Fatigue shadowed his eyes; he was likely tired after the long journey. Even so he looked remarkably handsome.

Was she staring?

She very much feared she was.

With effort, she shifted her gaze and walked over to stand beside him.

For a moment, she stood silently, solemnly regarding the headstone and its epitaph.

Katrin McKay Henshall
Beloved Wife and Mother
Forever in Our Hearts

According to the engraved dates, she had been gone over four years now, a year longer than Peter, her former betrothed, who had died of yellow fever during a journey to the West Indies.

After a few quiet moments, he said, "Ye canna imagine how sorry we were to return home and learn we had missed ye."

Oh, Sarah could well imagine it. "We were quite disappointed as well. I did receive your letter of explanation but have yet to reply. Now I suppose I need not. Thank you for writing; I was sorry to hear Effie's grandfather fell ill."

"He seems quite recovered now."

"Good."

He nodded, and an awkward silence followed.

She looked around the churchyard. "Did Effie not come with you?"

"To Sidmouth, aye. Still not keen to visit her mam's grave, however. I left her quite happily eating cake in the York Hotel."

"The York Hotel?"

"Aye. We didna wish to presume. . . ."

"There they are!" Georgie called from the gate, striding into the churchyard and all but dragging Effie by the hand behind her. Noticing the graves, Effie pulled away and hung back.

In the year and a half since they had last seen Effie, she had grown markedly taller. Even so, the two-year difference in the girls' ages had become even more evident. Seeing them side by side, Sarah saw with new eyes how much Georgiana had grown up. She looked like a young woman next to slender, coltish Effie, whose ginger hair hung loose around her narrow, freckled face, ears protruding through the fine strands. By comparison, Georgie had womanly curves, thick brown hair pinned back, blue eyes like Sarah's, and a pretty face with high cheekbones.

Now Georgie beamed. "Look who I found at the York Hotel!"

Moving toward the girl, Sarah gave her a gentle smile and laid a hand on her shoulder. "Effie. How good to see you again."

"And you, Miss Sarah."

"You've grown! You're nearly as tall as I am."

The girl looked down self-consciously. "Aye. Had to have new clothes made."

Georgie said, "Effie says they are planning to stay at the hotel, but I said, 'Don't be silly; you must stay with us.' Right? They must, mustn't they?"

"Um, well, yes. That is, I would like that very much."

"Would ye?" Mr. Henshall asked softly.

Sarah glanced at him, and her breath hitched. "I would."

For a weighty moment, his sea-green eyes held hers. Then he released a long breath. "I'm glad. I shall inform the hotel of our change of plans, collect our bags, and be there shortly."

Sarah smiled, her mood brighter than it had been in weeks. "Excellent."

Georgie insisted on returning to the hotel to help with their baggage, so Sarah walked ahead to Sea View alone, heart light. Surely he would not travel all this way were he really courting another woman. Might his coming here mean . . . ?

She would not presume, of course, but if so . . . were not things running smoothly at Sea View these days? With Mamma feeling strong, healthy, and able to oversee things, as well as Emily and James living with them and lending a hand when needed, not to mention Georgiana, the servants, and especially Mr. Gwilt? The latter had assumed the roles of bookkeeper, butler, and porter, especially as their elderly manservant, Lowen, was less able to carry heavy guest bags or buckets of water.

Then, despite these inner assurances, her mind began to whirl with all she had to do. Were the sheets fresh? Would there be enough food for two extra at breakfast?

Reaching Sea View, she hurried into the parlour and interrupted what appeared to be a rather serious meeting.

Emily, James, and Mamma sat together in quiet conversation. Mamma's new favorite novel, *Sense and Sensibility*, lay nearby, but was, for once, closed.

Mamma looked up. "Ah, Sarah. You are just in time. Emily and James have come to a decision."

"What decision?"

Emily explained, "We waited until you returned from Scotland. But poor James. Yes, Sir Thomas has lent him a horse and carriage to travel to and from Killerton, but it's over thirteen miles away. Even with a spry horse, the trip takes more than an hour each way—longer in bad weather—and so much time on the road has begun wearing on him. While you were gone, James stayed at

Killerton House for several nights in a row before returning to Sea View, but I could not bear to be parted from him so long.

"Now we have agreed to a new arrangement: Sir Thomas and his wife have generously invited us to use one of their guest rooms. We shall spend five nights a week at Killerton and spend the other two nights at Sea View. I can write and edit for Mr. Wallis anywhere, so it seems a reasonable solution."

Sarah stared at her, stomach sinking. But Emily went on before she could fathom a reply.

"Now that Mamma is feeling better, she has taken over much of the correspondence I was responsible for. Perhaps in time Georgiana might assist with that as well, although her handwriting is still rather poor."

Sarah felt the light go out inside her. She looked dully ahead, feeling numb. "Y-yes."

"And now you're home," Emily concluded, "I am not truly needed."

"I . . . see. I am sorry I didn't consider the wear on you, James, with so much time on the road. A perfectly logical decision, especially with winter soon upon us."

James nodded. "Thank you for understanding."

Emily studied her face. "You seem unhappy. Are you? Honestly, I did not think you would mind."

"I . . . I don't. Of course not. You must do what is best for the two of you."

Mamma also studied her in concern. "Sarah, what is it?"

At that moment, the door banged open and Georgie sailed inside, a more reserved Effie and Callum Henshall in her wake, valises and guitar case in hand.

"Look who has come!" Georgie announced. "And just in time for Christmas. Is it not grand?"

"Mr. Henshall and Effie!" Mamma rose and greeted them warmly. "How lovely to see you again."

"They were going to stay at the York Hotel, but I told them they must stay with us. Do you not agree?"

"Of course," Mamma said. "Effie, my dear." She opened her arms, and the girl melted into them, clearly relishing the maternal embrace.

Releasing Effie, Mamma turned to Mr. Henshall to introduce the new-wed couple. "You remember Emily, I trust."

"I do indeed." He bowed.

"And this is her husband, James Thomson."

"A pleasure." The two men shook hands.

Mamma said, "Would you like your former rooms? That is, unless you object, Sarah?"

"Not at all. I was about to suggest the same." Sarah managed a smile, even as her hope faded. When Mr. Henshall had turned up in the churchyard, she'd briefly believed there might be a future for them, but now the reality of her family's situation came rushing back.

She noticed Emily watching her, realization dawning.

"Sarah, you should have said something. Perhaps we can wait a bit longer or . . ."

Mamma interrupted her with a single clap of her hands. "Well now. Let's get our guests settled. The keys, Sarah?"

Clean towels in hand, Sarah led the Henshalls up to their rooms, Georgie tagging along.

When they reached the door, Mr. Henshall paused to regard the placard beside it. "This is new." He ran a finger over the carved words: *Scots Pine*. Then he turned to her, brows high in question.

Sarah felt her face heat.

Georgie grinned. "We named it in your honor!"

"Did ye indeed?"

"Um-hm."

Sarah opened the door and stepped inside, setting the towels on the washstand. The two young ladies disappeared into the adjacent room—Effie closing her door none too softly—leaving Sarah alone with Callum Henshall. In a bedchamber. She swallowed hard and reminded herself she was there in a business capacity only.

He set down his cases, turned to her, and sank his voice. "I hope you don't mind us coming to Sidmouth like this, unannounced. When we learned you'd come all the way to our house, I felt I had to see you. Even Effie, who despaired of the long journey after our last trip, wanted to come."

"*I had to see you.*" Sarah's nerves thrummed at the words, even as she told herself to be practical, to remember she was content as she was. Useful. Needed.

"I don't mind at all," she replied. She thought of James and Emily leaving, and again her mind ran through her lists, her plans, her tallies. She had accounted for a certain number of people for Christmas Eve, Christmas dinner, New Year's, and Twelfth Night. Would the plum pudding be large enough? Perhaps she should have ordered a larger goose. . . .

The next moment, all of those practical concerns fled. To travel all this way, and at Christmastide yet—what did it signal? How was she to respond? With cool officiousness, as though he were just another return guest, or at best, a family friend joining them for the holidays? Should she pretend to be unaffected by his arrival when every inch of her being was acutely aware of his presence?

She glanced up and was surprised to find him so near. Had he stepped closer, or had she?

He said, "When we met in the churchyard, ye seemed happy to see me. Has something changed?"

"Oh, um . . ." What to say? "It's only the busyness of the season. And Emily and her husband will be spending more time away from home, so there will be her duties to take care of as well. Nothing's wrong, just . . . a lot on my mind."

"And we have added to your duties by being here, especially at Christmastime."

"I didn't mean . . . It is not a problem, truly."

"We shan't expect any special treatment. Well, I shan't. I canna speak for Effie." He gave her a half grin. "For instance, I recall ye don't serve dinner to guests on Saturday and Sunday evenings. Don't make an exception on our account. We can easily go to one of the hotels."

Sarah considered. "We do have two other guests with us presently, and they might notice if we made an exception for you. But when they leave in a few days, I can easily modify the menus and shopping to include you and Effie as well. And you must join us for all the meals during Christmas week. I have promised Georgiana dinner parties and evening parties and every festivity I can think of. Last Christmas was a sad disappointment to her."

"We shall happily join you, then. In the meantime, perhaps I might take Mr. Hornbeam out for a meal. Is he still with you?"

"He was until a few months ago. He recently married."

Mr. Henshall's golden brows again rose high. "Ye don't say. That is excellent news. Yet another marriage since I was last here."

"Y-yes."

"And who is the lucky lady?"

"Her name is—was—Miss Reed. I don't know if you would remember her. I doubt you would recognize her as the same dour woman from the night of the flood. They are so very happy together."

He looked into her eyes and said softly, "Imagine that."

Sarah looked away, clearing her throat. "The two have moved into a lovely cottage only a ten-minute walk away. I am sure he'd be delighted if you stopped by." She smiled. "Perhaps play another game of chess?"

"I would like that. Although he'll no doubt win, as he usually did. Are we quite certain he's blind?" He winked.

"Oh yes. Though somehow he manages to see more than the rest of us do."

"I agree."

Sarah hesitated. She was drawn to this man, wanted to stay there with him, yet at the same time felt pulled in the opposite direction by the demands of propriety and duty.

A burst of giggles erupted from the adjoining room, recalling Sarah to her surroundings.

She retreated to the door. "Well. I shall leave you to settle in."

SEVEN

Mirth and laughter wild, free and sportive as a child.
Hope with eager sparkling eyes, and easy faith, and soft surprize.
—Charles Hague, *Glees, Rounds & Canons*

On Monday afternoon, Sarah and Viola walked to the London Inn to attend the committee meeting of the Poor's Friend Society.

With St. Thomas Day rapidly approaching, the ladies of the charity had decided that instead of the parish's elderly widows having to go around town as "mumpers," seeking gifts of food and coins as was done in many communities, the community would go to them.

After the formal meeting with the governors, the ladies reconvened at Sea View, where Mamma and Emily joined them. Over tea and fruit tarts Sarah had made, they reviewed and divided the names of the elderly poor between them. They made plans to deliver food, warm clothing, and a few coins to each person on the list.

Sarah and her family were happy to do their part, claiming the residents of the poor house for their special attention.

Noticing a familiar name on the list, Mamma offered to visit an additional widow who, according to Mrs. Fulford, was not only poor but also in poor health.

"Do you know her, Mamma?" Emily asked.

"I am not sure, but I once knew a *Miss* Limbrick, so I am

curious. It's a surname I heard often when we lived in Gloucestershire but not since. It's possible Mrs. Limbrick is related to her. Has she been in Sidmouth long?"

"About a year now, I believe," Mrs. Fulford replied. "Perhaps a bit longer. She came here as an invalid, hoping for a cure, as many do. Sadly, she has been primarily housebound since the summer."

"I see. Has she no family?"

"Only a granddaughter, as far as I know. Attends the Sidmouth School."

"Well. I shall look forward to meeting her."

During Claire and Sarah's trip north, Viola and Mamma—with a little, albeit imperfect, help from Emily and Georgiana—had already knitted scarves, mittens, and wool stockings, much as they had for the school children. Sarah now got busy in her workroom off the main kitchen, and over the next few days prepared doughs and fillings for biscuits, sugar cakes, gingerbread, and mincemeat pies, which she would bake fresh in advance of the big day.

Claire came over while she worked and watched, impressed, as Sarah measured, stirred, kneaded, and divided the different batters.

With a glance toward the door to make sure they were alone, Claire began, "So Mr. Henshall came here for Christmas. Is that not wonderful?"

"I suppose Georgie told you. Or Emily?"

"He told me himself. Paid a call at Broadbridge's to meet William and me. I imagine Georgie told him where to find us."

"Did he indeed?"

Claire nodded. "Said he wanted to thank us for calling at his home in Scotland, and to apologize for not being able to receive us."

"Goodness."

"And he is just as handsome as Emily described." A playful grin teased Claire's lips. "How is it going with him staying here?"

"Oh. Fine. He's . . . a very easy guest."

"Easy? Is that all you have to say?"

Sarah had half expected Mr. Henshall to hover nearby, seek her out often, and make his presence felt, but he and Effie kept busy shopping, sightseeing, treating Georgie to tea and cake at the York Hotel, visiting Mr. and Mrs. Hornbeam and being invited to stay not only for a game of chess but also for a meal, and now, she learned, paying a call on Claire and William as well.

Sarah shrugged. "We don't see as much of him as I might have thought."

Claire's fair eyebrows rose. "Really? I wonder why?"

Sarah wondered as well. Was he having second thoughts now that he had returned? "Well, I did tell him I would be busy preparing for Christmas."

Claire clucked her tongue and shook her head. "Sarah, Sarah, Sarah . . . Come now. It's me. Tell me what is going on in that head of yours."

Sarah considered. "When he first arrived, I was stunned and pleased and hopeful. I thought there might be a future for us. That I might be able to leave here and . . ." She broke off. "Then I learned James and Emily will only be here two days a week in future, so we will have far less of her help. And I keep thinking about how far away Scotland is. How long it would take to get here should something happen."

"But how do you feel about *him*?"

"I . . . admire him and am certainly attracted to him. But how well do I really know him? It's been a year and a half. Perhaps his sister-in-law was right and he is pursuing a neighbor of theirs."

"Have you asked him?"

"No."

"Well, even if he was interested in someone else, he's surely thought the better of it to come all this way."

"I hope you're right. Even so, I feel like I need to become better acquainted with him." To herself, Sarah added, *Before I risk moving so far away.*

"That's only natural," Claire replied. "And now he's here, you shall have the opportunity to do so—if you stop working now and then to spend time with him. How long is he planning to stay?"

"Through Epiphany, I believe. I did not like to press him."

"My guess is that he'll stay as long as it takes."

"As long as it takes to . . . what?"

"To win your heart." Claire cocked her head to one side and narrowed her eyes in thought. "Though I doubt your heart will be the problem. Your practical mind and sense of family duty shall pose the bigger obstacles."

Sarah slowly shook her head. "You know me too well."

Their other guests had departed earlier in the day, so that evening, Mr. Henshall and Effie joined them for dinner. They were a relatively small group with only seven around the table: Mamma, Georgiana, Mr. Henshall and Effie, Emily and James, and Sarah—if she ever sat down long enough to eat.

"Do sit, Miss Sarah," Mr. Gwilt gently insisted, taking a serving dish from her. "Jessie and I can manage, we can."

"Very well. Thank you, Mr. Gwilt."

She noticed Mr. Henshall and Effie eye the small Welshman with interest. Mr. Gwilt had not been in their employ when last they were here. He had been a fellow guest, and an odd one at that. He'd arrived at Sea View with a stuffed parrot in a cage and had the disconcerting habit of speaking to it as though it were still alive. Thankfully that tendency had diminished over the last year as Mr. Gwilt found his place at Sea View.

Mr. Henshall nodded to him. "Mr. Gwilt. A pleasure to see ye again."

"And you, sir. And Miss Effie as well."

"You're a servant here now?" Effie asked, with her usual bluntness.

"That I am." He displayed no embarrassment at having moved from guest to retainer. In fact, he looked rather proud.

"We quite depend on Mr. Gwilt," Emily said. "He's practically one of the family."

Mr. Gwilt beamed.

"And where's Parry?" Effie asked.

"In my room belowstairs. Snug as a bee in a box, he is. And so am I."

Emily added, "Mr. Gwilt has written a wonderful children's book of Parry's adventures. No doubt to be published one day."

"Oh, now. That was Miss Emily's doing, mostly. I don't expect anything to come of it, I don't. But a pleasure to put it down in writing, all the same." He smiled and finished serving the meal.

As they ate, Sarah gazed across the table at Callum Henshall and felt almost dizzy, as if she had walked up from the kitchen in December 1820 and stepped back in time to the dining room from the summer of 1819.

Mr. Henshall met her gaze. "Like old times, aye?"

Had he read her mind?

He turned to include the others, adding, "It's good to be at your table again. Thank ye for havin' us."

"As long as ye don't start telling all them old legends about Vikings and thistles and such," Effie warned.

"Ah! Thank ye for remindin' me. That brings to mind another tale—"

"Oh, no ye don't." Effie raised a bread roll as though to throw it at him, her threat clear.

He raised a placating hand. "Very well, then. I shall have mercy on ye tonight. But no guarantees come Christmas, ye ken? And then Hogmanay! Prepare yourselves."

"What's Hogmanay?" Georgie asked around a bite of bread.

Effie groaned and shook her head. "Don't get him started!"

With a tolerant grin at his stepdaughter, he replied, "For poor Effie's sake, I'll say only that it refers to the Scottish New Year. In Gaelic it means something like 'New morning.' An important holiday in our homeland."

"And how do you celebrate it?"

Mr. Henshall glanced at his stepdaughter again and then sent Georgiana a conspiratorial wink. "I shall tell ye later."

Remembering her talk with Claire about becoming better acquainted with the man, Sarah said, "I think we all enjoyed hearing about your life in Scotland last time. Perhaps just one story?"

"No legends, though!" Effie insisted.

Mr. Henshall considered, fair eyes alight with nostalgia. "Well, I doubt it's diverting, but I shall describe a memorable Christmas from my boyhood. My aunt, uncle, and cousin Alistair arrived for the holiday just as a winter storm struck. Snow and ice and so cold the streams froze over and the pump too. We had to carry in buckets of snow to melt for washing and cooking. It was too icy to risk riding the horses into town to visit the butcher or baker or chandler. No delivery wagons went out either. We made do with what we had in the larder and conserved our candles by spending a great deal of time together at one table. Instead of gifts from the shops, we told tales and shared favorite memories. There were no carolers or mummers that year, but we played our instruments by the fire and games by candlelight. On Christmas Day, Da' read from the Bible and we all sang carols. How we could harmonize. Mam even danced a jig right there in the parlour."

He chuckled at the memory. "We had no Christmas goose, no oranges or peppermints. No sallying forth for parties with friends or services at the kirk. Yet it lives on in my memory as one of the best Christmases of my life."

Mr. Henshall stopped speaking, although his gaze remained distant. A reverent silence followed. Then, recalled to his surroundings, he looked at Georgiana and said, "Though this year will no doubt be just as memorable."

Sarah sent him a grateful look.

Effie sighed. "I wish I had known your parents."

"So do I. Ye would have liked them, and they would have doted on ye."

Sarah asked, "Your cousin Alistair . . . Is that the cousin you mentioned who will inherit Whinstone Hall one day . . . ?" She bit back the words *barring a son of your own.*

"Aye."

Sarah nodded, then let the subject drop.

After dinner, James and Emily retired, since James had to rise early to make the long drive to Killerton. The couple had decided to continue living at Sea View until after the New Year, despite Sarah's protests that they need not delay on her account.

The others moved into the parlour. Georgiana and Effie sat at the table playing a game of draughts, while Mamma sat with a cup of tea and chatted with Mr. Henshall. After Sarah helped tidy up, she joined them.

Mamma said, "Sarah mentioned your sister-in-law lives with you, and serves as your housekeeper. Was she not sad to be left alone at Christmastime?"

"She's not alone. Isla had been estranged from her father, which is why she came to live with us in the first place, but he recently extended an olive branch and invited her to come back. Apparently their rift is at an end." With a glance at the girls enmeshed in their game and paying their conversation no heed, he added, "And despite her fondness for Effie, she was eager to return home."

"Good for her, but not for you," Mamma said. "I imagine you were sorry to see her go."

With another glance at the girls, he lowered his voice. "Effie was sorry. I was . . . less so."

"Might I ask why?"

He shifted uneasily. "I don't wish to speak ill of Effie's aunt. She is well-intentioned and truly wanted to help. But she was neither organized nor good with the servants, sorry to say. Between us, her departure is something of a relief. Though we will of course visit her when we can."

Sarah nodded her understanding but remained silent. She felt oddly relieved at the news but could not say why. Or at least she refused to admit the reason even to herself.

EIGHT

Christmas is a-coming, the goose is getting fat. Please put
 a penny in the old man's hat;
If you haven't got a penny, a ha'penny will do, If you
 haven't got a ha'penny then God bless you!
 —Old English Christmas song

The following day, Viola, Claire, and Mira joined them at Sea View. They all gathered in the dining room to assemble their St. Thomas Day gifts for the poor-house residents: brown paper parcels of Sarah's baked treats tied with ribbon and sprigs of holly. The knitted scarves, mittens, and stockings, and small pots of preserves. Emily also planned to buy imported sweet oranges to add to their offerings as soon as she finished an editing project for the local publisher.

They had decided to include simple cards, so artistic Claire had brought over her art supplies to help with the project. While Claire drew the outlines of holly, ivy, and candles ringed in evergreens, Georgie, Effie, and Mira happily colored them in and folded the cards.

They made extra to take to ailing Mrs. Limbrick. They added a few additional items, including a quantity of wheat, which was quite expensive, to this final basket that they would deliver to the woman that very day.

Mr. Henshall assisted them throughout, carrying trays of baked goods from the workroom belowstairs, sorting supplies, and tying parcels. Without fanfare, he contributed coins for the enterprise as well.

Sarah was impressed. "Very generous, thank you."

He shrugged off her praise. "'Tis only a trifle."

"Not to them, it won't be. And not to me."

He held her gaze. "Then I am glad to do it."

She became aware of her sisters watching them with eager expressions and turned away to busy herself elsewhere.

While the others finished the preparations for the poor house, Georgiana and Mamma set out to visit Mrs. Limbrick. Georgiana carried the basket, and Chips trotted along at her side.

The woman lived in The Retreat, a lodging house on Church Street in a less affluent part of Sidmouth with no view of the sea.

Inside the house, the smells of damp and cabbage met them. They found the door marked *D* at the end of the passageway and knocked.

The door opened more quickly than Georgiana would have expected. A young girl stood there, looking up at them in surprise. A familiar girl.

"Cora? What are you doing here?" Georgie asked. "Should you not be at school?"

"Stayed home today. My nan is feeling poorly."

Georgie turned to introduce her companion. "This is my mother, Mrs. Summers. Mamma, this is Cora. Mrs. Limbrick's granddaughter."

"Ah, Cora! Georgiana speaks of you often and fondly."

Cora gave her a shy smile, although worry still shadowed her eyes.

Georgie lifted the basket. "We've brought some things for your grandmother. But if she is not equal to visitors . . . ?"

"I dunno. I shall ask her." The girl turned and dashed into the next room, leaving them standing in the dank passage.

They heard "Nan? Miss Georgie and her mum are here. Can they come in and see you? They've brought you something."

"Yes, of course. Show them in, although I no doubt look a fright."

Cora returned to them. "She says come in."

As they stepped inside, Georgie closed the door behind them and took in the small parlour—not squalid but certainly humble. Chilly as well.

They followed Cora to the open door of the bedchamber, which held two narrow beds. An elderly woman lay in one, covered with several blankets.

They introduced themselves and made polite conversation, asking how long the two had been in Sidmouth and where they were from originally.

The woman replied, "Over a year now. Came from Longhope, in Gloucestershire."

"Ah! We are from May Hill," Mamma replied, expression brightening. "A small village three or four miles north of there."

"Oh yes. I remember visiting the hill as a girl."

Mamma said, "I went to school with a Miss Esther Limbrick. Any relation?"

A smile broke over the woman's face. "You never! Esther was my daughter. And Cora's mum. Sadly, we lost her and her husband several years back."

"I am terribly sorry for your loss. Both of you."

The woman nodded. "It's been hard, I can't deny. But at least Cora and I have each other." She sent her granddaughter a fond look.

Cora came over and took her hand. "That's right, Nan. We get on perfectly well, the two of us."

Mamma studied Cora and said, "It has been many years, but seeing you . . . yes. There is a marked resemblance to the young lady I remember."

"I look like her?" Cora asked.

"Indeed you do."

"I am glad."

Mamma turned back to Mrs. Limbrick. "Cora is so young, while my youngest here is already seventeen. Hard to believe her mother and I were at school together."

"You married quite young," Georgie reminded her.

"True. And as I remember, Esther was determined not to marry for any inducement other than true love."

Mrs. Limbrick nodded. "That was my Esther. She waited many years to find her Mr. Griffith, and how she loved him."

Silence fell after that, and to fill it, Georgie gestured toward the items in the basket. "We've brought some bread rolls and preserves. Oh, and this is a jar of Mrs. Besley's chicken soup, which always makes me feel better when I'm poorly. And some nice warm stockings and mittens too."

"Thank you, my dear. Very kind."

Cora accepted the basket on her behalf and carried it into the other room.

"Is there anything else you need?" Mamma asked. "Some tonic from the apothecary, perhaps? Or we could ask Dr. Clarke to call?"

"No need. I saw him shortly after we arrived. He recommended sea air and sea bathing. I did try them, to little effect."

Georgie nodded. "He recommended the same to Mamma, and though she was reluctant, sea bathing helped her a great deal. Long walks too . . ." Taking in the woman's pallor and frailty, she swallowed and amended, "Although, of course, it does not help everyone."

They left a short while later, Georgie's usually buoyant spirits dampened by the visit, her heart going out to the woman. Going out to them both.

"I wish there was more we could do for them," Georgiana said.

"So do I, my dear. So do I. For now, let's pray for Mrs. Limbrick, shall we?"

Georgiana nodded and took her hand. "Yes, let's."

Late that afternoon, Emily came into the library carrying a manuscript. "I have not yet bought oranges for the poor house." She lifted the stack of pages in her hands. "I am still editing this for Mr. Wallis, so I can't go myself. Would you mind? Russell's has them three for a penny."

Sarah rose with a sigh. "I suppose not. Though I wish you would have asked me earlier. It will be dark soon. Will one for each resident suffice?"

"Yes, thank you."

Sarah donned a warm pelisse, bonnet, and gloves and set out, market basket over her arm.

She walked into the eastern town and through the marketplace until she reached their favorite fruiterer, the shop marked by a hanging-melon trade sign. Lamplight illuminated the shop's interior. Its window displayed pyramids of imported oranges and lemons, fruit-basket gifts, and even a prized pineapple. In front of the small shop sat baskets of apples and pears, which were no doubt taken inside when the weather turned too frosty.

Through the window, she recognized a familiar figure standing near the oranges. He looked up as if aware of her gaze, and a warm smile transformed his face.

She stepped inside, the shop bell jingling in her wake.

"Mr. Henshall! I am surprised to find you here. I am not following you, I promise. Emily sent me here on an errand."

"That's odd. She asked me to do an errand for her as well."

"To buy oranges?"

"Aye. In fact, she made a point of telling me the oranges in this shop were the best in town."

"What a schemer!"

He chuckled. "Apparently your sister is in favor of a . . ." With a glance at the shopkeeper and the few milling customers, he broke off.

A . . . what? Sarah wondered what he'd been about to say. *A match between us?*

He stepped closer and lowered his voice. "Of you and I spending time together."

Sarah felt her neck grow warm. "Perhaps, though I really do think she wants oranges for the poor house."

"Not a complete ruse, then? I shall purchase them, if ye don't mind. I said I would and am happy to do so."

"Very well."

A few minutes later, they exited the shop, a mound of oranges in Sarah's basket, which he offered to carry for her.

Glancing up the street, she noticed a crowd standing outside one of the shops. "I wonder what is going on there?"

He followed her gaze. "Shall we walk over and see? I am not in a hurry, if you're not."

"I own I am curious." Together they strolled up the street.

"Oh!" Sarah said as they drew nearer. "That's the print shop. Emily mentioned a new window display for the holidays."

They waited their turn to step close and look at the "illuminations" in the panes of the print-shop windows. The translucent colored prints had been varnished and lit from behind, causing the scenes to glow with light and life, drawing admirers and shoppers alike.

Sarah recognized the ruins of Tintern Abbey by moonlight, a London street scene, and another depicting fireworks in Green Park to celebrate the Treaty of Paris.

"This is Tintern Abbey." She pointed to the image. "We stopped there during our journey north."

He bent to look more closely. As he straightened, another caught his eye. "Ah. And here is the Palace of Holyroodhouse by night."

Someone had painstakingly cut out dozens of tiny windows, and the light shone through them in a bright, realistic way.

"We visited the palace when we were in Edinburgh," Sarah said.

"I wish I had been there with ye."

"So do I."

When he was silent, she glanced over and found him standing close, looking at her instead of the illuminations.

She swallowed. "Well. The palace looks lovely by lamplight."

His focus remained on her. "So do you."

Gratification warmed Sarah's heart.

He offered her his free arm. "May I walk ye home, miss?"

She smiled softly in reply and laced her arm through his. "You may."

On St. Thomas Day, Sarah and the others gathered in the hall, waiting for Viola and Jack to come from Westmount in their carriage. When they arrived, Jack helped Mr. Henshall and Mr. Gwilt carry out the heavier baskets, while the others carried the lighter items. Mamma, however, had decided to stay home and rest. She said she was feeling tired after a poor night's sleep. Sarah hoped that's all it was.

Viola and Effie rode in the carriage with the gifts, while Jack, Sarah, Georgie, and Mr. Henshall walked, the Scotsman carrying his guitar case. Thankfully the December day was temperate and sunny, far milder than the bitter cold and heavy snow of the previous winter.

Arriving at the poor house, they all helped carry the gifts inside while Effie held the door.

Miss Reed was no longer in residence, having married Simon Hornbeam, but their dear friend Mrs. Denby was still there, as were two retired fishermen, and a few new residents they had yet to meet.

Viola went around knocking on the residents' doors to announce their arrival and came back pushing Mrs. Denby in her wheeled chair.

When all had gathered, they passed out gifts to sincere exclamations of appreciation, and Sarah noticed one elderly man discreetly wipe a tear from his eye.

"I don't suppose you'd care for a song?" Mr. Henshall asked with a lift of his instrument case.

Mrs. Denby answered for them all. "Indeed we would. What a treat!"

He opened his case, and one of the old fishermen asked, "What's that, then?"

"A Scottish *guittar.*"

"Never heard 'a one of them. Let's hear it."

He led them first in an old Christmas carol sung in the West Country for hundreds of years.

> "The first Nowel that the Angel did say
> Was to certain poor Shepherds in fields where they lay;
> In fields where they lay, keeping their sheep,
> In a cold Winter's night that was so deep.
> Nowel, Nowel, Nowel, Nowel, Born is the King of Israel."

The residents joined in, warbly voices and shining faces raised. When the song ended, everyone applauded, and Mrs. Denby asked for another. Mr. Henshall led them in another traditional carol, "God Rest Ye Merry, Gentlemen."

As he played and sang, Sarah admired his handsome face earnestly intent on his song, and his rich, pleasing voice. His fingers moved skillfully over the guitar strings, and she recalled him trying to teach her to play at a summer picnic during his last visit. He'd knelt behind her, his arms around her, his hands on hers, guiding her fingers to the strings. She'd felt his breath tickling her ear, and the warmth of his chest at her back, the close position strangely intimate and thrilling. . . .

People around her began clapping, which yanked Sarah from her reverie back to the present. She belatedly joined the applause.

After the singing, they remained awhile longer to chat with the residents. Mrs. Denby summoned Sarah over and asked to meet "your young man."

Hoping he did not notice the flush surely moving up her neck, Sarah introduced the two.

"Ah yes," he politely replied. "We met in passing the night of the flood, though I don't believe we were formally introduced. An honor, ma'am."

"You're a handsome one. Fine voice too. And a keen eye if you've taken notice of our Sarah here. What a catch she would be, pretty and kind and an excellent baker too. . . ."

Supremely self-conscious to be praised in Mr. Henshall's hearing, Sarah felt the flush scald her cheeks now as well.

"I have indeed taken notice, and I wholeheartedly agree with ye." He gave the woman a crooked grin.

Pleasure flowed through Sarah at his words, and Mrs. Denby giggled in delight. Though her laughter ended in a cough.

Viola was instantly at her side. "Are you all right?"

"Oh yes. Throat's a little dry from all that singing."

Then, after wishing them a happy Christmas, they bid the dear folks farewell. Viola helped Mrs. Denby back to her room, with a promise to collect her for the Christmas services followed by dinner with the family.

As they left, Sarah walked beside Mr. Henshall. "Thank you. Music was an excellent addition to our gift giving, and we all enjoyed hearing you play."

"My pleasure, Miss Summers. Any time."

When Sarah returned to Sea View, she went belowstairs to see if Mrs. Besley had started a batch of wassail, but their cook was not in the kitchen. Lowen was sitting in a chair in the corner, peeling parsnips. He said, "She's feeling poorly today. Went back to her room."

"Oh no, what's wrong?"

He hesitated. "Better ask her."

Although the two elderly retainers were of similar age, usually it was Lowen who was laid low with some ailment or another. Mrs. Besley had remained hale and spry, at least compared to him.

Concern flaring, Sarah went down the passage and knocked on the door to the cook's bedchamber.

"Come in."

Sarah tentatively opened the door and was disconcerted to see Mrs. Besley in bed during the day, something Sarah had never witnessed before. Her foot was wrapped in flannel and propped on a pillow.

"Sorry, Miss Sarah. This foot is paining me something fierce."

"Oh dear. Did you injure it somehow?"

"No, miss. I'm embarrassed to say it's an attack of the gout. Plagued my mother too, when she was even younger than I am. Thought I'd escaped it, but no."

Sarah's concern mounted. Gout could be debilitating. "Are you sure that's what it is? I thought only men suffered from gout."

"More men, yes. Though women too. Runs in my family, sad to say. No doubt all the rich food I prepare and partake of here does not help."

"Shall I call for the doctor?"

"No need. Though if someone could find the Epsom salts and

76

perhaps buy some oil of wormwood from the apothecary? And goutweed, if he has any?"

"Of course. Straightaway."

Sarah tasked Mr. Gwilt with the errand, then returned to her workroom, thoughts in a tangle. First Emily leaving and now their cook laid up? Was God trying to tell her something? She pushed the unhappy notion aside and began preparing the batch of wassail—spiced cider topped with roasted apple slices—as well as gingerbread and small mince pies. She knew some groups of men or lads went "wassailing" on St. Thomas Day, while others did so on Christmas Eve, Christmas Day, or even Twelfth Night. Either way, she wanted to be prepared.

Since moving to Sidmouth, Sarah had learned that in cider-producing counties like Devonshire and Somerset the old wassailing tradition also included blessing the apple trees in local orchards in hopes of an abundant harvest in the coming year.

Sure enough, at dusk, a group of young men and boys came up Sea View's drive, their leader carrying a lantern. Sarah recognized the apprentice Billy Hook among them—the lad who shot through Woolbrook's nursery window during the Duke and Duchess of Kent's stay last year.

The group sang,

> "Wassail! Wassail! All over the town!
> Our toast it is white and our drink it is brown; Our bowl
> it is made of the white maple tree; With the wassailing
> bowl, we'll sing to thee."

And,

> "Here we come a-wassailing
> Among the leaves so green;
> Here we come a-wand'ring
> So fair to be seen.
>
> Love and joy come to you,
> And to you your wassail too;
> And God bless you and send you a Happy New Year."

Drawn by their singing, more boisterous than melodious, people from around the house gathered at the door. Georgie opened it and stood there listening, arms crossed.

When they finished singing, they held out earthenware cups, which this group carried instead of one large bowl.

Georgiana said, "You're a bit early, Billy Hook. Are you not?"

"Not a bit of it. It's the day for charitable giving, after all." He winked and held forth his cup.

Sarah brought out the gingerbread and mince pies, while Mr. Henshall carried the heavier pitcher of cider. Together they walked among the group, distributing their rewards. Mr. Henshall paused to clap one youth on the shoulder, saying, "Fine voice, lad."

The ginger-haired boy flushed as red as his hair with equal parts pleasure and embarrassment.

The revelers wished them prosperity, drank to their health, and then moved on to another house.

Sarah watched them go, then turned to Mr. Henshall. "After that raucous music, I think we need something pleasanter to ease our ears. Will you oblige us?"

"Twice in one day?" he asked, brows high. "I don't wish to weary ye with my simple songs."

"Not at all," Sarah encouraged him. "I for one should never tire of hearing you."

He looked at her quickly at that, as did the others. Sarah's ears heated. *Ease our ears*, indeed. She attempted an unaffected smile and gestured them all into the parlour.

NINE

No lace. No lace, Mrs. Bennett, I beg you!
—*Pride and Prejudice* (1995 screenplay)

The next day, Mr. Henshall came and found Sarah in the library-office. "I wonder if ye might help me with something?"

"Of course, if I am able."

"I face a feat nigh on impossible. One that has defeated many a man before me."

"Good heavens. As bad as that?"

"Aye." Grim humor glimmered in his eyes. "For I risk fierce censure from a treasured female should I fail."

A treasured female? Was he referring to her? Or to someone else? Her mouth dried. She swallowed and managed, "Go on."

"Will ye help me choose a gift for Effie?"

"Oh." Disappointment flared, then quickly faded as he continued.

"Last year's wool stockings and Fair Isle *kep*—a knitted cap— earned me a week's cold shoulder. She accused me of trying to dress her like a cod fisherman."

"I see." Sarah bit back a smile. "Practical choices to be sure."

"I thought so. Though clearly not what a girl wants. So will ye help? I took her to a few shops here hoping she would take interest in something and give me a clue. But little seemed to please her."

"I am not sure I shall succeed in pleasing her either, but I will certainly offer what assistance I can."

"I'd appreciate it. When might ye have time?"

With their cook ailing, Sarah really shouldn't go but found she could not resist. "How soon were you hoping to give her a gift?"

"New Year's Day, or Twelfth Night, perhaps? What is customary here?"

"Varies by family. But we can surely find something before then. Shall we say this afternoon?"

"Perfect."

Georgie returned to the charity school that day, and Colin Hutton tagged along, saying he was on his way to the eastern town anyway to do some errands.

On this visit, they did not see scrappy Cora among the children playing in the schoolyard, and Georgie wondered if she had stayed home with her ailing grandmother again.

When Mr. Ward stepped outside, Georgie asked him, "Where is Cora?"

He winced and pointed inside. They looked through the door and saw Cora huddled in a corner, sobbing. A few girls were gathered around her, trying to comfort her.

"What's happened?" Colin asked.

"Her grandmother died," Mr. Ward replied. "Her last living relative, as far as we know."

"Oh no. What will become of her?"

"We shall meet with the governors to decide what is best to be done. We shall likely have to send her to the orphanage in Exeter. The vicar has offered to give her a place as a scullery maid, so that is an option as well."

"Surely she is too young to enter service," Colin said. "She is only, what, eight or nine?"

"What else would you suggest?"

"I . . . well, there must be something. Orphanages are rather bleak prospects, are they not?"

"Some are, yes. And all the more for a gentlewoman's granddaughter."

Colin asked, "How did Cora's parents die?"

"Carriage accident. Cora has lived with her grandmother since then. Or had."

"How dreadful."

"Yes. Life is often difficult. Especially for vulnerable children."

"Poor Cora," Georgie murmured.

"Indeed. I am surprised she is here," Colin said, "given her recent loss."

"Are you? When she has friends and a warm fire here and an empty pair of cold rooms at home? I know which I would choose."

Georgie nodded. "Good point. So would I."

Mr. Ward opened the door for them. Seeing the visitors enter, the other girls moved back to give them room. Georgie sat on one side of the grieving girl, Colin on the other.

"We are so sorry to hear about your grandmother."

Still sniffling, the girl nodded, head bowed. "She was all the family I had. And very good to me she was too."

"I am truly sorry," Georgie repeated. "We both are. And we can relate, at least in part. I've lost my father, and Colin here, his mother and brother. Are you certain you have no other relatives? An aunt or uncle or cousin?"

"Not that I know of."

"Don't lose heart, Cora. You are not alone. You have friends like us, not to mention your schoolfellows."

"Not the same, though, is it? As having someone who loves you and cares for you?"

"No, I suppose it is not."

They stayed for several minutes longer. Then Colin excused himself to continue his errands. Before he left, they made plans to return to the school the next morning to see how Cora fared.

Georgie did not really feel like playing ball after learning of Cora's loss, but the other students cajoled her into joining them for a game, which with Georgie was rarely difficult to do. Her spiritless opening kick quickly blossomed into an energetic, full-blown match.

Soon Cora came out to watch. When a ball rolled in her direction, she instinctively chased after it at the same time Georgie did.

Georgie raised her hands to try to prevent a collision, but the two ran into each other. Cora fell into her arms and held on tight.

For several moments, they stood that way, Georgie patting the girl's back. Then Cora straightened, wiped a sleeve over her eyes, and said, "Now, let's play."

On their shopping excursion that afternoon, Sarah and Mr. Henshall stopped first at Wallis's Marine Library, a circulating library that also sold prints, local guides, sheet music, and more.

"You mentioned Effie plays guitar and mandolin, so perhaps sheet music?"

"Good idea, although she mostly plays by ear. And no books, or she'll accuse me of trying to make her learn something. She's still opposed to more schooling."

"Very well. Let's move on."

They next visited a modiste and milliner.

"Perhaps ruffles, to add to a dress?" Sarah suggested.

He shook his head. "If I bought her something as impractical as ruffles, she would die of shock—and know straightaway I had not picked them out."

Sarah chuckled and could not contradict him.

He then inspected an embroidered handkerchief, but Sarah told him she could make one finer for a fraction of the price.

Sarah hesitated at a selection of embroidered dancing slippers. "These are lovely. And I recall you saying Effie likes to dance."

"Aye. She's a bit young to attend formal balls, but she loves to dance at neighbors' parties or *cèilidhs*."

Sarah tried the foreign word, "'Kay-lees.'"

He nodded. "Although Effie is often mortified by all my boisterous stomping and whooping."

"In that case, should we avoid dancing at our Twelfth Night party?"

"Not on my account. I wouldna suspend your pleasure for worlds."

"It's Georgie who requested dancing. And I'm determined to give her a festive Christmastide if it kills me."

It was his turn to chuckle. "Now that I wouldna like."

They continued through town, looking in windows at displays of elaborately decorated Twelfth Night cakes, star-shaped iced biscuits, and other pastries at the bakery, and every sweet dainty imaginable at the confectioner's. They stopped at a jeweler's and admired the gold chains, earrings, brooches, and rosewood jewelry boxes on offer.

"I know she already has her mother's necklace and earrings," Sarah began. "But perhaps something simpler for daily wear like this gold cross or this one of amber?"

He bent to look closer. "Both are nice. Which do ye prefer?"

"I like the simple gold cross, but I don't know that Effie would share my taste."

"I shall give it some thought before I decide."

In the stationer's they looked at embossed writing paper, memorandum books, ink, and other supplies.

He picked up a penknife.

Sarah shook her head and gently took it from him, returning it to the shelf. "Too practical."

They stopped next at the Nicholls lace shop. They looked at the finished articles of lace in the display window, including collars, fichus, and handkerchiefs edged in queen shell lace.

"Devonshire is famous for its lace, but I suppose it's a bit dear."

"Lovely work, though I wonder if Effie is old enough to appreciate all the fine skill and time that goes into making something like that."

They moved on. Passing a secondhand shop, Sarah spied a tambourine in the window. "I don't suppose Effie would like that?"

"She might indeed." He grinned. "But would the rest of us like the clatter?"

"Good point."

In the end, he purchased a plain pair of dancing slippers that Sarah assured him she could embroider by Twelfth Night.

"With everything else ye have to do?"

"It will be my pleasure."

"In that case, may I treat you to some refreshment? Georgiana and Effie tell me the cakes at the York Hotel are excellent."

"I am not hungry, but tea sounds heavenly. Thank you."

When they reached the hotel, a waiter seated them and took their order. While they awaited their tea, Sarah realized a few of her female acquaintances were there and watching them with interest. And one, Mrs. Robins, with disapproval.

They were doing nothing untoward, Sarah reminded herself. A public place. A family friend . . . And as she and Mr. Henshall began relishing their tea and conversation, Sarah forgot to care about what anyone else might think.

"You mentioned Effie is opposed to more schooling?"

"Aye. We had a few governesses in the past. She found fault with every one of them and none lasted long. I suppose I should try again. She is also opposed to the idea of going away to a girls' school, and after losing her mother, I didna have the heart to insist. Katrin's sister offered to take Effie's education in hand, but I wasna keen on the idea. She is well-intentioned, as I've said, but a bit—what is the term here—scatterbrained?"

Sarah nodded. "When we visited, I noticed she had a slight limp."

"Did she? It was gone by the time we got home. The woman is forever striking her toe on something. Forgets to look where she's going."

"Oh."

"I hope ye don't think less of me for saying so."

"And I hope you don't take a severe view of women in general."

"I do not. In fact, I am thoroughly impressed with you, Miss Summers. You're gracious and capable, kind and lovely, and"—he smiled softly—"not scatterbrained in the least."

Sarah smiled in reply and finished her tea. Then she glanced at the clock in the corner and was startled to see the time. The errand had taken longer than she'd realized. She set down her cup and said, "And now I really must return home. Mrs. Besley is unwell, and I need to assist her in the kitchen."

She rose, and he followed suit.

"Might I lend a hand? I would be happy to help."

"And I would be happy to accept, thank you."

On her way home from the school, Georgiana walked down Fore Street, past several shops, still having no idea what she might buy for her mother and sisters for Christmas, and still having no money to buy anything even had she an idea.

She thought she glimpsed Sarah and Mr. Henshall walking down a side street together but they were too far away to hail.

She looked ahead, and her steps faltered. There stood Colin Hutton talking with Miss Marriott outside a millinery shop.

For a moment, Georgiana considered cutting through an alley to avoid them, but she trudged on, continuing along her intended path home.

At the sound of her footfalls, Miss Marriott turned. Colin, meanwhile, seemed oblivious to anyone but the elegant Eliza.

"Good day, Georgiana." The young woman's gaze fell to her hems. "You have been . . . enjoying the outdoors again, I see."

"I've just come from the school," Georgie replied. "Played ball with the children there, as I often do." She gave her skirt a few downward tugs, trying to hide her muddied petticoat.

"I'm surprised they played today. Mr. Hutton was just telling me about the poor orphan girl there."

"I think the game cheered us all. Even Cora."

Eliza went on as though Georgiana had not spoken. "I admit her loss reminds me of my own dear Mamma, gone these many years."

"I am sorry," Colin said. "And I quite understand."

After a few moments' silence, Eliza regarded Georgiana once more. "How good you are. How . . . playful. Though I suppose you are still practically a child yourself."

"I am not a child, Miss Marriott."

Colin said, "Though you are indeed a sportive girl, Miss Georgiana. I have often said so."

"I admire your freedom," added Miss Marriott. "My stepmother would never approve of me running wildly about like that. I fear she would call me a hoyden."

Eliza nodded toward the shop window. "She is in there now, selecting a new white fichu or tippet for my Christmas gift. I shall pretend to be surprised, of course."

She turned back. "And you, Miss Georgiana. Have you settled on gifts yet for your mother and sisters?"

"Not yet."

"I have decided to follow the lead of Mr. Hutton here and purchase cologne for my father and perfume for my stepmother."

"How nice."

"And how will you celebrate the holidays?" Colin asked Eliza.

"Oh, just a quiet observance with my father and stepmother. Church, a good dinner, and a few gifts."

He smiled. "That does sound . . . pleasant, although quiet indeed. We have all been invited to Sea View. There's to be an evening party on Christmas Eve and a party on Twelfth Night as well. You ought to join us. Your family would not mind, would they, Miss Georgiana? I know it's not my place to extend an invitation, but they have made me feel like almost one of the family."

"I could not," Eliza demurred. "I would not wish to intrude."

"Your feelings do you credit. Leave it with me. I will talk to Mrs. Summers and fix it up. Temple Cottage, you said? If you will allow me, I shall pay a call soon."

"Very well. Now I had better rejoin my stepmother. Good day, Mr. Hutton. Georgiana." She turned and entered the shop.

When the door closed behind her, Colin sent Georgiana a sidelong glance. "I hope you don't think that was terribly presumptuous of me. But your lovely friend looks like she could use some enjoyment in her life."

It was on the tip of Georgiana's tongue to retort that Miss Marriott was not her friend, but she resisted. That would be petty of her, quite unlike herself, and not completely true. What was wrong with her?

When Georgiana returned home, she went looking for her mother and found her belowstairs with their cook. Mrs. Besley was sitting in a chair, soaking her gouty foot in a tub of warm Epsom-salt water while Mamma sagged against the worktable, displaying none of her usual excellent posture.

Georgie told them what she'd learned about Cora.

Mamma turned to Mrs. Besley to explain who Cora was, and the woman nodded and said, "Oh yes, I've heard Miss Georgie speak of her. And I sent chicken soup for the girl's grandmother, remember? God rest her."

Mamma turned back to Georgie. "How very sad, my dear. And how kind of you to take an interest."

"I wish there was more we could do."

Mrs. Besley clucked her tongue in sympathy. "Has she no other family?"

"Apparently not."

"Where is she now?" Mamma asked. "I do hate the thought of a girl like her, so recently bereaved, spending Christmas on her own."

"Mr. Ward said the governors will have to decide whether to send her to the Exeter orphanage. Otherwise, Mr. Jenkins has offered her a situation as scullery maid."

Mamma frowned and straightened. "A scullery maid! Esther Limbrick's daughter? I think not."

Mrs. Besley said, "I don't like to speak ill of anyone, missus, and the vicar and his wife seem kindly enough, but their cook?" She adamantly shook her head. "I'd not send a sweet little girl into Beulah Browland's kitchen for worlds."

"Good heavens. As bad as that? We can do better for the girl, I hope." Mamma turned back to Georgie. "When are the governors meeting?"

"I'm not certain," she replied. "But I will find out tomorrow."

"Be sure you do," Mamma said sharply.

Georgiana reared her head back in surprise. It wasn't like her mother to be snappish.

Noticing her reaction, Mamma said more gently, "Sorry, my dear. It's only that I am anxious for her."

"I understand."

Sarah came in, followed by Mr. Henshall.

She looked from Georgie to their mother and said, "Ah, good. Reinforcements. You will both help us prepare dinner, I trust?"

After dinner that evening, Sarah overheard Effie and Georgiana talking—arguing, really—and crossed the hall to the parlour to see what was wrong.

Effie stomped out past her and started up the stairs.

"What is it, Effie? What's happened?"

"Georgie thinks she's too good for me now. Too grown-up."

That did not sound like her little sister. "I am sure that is not so. . . ."

But the girl continued her march up the stairs.

Sarah went into the parlour and found Georgie slumped in a chair near the fire, a tangle of needlework on her lap. Needlework! And with Mamma not present to insist?

"What is it? Effie is upset, and you don't look much happier."

Georgie sighed. "I did not mean to anger her or injure her feelings. She wants to put on another play, like we did when she was last here, maybe recruit Mr. Gwilt to help us again."

"That sounds . . . diverting. You enjoyed it the last time, I recall."

"I did. But perhaps it's time I outgrew childish things like play-acting."

Sarah watched her usually cheerful, carefree sister in concern. "Has someone said something to make you think that? Made fun of you, or teased you unkindly? I believe you saw Colin Hutton earlier today. Did he . . . ?"

"No. Though I passed him and Eliza Marriott chatting on the street and . . . She said nothing wrong either. In fact, she was perfectly polite. Perfectly ladylike and elegant. And there I stood with my petticoat six inches deep in mud after playing with the schoolchildren—as though I were a child myself."

"Ah. I see." Understanding dawned. "She is several years older than you are," Sarah gently reminded her. "You needn't compare yourself to her."

"I know. She is nearer to Colin's age than I am. And how he admires her." Georgie shook her head.

"Do you think . . . Well, do you think it's possible you've unintentionally made Effie feel a little like Miss Marriott made you feel?"

Georgie gaped up at her, realization widening her eyes. "Oh no, I'll wager I did! Never meant to, though."

"I know you are growing up, but you are never too old to do something you love."

Even as Sarah said the words, the irony struck her. Apparently her sister noticed as well.

"What about you?" Georgie looked at her thoughtfully. "You never do childish things or indulge in pastimes you enjoyed in girlhood. Or are you telling me you were born hardworking and practical?"

Had she been? Or had she felt duty bound to become that way?

"Sometimes I think I was," Sarah replied. "But you're right. I don't take time to enjoy things I used to as much as I ought. Except needlework. I've always enjoyed that."

Georgie rose and handed Sarah her tangled thread and fabric. "Then you may have mine, and good riddance. And I shall go and apologize to Effie and ask what sort of play she wants to perform."

Sarah patted her arm. "Well done, my dear."

As her sister walked away, the irony lingered. Perhaps it was time Sarah began taking her own advice.

TEN

This is quite the season indeed for friendly meetings.
At Christmas everybody invites their friends about them,
and people think little of even the worst weather.

—Jane Austen, *Emma*

The next morning as previously arranged, Colin met Georgiana on Glen Lane, and the two set out for the school together. As they walked along the esplanade, pretty Miss Marriott came up from the beach, basket in hand, and waved to them.

"Ah, Mr. Hutton, a pleasure to see you again so soon. And you, Georgiana."

Colin bowed. "Miss Marriott."

"I was just telling my father about you over breakfast. Now he is eager to meet you, being some acquainted with your brother. Won't you walk with me to our house? You could also view my conchology collection while you're there."

Colin hesitated. "We were on our way to the school, but I . . . suppose I could always go there later. I would enjoy seeing your collection and meeting your father. Thank you. You don't mind, do you, Georgiana?"

"Not at all," Georgie lied.

"Capital. That's sporting of you."

With a vague nod to her, Colin offered the enchanting Miss Marriott his arm, and the two walked away together.

With a little huff, Georgiana watched them go. Then she continued on to the school alone to ask Mr. Ward about the meeting and to see how Cora fared.

But Cora was not there.

"What do you mean Cora is not here?" Georgie asked.

"She has moved into the vicarage. I believe I mentioned that might happen?"

"Y-yes. Though I didn't realize you meant so soon. Have the governors already met?"

"No, they meet this evening. But the landlord rented her grandmother's apartment to someone else. Cora needed somewhere to sleep."

"Will she be able to attend school?"

"Not while in service, no. If it is any comfort, I doubt she would be well educated in the orphanage either."

"How sad. She loves it here."

"Yes, but a good situation is worth a great deal in this day and age."

"I . . . suppose," Georgiana replied, although she was not convinced.

Disheartened by the news, Georgie did not remain long at the school, and instead trudged home. Soon after she returned to Sea View, Colin came over fresh from his visit to Temple Cottage to apologize.

"Sorry about that. I hope you truly did not mind?"

"Of course not. I've been visiting the school on my own for months now. How did you find the shells?"

"Multitudinous. Who knew there were so many kinds? Her parents seemed nice, though. How is Cora?"

Georgie explained all he had missed that morning.

"Poor girl."

"Yes, although I believe the vicar and his wife will be kind to her."

"Still . . . to be thrust into service, at her age?"

"I know. I have to clean our water closet and make my share of beds, but at least what I do helps my family, people who love me."

He slowly nodded, expression troubled. Georgie knew how he felt.

Mamma invited Colin to stay for luncheon. He agreed and sat down with the Summerses, along with their guests. Throughout the meal, Georgiana noticed Colin glance from Sarah to Mr. Henshall more than once.

Afterward, Colin followed Georgie out of the dining room and asked in confidential tones, "So what's going on with your sister and this Scottish chap?"

Georgie shrugged. "He likes Sarah and she likes him, but I doubt she'll trade her responsibilities here for something as trifling as romance."

"Not a romantic yourself, Georgie? That will disappoint the local lads, I don't doubt."

"Ha."

Colin glanced back into the dining room, where Sarah lingered with Callum Henshall.

"I remember him from that cricket match against the Sidmouth fishermen. He was on the visitors' team with us. Good man to have on the pitch."

"That's right."

He looked at her, and his eyes softened in memory. "I also recall you filled in for me when we had to rush Vi to the doctor. The Scotsman insisted you be allowed to play, when others were opposed to a girl joining the game. And from what I heard afterward, you won the naysayers over with your skill."

Another shrug. "We still lost."

"Most impressive even so."

She narrowed her eyes at him. "Why are you being nice to me all of a sudden?"

He barked in laughter. "Am I usually rude or something?"

"You are usually too busy teasing and roasting me."

"True enough. At all events, do you like this man? For Sarah, I mean."

"I do, yes. If she were to marry, she could pick a far stupider person. And he did travel an awfully long way to see her again."

"Needs a little encouragement, does she?" Colin's eyes lit with mischief. "I have an idea. Why don't we help them along?"

"Help them? How?"

"Spark a little romance." He waggled his fair eyebrows.

"How on earth would we do that?"

"Poor Georgie. You truly aren't a romantic, are you? I will have to give the scheme more thought, but a few ideas spring to mind. We could make sure the two of them dance together at one of the parties your family's planning. And subtly hint that we've noticed how much the one admires the other. Oh, and of course, there must be a kissing bough. My personal favorite Christmas decoration. Does mistletoe grow around here?"

Georgie's mind reeled to keep up. "I . . . don't think so. Oh, wait! I saw a big clump of it during one of my rambles. In a tree on Vicarage Road."

He grinned. "There, you see? I knew you'd be the perfect partner in this plot. And no time to waste. Christmas Eve is tomorrow. Can you take me there now?"

"Certainly. It's a bit of a walk, though." She looked skeptically at his shiny black shoes with crimson ribbon ties and red leather heels. "You've already walked to Temple Cottage and back. Are you sure you can walk nearly the same distance again in those pointy shoes?"

"Ah. I think you mean these very stylish shoes, perfect for a pink-of-fashion like me. Would you have me be an old-fashioned square-toes?"

Georgie looked heavenward and shook her head. "Let's go. Just no complaining if your feet hurt."

She led the way across town, past the church and eventually the vicarage, which stood near the north entrance of town. The vicarage house was old but had recently been enlarged and improved.

When they neared, they saw Cora sitting on a stool outside, wearing a maid's apron and mobcap. They waved to her, and she waved back before returning to her task of plucking a chicken.

The sight saddened Georgiana.

As they passed, Colin shook his head. "To go from living with a loving grandmother and attending school to this . . . ? Can nothing be done?"

"The governors will meet tonight to decide her fate officially. I believe Mamma plans to attend and speak up on Cora's behalf. But this looks to be her future if nothing changes."

He blew out a deep breath and paused to look back.

For a long moment, the two stood there, watching the girl gingerly pull feathers from a chicken, perhaps for the first time in her life.

Then Colin said, "I suppose we had best get on."

"Yes." Georgie hesitated. "Though I've realized we might need a knife. Perhaps we could borrow one from the vicarage kitchen instead of walking all the way back for one."

"My pointy shoes approve of that plan."

They retraced their steps and asked Cora if they might borrow a knife.

"I don't know. I don't want to get into trouble. . . ." The girl worriedly chewed her lip. "But you've been so kind to me. Just one moment." She darted inside before Georgie could stop her.

"I hope she does not get into any trouble on our account."

Cora reappeared and handed them a sharp knife. "You will bring it back?"

"Of course we shall. Never fear."

Promising Cora they'd return as soon as possible, the two continued up Vicarage Road.

"There it is. See?" Georgiana pointed high into a lime tree's canopy, to a roundish bunch of green visible in the winter-bare tree branches.

He let out a low whistle. "That is higher than I imagined. How will we get it down?"

"I think there are two options. If we had a gun, we might be able to blast it down. Sadly I have no gun."

"I should hope not!"

"Have you?"

"Jack has a few, but he'd not let me anywhere near them."

"Wise man."

"And our other option?"

Georgie waggled her brows, clamped the knife between her teeth, hiked her skirts, and began climbing the tree.

"Georgie, no!" Colin called. "It's too high! If you break your neck Jack will break mine—if your sisters don't do so first. I did not mean that you should climb up."

Reaching a *Y* of the trunk that allowed her to sit, Georgie momentarily removed the knife with one hand, still holding on to a branch with the other. "Well, you were not going to do so. Not in those silly shoes! At least I'm wearing sturdy half boots."

"And a skirt! Come down, I beg of you."

"I shall. In just a few minutes more."

Clamping the knife between her teeth again, Georgiana continued the climb, more for the thrill of the challenge than any fondness for kissing boughs.

Reaching the important branch, Georgie edged her way out on the limb, which swayed beneath her weight.

"That branch is not strong enough. Stop!"

Georgie did not stop. Instead she reached out, grasped a vine-like shoot of the stuff, and yanked it closer to the trunk. Wrapping one arm around the tree for balance, she then began sawing at the mass.

Finally a tangle of mistletoe fell. Then another.

"That's enough!" he shouted up to her. "We don't need enough to have the whole town puckering up!"

The branch made an ominous cracking sound beneath her.

"Oh, Lord help us," he cried.

"I'm all right." George returned her weight fully to the trunk and then slowly and carefully made her way down, muscles trembling from the effort and the near fall.

She leapt the last few feet and landed with a *thwump* and a rush of satisfaction.

A moment later, Colin's arms were around her in a fierce hug. "You foolish, headstrong girl. You scared the life out of me."

Georgie blinked in surprise at the unexpected embrace but did not push him away.

"What are you doing?" Cora's voice called from behind them. The two quickly parted.

Colin recovered first. "The question is, What are you doing here?"

"I followed you. Had to see what you needed a knife for."

Georgie feigned composure she did not feel and pointed to the green vines on the ground. "For mistletoe, of course. Tomorrow is Christmas Eve."

"Is it? I did not realize."

Colin's usual good humor returned, and he grinned at the girl. "And will there be any festive doings at the vicarage, Cora?"

"Yes, sir. For the vicar and his wife. I think they are having some people in. Not for me, though. Except maybe a little something on Boxing Day."

Colin's grin faded.

"Well," Cora said, "I'd better get back before I'm missed."

Mistletoe in hand, they turned and walked back with her.

As they neared the vicarage, the sharp-featured cook, Mrs. Browland, met them, hands on hips. "There you are, Cora! I was about to send the constable after you. Thought you'd run off, and with my best knife!"

Colin strode forward, oozing gentlemanly charm. "Now, now, my dear madam. I take all the blame. Young Cora here was only being neighborly by helping us when I asked to borrow a knife. A thousand apologies if Cora's brief absence proved an inconvenience. And here is your knife." Never removing his focus from the woman's face, he extended a palm toward Georgiana. She paused only a moment to wipe the blade clean on her sleeve, then dutifully laid it in his hand.

"Here you are. Good as new. We sincerely appreciate your generosity and understanding. And may we wish you a happy and blessed Christmastide." He bowed to her, and the woman fairly blushed!

"Thank you, sir. Very obliging, I'm sure."

With a hidden wink at Cora, Colin walked away, Georgiana hurrying to catch up.

When they were out of earshot, she said, "Good heavens, you're a smooth-boots when you want to be. 'Very obliging, I'm sure . . .' One would think you'd given her the crown jewels instead of her own knife back."

Georgiana expected a teasing jibe in return, but Colin appeared pensive.

As if he'd not heard her, he said, "So no Christmas for Cora, then? No plum pudding or roasted chestnuts or mince pies? No carols around the fireplace?"

"I don't know," Georgie allowed. "I suppose it depends on the household and the generosity of the family. And not just for Cora but for everyone in service."

"But she's so young. It's not fair."

"No, Colin. It's not. Yet life isn't always fair, is it? I have been praying for her and will keep praying. What else can we do?"

"I don't know. I shall pray as well."

Later that afternoon Mr. Henshall found Sarah in the library-office. "It's a beautiful day," he said. "Might we go for a ride? Effie and I hired two decent mounts from the local livery when last we were here."

"I remember." He had cut a fine figure in his riding attire too, as she recalled. "Do you ride year-round at home?"

He nodded. "Except when icy conditions might endanger my horse. If we rode only on warm, dry days, we'd ride very rarely indeed, so we simply dress for the weather. We Scots are a hardy breed—our horses too. But even English horses need exercise." He grinned at her. "English ladies too."

She raised her chin. "I take plenty of exercise, with my duties around the house. Though admittedly less in the winter, since there is little gardening to do."

"I recall you mentioning you used to ride."

"Yes, but not since I was Effie's age or a little older."

"You also said you like horses."

"Goodness. You have quite a memory."

"Where you are concerned, I do indeed."

Self-conscious pleasure flowed through her. Sarah said, "Papa kept a fine stable at Finderlay. He rode regularly as a younger man. I often went with him."

"Your sisters too?"

Sarah thought back. "No. Claire was not fond of riding, and the other girls were so much younger. Emily did ride with our neighbor Charles on occasion, but by then I had given it up."

"May I ask why?"

A dull, familiar ache rose in Sarah's chest. "When our mother became ill, Claire and I assumed many of her responsibilities. Claire took charge of our younger sisters, and I helped with her duties as mistress of the house—meeting with cook and house-keeper, keeping Mamma's prized garden in order, and visiting elderly and infirm neighbors. I became too busy to ride. And then after Papa died, we had to sell the horses."

"Would you like to start riding again?"

Sarah considered. "We are in a better position financially than we were even last year, yet we are a long way from being able to afford to keep a horse."

She exhaled a deep breath. "Still, it's interesting you should ask me now. Georgiana recently spoke with a young lady a few years older and quite refined, and felt immature by comparison. When Georgiana came home, Effie suggested performing another play, and it suddenly seemed juvenile to her. I gave her some speech about never growing too old to do what you love. Even as I said the words, the irony struck me. I have given up a pastime I once loved too. Become increasingly consumed with cares and responsibilities. My parents did not tell me I had to give up riding. I did that myself."

His eyes softened in understanding. "There is nothing wrong with being responsible, Sarah. Though you are the last person I need to say that to." He reached over and took her hand. "Still, I am sorry you bore so much while you were so young. You have sacrificed a great deal for your family."

Unexpected tears heated her eyes. "Thank you. Yes, I grew up quickly. Too quickly, maybe. But there's still time for Georgie. I don't want her to rush into adulthood and lose her spark in the process. Pardon me. I am talking too much." Sliding her hand from his, she pressed her fingers to her mouth.

"Not at all. I like hearing what you think." He paused, then added with a mischievous grin, "And what I heard was that you have clearly realized the error of your ways and shall not miss an opportunity to ride with a visiting friend."

Sarah hesitated. "Even though I want to, I could not."

"Why?"

"With Mrs. Besley laid up, I have more to do in the kitchen. Besides that, I have no riding habit, and—"

"You may borrow my new one," Effie said, popping her head into the room with a smile. "You said it yourself, we are nearly the same height now."

"That does not mean it would fit . . . elsewhere."

With a frown, Mr. Henshall asked, "Effie, were ye eavesdropping?"

"It was easy enough to hear ye from the next room! And besides, it's for a good cause. I want Sarah to go riding too."

Effie turned back to Sarah and urged, "Ye can at least try on my habit, can ye not? And if it doesna fit, perhaps ye might borrow one. Maybe your mam has an old one somewhere?"

"If Mamma had one, it would be rather ancient by now. Not to mention moth-eaten."

Effie gestured to her stepfather. "Then lucky for us, this wise man insisted the habit maker allow for future growth, so there are laces at the back of both jacket and skirt. Habits are expensive, apparently."

"Ye didna think I was so wise at the time," Mr. Henshall dryly replied. "I recall the term *skinflint* being tossed at me."

"In hindsight, your miserly ways have worked out well this time. Now do come, Miss Sarah, and try it on. I'll even help in the kitchen while you're gone, if that will convince ye."

"Oh, very well," Sarah reluctantly agreed and allowed Effie to lead her away.

Over her shoulder, the girl said, "I'll get her into a riding habit one way or another while ye change and see about the horses."

A few minutes later, the two met in Sarah's room, since it was larger than Effie's. Effie carried in her new habit and spread it across Sarah's bed. The tailored jacket of sapphire blue wool was adorned with braiding on the front and the promised laces at the back. The matching skirt had a train long enough to cover the legs modestly while riding sidesaddle.

"It's lovely, Effie."

"Now to see if we can get ye into it."

The girl helped Sarah dress. The habit shirt—a short cotton chemisette with frilled collar—was loose and went on easily. The jacket was a little tight at the waist and extremely tight at the bosom, but with strenuous tugging on the laces of Sarah's long boned stays, followed by loosening the jacket laces, Effie managed to do up the fastenings. The similar lacing at the back of the skirt allowed Sarah to don that as well. She wore her own gloves and half boots, although Effie insisted Sarah wear her rather masculine-looking hat, which Effie placed atop her head and pinned to her hair.

When she was fully dressed, Sarah regarded herself in the long mirror.

"It is very becoming, Effie. But don't you wish to wear this and ride with Mr. Henshall yourself? I remember how happy you were to ride with him the summer you were here."

"I would be. Though not today. I'm . . . Well, remember that certain female affliction ye explained to me during our last visit?"

"I do."

"Well, it's upon me now, and I don't feel equal to riding. So please do go with him."

"If you are certain . . . ?"

"I am. In the meantime, I will help in the kitchen—at least until Georgie returns from wherever she went. Then she and I plan to begin writing our new play."

Sarah looked at her in surprise. "I am glad to hear it. I shall look forward to seeing it."

Effie smiled at her. "And I look forward to seeing ye enjoy yourself."

The two went downstairs together, Sarah feeling uncomfortable in the form-fitting habit and nervous as well.

From the window, she saw Mr. Henshall ride up the lane atop a chestnut horse, leading a smaller dappled grey by a lead.

Sarah went outside to join him. As he'd said, the afternoon was brisk and sunny—a typical December's day on the south coast of Devonshire.

He had changed into riding clothes before leaving the house, and once again she noticed how striking he appeared astride his horse, his posture excellent, his shoulders broad, his manner confident. In his cutaway riding coat and black boots with tan cuffs, he looked so handsome and masculine that Sarah's stomach seemed to somersault inside her.

Mr. Henshall dismounted and tied the horses to a nearby post, then turned, his gaze lingering on her face and figure. "You look lovely, Sarah."

"Thank you."

He raised a gloved hand to salute Effie, hovering in the doorway to watch them depart. "Well done, lass."

The grey mare wore a sidesaddle and regarded Sarah with part wariness, part resignation. Sarah gingerly approached and stroked her velvety muzzle, whispering, "I know how you feel."

Would she remember how to do this? Sarah hoped she neither injured nor mortified herself.

Mr. Henshall came and stood beside her. "There's an old mounting block there, or I could give you a leg up?"

"Perhaps both?" Sarah stepped atop the mounting block, and from there Mr. Henshall assisted her up into the sidesaddle. Once seated, she hooked her right knee over the pommel, while he guided her left half boot into the single stirrup. Her breath caught to see his gloved hand on her ankle.

When he'd finished, Sarah rearranged the long train of the habit, making sure her legs were fully covered. Then she picked up the reins.

The horse shied, probably unnerved by Sarah's ungainly mounting. "Easy, girl. You're all right." Sarah reached low and stroked the sleek neck, and the mare seemed to calm.

Once she was ready, Mr. Henshall remounted his own horse.

Gathering the reins, he said, "Let's start slow, till ye grow accustomed to being in the saddle again." He clicked his horse into a walk back down the drive, and the mare followed after the merest touch of the rein.

"All right?" he asked.

Sarah nodded. "So far."

To avoid busier Peak Hill Road, they rode inland, going up Glen Lane. When they had passed Westmount, he asked, "Shall we try trotting?"

"Very well."

He signaled his horse into a trot and hers reluctantly followed suit. Memories came back to her of all those long-ago rides with her father, first on a stubborn pony and later on a bay gelding.

As Sarah bounced along at a trot, she was suddenly grateful for her supportive stays.

"May we canter instead?" she asked.

"If you're ready."

"I am." She urged the mare into a canter, and this time it was his horse who followed suit. Soon, Sarah was rising and falling with the rolling gait. As she settled into a smooth rhythm, pleasure filled her. She smiled over at him. "I have missed this. Thank you for suggesting it."

They turned onto a quiet bridle path he had discovered during his previous visits to Sidmouth. As they rode along it, her trepidation faded, and she relished the exhilarating freedom of riding companionably on a sweet, well-trained horse. How could she have forgotten?

She looked around as they rode. Even in December, the hedgerows were still green, and hardy birds that stayed all year sang in the trees, some tenaciously holding on to their leaves, and the occasional Scots pine standing green and regal among them.

The sky above was a glorious clear blue. Even though the day was mild for winter, the brisk air made her eyes water and her cheeks tingle with cold.

As they rode along the path, a quail flew up, its beating wings startling the mare. Sarah managed to keep her seat, and again calmed the horse with soothing words. "You're all right. Just a little bird. More afraid of you than you are of him."

They rode on, trotting up a gentle rise until they reached a small grove of trees partway up Peak Hill.

"We had a picnic here that summer," she said.

"I remember."

They reined in their horses next to each other, the train of her skirt brushing his leg.

"You tried to show me how to play your guitar."

"An excuse to be close to ye, as ye probably guessed."

Was it? If that had been his aim, it had certainly been effective.

"How often do you play at home?" she asked.

"Daily, if I can. Music brings me peace as well as pleasure. Even when my life with Katrin was in turmoil"—his eyes took on a distant look—"I felt God's presence when I played."

Sarah thought for a moment, then confessed, "I have not often felt God's presence these last few years. I know He has not changed. I'm the one who has grown distant, busy trying to manage everything and everyone on my own." The truth of the admission pressed hard on her heart. "And yet, I have also seen God's provision in ways I never would have asked for or imagined. He is faithful, even when I am not."

Callum Henshall held her gaze, slowly nodding his understanding, and for a moment, the silence between them hummed with possibility.

Being alone with him there felt intimate and exhilarating. They were close enough to touch. Maybe even to lean across and . . . Guilt pricked her. Was it wrong to be here enjoying herself while Mrs. Besley was in pain and Effie, a guest, was at home helping her?

A squirrel scampered through the leaves, and the mare snorted and sidestepped.

Sarah pressed her lips together. "Perhaps we had better head back."

"If you wish."

As they returned to town, Sarah insisted on riding with him all the way to the stables. When they reached the livery, Mr. Henshall helped her dismount. Her legs were like jelly and nearly buckled beneath her.

He quickly put his arms around her to support her. "Careful."

"I feel like I'm still riding."

"You will regain your land legs in time."

A groom came out to take the horses.

"Why don't we sit?" Mr. Henshall suggested, pointing to a bench. "Rest a bit before walking back?"

"Actually, I think I've been sitting too long as it is. But might I take your arm until I am feeling steadier?"

"Certainly, my Jo."

She looked up at him, surprised and uncertain. Why had he called her Jo? Had he mistakenly called her by another woman's name?

As she placed her gloved hand on his sleeve, he covered it with his own and said, "I am yours to command."

And the way he said *"I am yours"* made her breath hitch.

A stagecoach rattled into the stable yard, and the guard blew a loud blast on his horn.

Sarah lurched back, hand to her racing heart. "That scared me."

But whether the horn or Callum Henshall's words had startled her more was difficult to say.

After Colin returned to Westmount to begin crafting his kissing bough, Georgie had sneaked back and climbed the lime tree again, returning home with scraped hands, streaked knees, and money in her pocket. She hurriedly washed, changed, and spent some time discussing the play with Effie before the meeting of the governors.

Sarah had not been involved at the school, so she volunteered to remain at Sea View with the Henshalls. And James was working late at Killerton. That left Georgiana, Emily, Mamma, Viola, and Jack to attend the meeting of the subscribers of the Sidmouth charity school. The special meeting was held in the school room, and the purpose was to resolve what should be done with former pupil Cora Griffith.

The vicar, the Reverend Mr. Jenkins, served as the committee's spiritual governor. Vice presidents and committee members included his wife as well as Mrs. Fulford, Lady Kennaway, Sir John Kennaway, and Sir George Cornish, among others.

The schoolmaster began by explaining the situation for those not yet informed, and then read a paragraph from Mrs. Limbrick's will, which confirmed that Cora had no other known relatives yet living. She was, as far as anyone knew, an orphan. And an impoverished one at that.

Then began a debate over the merits of sending the girl to the orphanage in Exeter compared with allowing her to remain in service at the vicarage.

Mr. Jenkins spoke of his willingness to house and provide for the orphan under his roof and under the guidance of his cook, Mrs. Browland.

That woman nodded her flinty face. "That's right. A firm hand is what's needed for young chits like her."

Georgiana huffed, incredulously and audibly. Emily's mouth fell open, and she turned on her chair, looking ready to object. Mamma, seated beside them, stood abruptly and addressed the governors. "I wonder if I might offer an alternative living situation?"

"Better than in service to our good vicar?" Mrs. Browland asked.

"I have no wish to cast aspersions on you or Mr. Jenkins, but yes. I was at school with Cora's mother. I know firsthand that theirs was a genteel, upstanding family, despite recent financial hardships. And as someone from the same parish, and well acquainted with the girl's mother, I put myself forward as a suitable guardian. I am willing to bear the responsibility of Cora's care and upbringing until she reaches her majority, and beyond that if she wishes."

Georgiana stood and clapped. She had never been so proud of her mother. Emily joined in her applause while others in attendance talked among themselves.

Viola gently pulled Georgiana back into her seat.

"Quiet. Quiet, all," one of the vice presidents demanded. "This is a respectable meeting of the school's governors, not a beer house."

The vicar asked, "And you believe you are in a better position to offer this orphan a home and a future?"

"I do. We are not wealthy, but our guest house is financially sound. Moreover, I have raised five daughters, and while not claiming perfection by any measure, I believe I am qualified to guide another girl on to adulthood."

The vicar's wife spoke up. "But we have already taken her in. Mrs. Browland . . . we . . . have need of her. Previous girls have not stayed long. The last one did not last a week."

Georgiana could well believe it.

Mamma said politely, "I am sure your offer of employment was kindly intended, Mrs. Jenkins. Even so, your cook's difficulty in keeping a scullery maid does not make this the best situation for young Cora."

Now Mrs. Browland stood, jaw jutting hard. "You mentioned her grandmother's financial problems. You know all about falling into hard times, don't you?"

At this, Jack tensed, scarred cheek stretched tight, and looked ready to leap from his chair in defense of his wife's mother. Viola grabbed his arm to stay him.

Their mother did not need the major's protection. If this woman meant to humiliate or cow Eugenia Summers, she was to be disappointed.

Mamma lifted her chin and calmly replied, "Indeed. We lost my husband, and the estate, being entailed, went to a distant male relative. But my girls and I have made a success of the guest house here, thanks to the initiative of my daughter Sarah, and we have all lent a hand. There is no shame in expending effort to provide for one's family."

"So you want a cheap servant for yourself, is that it? Perhaps a chamber maid rather than a scullery maid. But in the end it amounts to the same thing."

Again Mamma managed a calm reply. "If Cora comes to live with us, she will be expected to help around the house just as my daughters and I do. But help is not what motivates me. If I simply wanted another servant, I would engage one older and more experienced."

Before the disgruntled cook could fashion another retort, Mrs. Fulford stood and gave an impassioned appeal on their behalf, describing the Summers family as most charitable and deeply involved with both the poor house and the school. Lady Kennaway seconded her appeal.

They were well acquainted with both Mrs. Fulford and Lady Kennaway, and Georgie had known they could count on their support. Of the others, she was less certain.

Cora, as a child, was not asked nor allowed to give an opinion. But Mr. Ward spoke on her behalf, confirming Cora's fondness for Georgiana as well as her sister Mrs. Emily Thomson and her husband, who all regularly visited the school to play games or read to the children.

The vicar asked, "Even so, has the girl even met Mrs. Summers herself, the one petitioning for custody?"

"She has, sir," Mr. Ward replied. "Cora told me with great satisfaction that Mrs. Summers and Miss Georgiana visited her grandmother recently to bring gifts of food and clothing. The only people to visit the ailing woman in several weeks, I might add." He did not glance at the vicar as he said it, but others did.

The vicar looked down.

While the governors conferred among themselves, Mamma, Viola, and Jack had a private conversation that Georgie could not hear.

In the end, the governors were swayed to grant temporary custody to Mrs. Summers, with the caveat that they would need to consult a lawyer to verify the legality of such an outcome.

But for now, Cora would move from the vicarage to Sea View.

ELEVEN

Thy welcome eve, loved Christmas now arrived,
The parish bells, their tuneful peals resound,
And mirth and gladness every breast pervade.
—RJ Thorn, "Christmas"

Mamma and Emily hurried home to alert Sarah and request her help in preparing one of the attic rooms near Georgiana's.

Meanwhile, Georgie, Viola, and Jack went to the vicarage to help Cora gather her things, and to protect the girl from any retaliation from the disgruntled cook.

They discovered that Cora had slept on a rough pallet on the scullery floor, which was propped against the wall when not in use.

The cook now stood in the doorway, arms crossed and scowling. "That pallet belongs to the vicar."

Viola said, "We have no intention of taking it, I assure you."

They gathered Cora's few belongings into her small valise, and then the girl, emboldened by the presence of supportive friends, asked, "Mrs. Browland, where is my grandmother's trunk?"

For a moment, the woman glared at her. "What need have you for a grown woman's things? Have I not undergone the trouble and expense of feeding and training you?"

"She has only been here a short time," Jack retorted. "Moreover, any expense was borne by the vicar, who compensates you for your *trouble*. If he wishes to present me with an accounting, I shall pay it, but we will have Mrs. Limbrick's trunk, and every single one of her and Cora's belongings." Major Hutton stood tall, shoulders back and presence commanding. He was every inch the military leader in that moment. And not a man to cross.

Cora stared at him, likely transfixed by the scars that webbed half his face and made him doubly intimidating.

Even so, Georgiana wondered if Colin's charm would have been more effective, or at least more pleasant. She was oddly glad the major's younger brother did not possess the same fierce bearing.

Viola, in conciliatory tones, added, "And we will happily reimburse you for any out-of-pocket expenses you have borne. Won't we, my dear?"

Jack's nostrils flared. "If and when every one of Cora's belongings has been returned to her."

For a moment cook and major squared off, but then the woman huffed. "The trunk is in my room. For safekeeping. There was no space for it in the scullery."

Jack followed the woman to her room down the passage and emerged a short while later carrying the trunk on his own. After a telling look from Viola, he set it down, begrudgingly removed a few coins from his purse, and handed them to the woman.

Then he summoned Taggart, and together the two men carried the trunk out and lifted it onto the Huttons' carriage. As Georgiana helped Cora climb inside, she heard Jack grumble, "Tell me why we gave that woman even a farthing?"

Viola patted his arm and replied, "Think of it as an offering to the church, my dear. For a bit more peace for the vicar and his wife."

Once they reached Sea View, Jack and Taggart hefted the trunk while Mr. Gwilt carried Cora's valise up the several flights of stairs to the attic. In a former servant's room between Georgie's own bedchamber and the old schoolroom, they found Sarah, Emily, and Mamma hard at work, sweeping the floor, smoothing fresh bedclothes onto the single bed, and arranging a hand towel, basin, and pitcher on the washstand.

Sarah, broom in hand, paused to eye the newcomer with interest. Sarah had often taken baked goods to the poor house but was less familiar with the pupils of the charity school.

"Welcome, Cora," Mamma began. "We hope you will be comfortable here."

Georgie added, "You know Emily already, and this is our older sister Sarah."

"Welcome," Sarah echoed her mother's greeting. "We've tidied up as best we could in the short time we had. We shall clean the windows and perhaps replace these old curtains in a day or two."

"That's all right. It's nice," Cora said.

"You don't . . ." Mamma hesitated, then asked, "That is, do you mind that we interfered and took you from the vicarage? They did not allow you to speak for yourself, so I hope you know we were acting from the best intentions. If you preferred to stay where you were, then . . ."

"No, ma'am. I did not want to stay there. I want Nan."

"Of course you do." Mamma braced an arm around her small shoulders. "I am sorry, my dear. I know you are grieving and maybe even scared. We will help you all we can. Won't we, girls?"

"Yes," Georgie said eagerly, and Emily echoed her reply.

Sarah nodded her agreement, even as her feelings remained unsettled. In truth, she did not know how to feel about it. Her mother, an invalid for many years, now making such a bold decision, one that might prove life-changing for Cora and, in some ways, for all of them. It was not that Sarah questioned her mother's state of mind in pursuing such a course. She knew her to be rational and kind.

And it made sense, to a degree. She had been a friend to Cora's mother, and the girl apparently had no family now that her grandmother had died.

Yet for years, they had all feared their mother might not survive much longer, and here she was, committing to care for a child at least until she reached adulthood, nearly a decade hence. Mamma had gained strength and shown signs of recovery in recent months, but would it last? And if not, which of them would care for Cora in her stead?

There was a time, not long ago, when Sarah had felt responsible for her mother. And now, here her mother was, vowing to take responsibility for someone else.

The thought left Sarah feeling oddly torn between admiration and unease. She hoped her mother would not live to regret her decision. That they all, Cora included, would not come to regret it.

A short while later, Georgie took Cora down to the kitchen for something to eat while Sarah, Emily, and their mother finished tidying the room.

Sarah realized Mamma was watching her in some concern. "Sarah? You are awfully quiet. Do you disapprove?"

"No. I am just surprised. And . . . thinking ahead to the implications. Her future. Ours."

"You need not worry about being responsible for her one day. Should something happen to me, Jack and Viola have offered to serve as guardians in my stead."

"Have they?" Emily asked. "How gracious of them."

"Yes," Sarah agreed. And how petty she felt for harboring reservations. "It was good of you, Mamma," she said. "Very generous."

Later that night, after the others had gone to bed, Sarah sat near the fire with Mr. Henshall, Emily, and James.

James had returned late from Killerton, so after bringing him some food, Emily explained the day's events to him, describing the meeting and its outcome. Mr. Henshall listened with interest as well. While the three of them conversed, Sarah took advantage of the quiet time to work on the dancing slippers for Effie.

James, clearly tired from his long day, soon bid them good-night. Emily followed. Sarah and Mr. Henshall, however, lingered in the parlour.

He asked what she thought of the day's developments.

Sarah reconsidered the situation, then admitted, "It's odd. I feel like I have been trying to take care of Mamma—of the entire family—for years. Especially after Claire left and Papa died. And now, well . . . perhaps this shows she does not need looking after anymore. And if so, that is good. And I am grateful. And yet . . . Oh, what is wrong with me?"

He reached over and took her hand in his larger, warmer one. "We all like to feel needed, important to those we love. It's only natural. And ye are important. To all of us."

Sarah's chest tightened and tears blurred her vision. "Thank you. That is kind of you to say."

For a moment she returned the pressure of his hand, but then she slipped her fingers from his and rose. "Now I had better go to bed as well. Tomorrow is Christmas Eve, and there will be much to do."

The next morning, Sarah rose early as was her custom and went downstairs to the library-office. She was surprised to find Effie already up, staring out the window toward the turbulent sea, expression troubled.

"Good morning, Effie. Everything all right?"

"Well enough, I suppose. Odd about your mam and Georgie bringing that little girl here to live, is it not?"

"Certainly surprising."

"What do ye think about it?"

"I hardly know. It's still so new. Why? Does it . . . trouble you for some reason?"

"I liked it better when Georgie treated me as her little sister."

Sarah's heart went out to her, and she stepped closer. "Oh, Effie. She is very fond of you as well."

Effie shrugged. "Then she'd be the first."

"That is not true. All of us care about you. And your stepfather and your aunt both love you deeply."

Another shrug.

"In fact, Mr. Henshall told me when you two were last here that although he is not your natural father, he feels as protective and fond of you as any father would—any good, loving father, that is."

When Effie remained quiet, Sarah laid a hand on her shoulder and said gently, "I am sorry your parents were not . . . all they might have been. Is that why you don't want to visit your mother's grave?"

Effie nodded. "I should have been here when she died. If I had been, perhaps . . ." She shook her head. "But she did not like me. Refused to bring me to Sidmouth with them, even though Mr. Henshall insisted he would welcome my company."

"Perhaps she thought you were too young to travel such a long way."

Again Effie shook her head. "I hoped she might warm toward me after my father died. But no."

"Mr. Henshall mentioned that her first husband was . . . difficult."

"Aye. He gambled away most of her valuables. Yelled vile things at her. Struck her."

"And you?"

"He didna strike me. Well, only with words."

"Those leave lasting wounds too."

"Now I don't even like bearing his surname. My aunt says I should use Mam's maiden name—her surname too—but I'm not sure. Mr. Henshall asked me once to adopt his name. I refused. This was a few years ago. I was mean and spiteful about it. Perhaps I really am my father's daughter."

"You were an angry adolescent, Effie. Not the first and not the last."

"Maybe. Yet I regret that now."

"Then talk to him. I'm sure it's not too late."

For a moment Effie said nothing. Then her discouraged expression brightened. She sent Sarah a mischievous sidelong glance and said, "I'll consider taking his name . . . if ye will."

Sarah blinked in surprise. If the girl was in earnest, it was quite a compliment, really. Yet Sarah thought it wiser not to reply. Instead she chuckled a bit awkwardly, squeezed Effie's hand, and excused herself.

Sarah had already begun working on the dancing slippers for Effie in her rare moments of spare time, embroidering a thistle design onto the toe of each: spiny green ball topped by a purple crown.

Now, as she did so, she found herself praying for the girl, praying that God would heal her wounded daughter-heart from past hurts and guide her into the future. That He would hold her in His mighty hand and, even when she stumbled, not let her fall.

"Please protect her, Lord, and direct her steps. Please direct mine too."

On Christmas Eve, the five bells in the parish church tower began to chime, calling the faithful to the traditional Christmas Eve service.

Sarah and her family set out together along with Cora, Mr. Henshall and Effie, and the Huttons. Mr. Hutton senior had recently arrived in Sidmouth and joined them as well. William, Claire, and Mira met them at the church.

The temperature had dropped, so they dressed warmly. In fact, Mrs. Denby had declined the invitation to join them due to the cold night and a persistent cough but had promised to come over for dinner on Christmas Day.

"I don't like that she has to live in that drafty building near the river," Viola said. "The damp there cannot be good for her."

As they walked up the churchyard path, Georgiana shivered and then sighed. "I had so hoped for snow. Not for a Christmas as cold as last year's, but a little snow would be nice."

Colin teased, "I shall put in a good word with Mother Nature. Women have always liked me."

"Ha!" Georgiana scoffed and slapped his padded shoulder. "You wish!"

"We had far more snow than usual last year," Emily said. "Can't expect that again."

Sarah added, "I am doing everything in my power to give you a festive Christmas, Georgiana, but the weather is outside of my control."

Together they all entered the church and processed up the long nave to their usual pews near the front.

During the service, they sang an old Christmas anthem that interwove Latin phrases with English.

> "Nowell sing we, now all and some,
> For *Rex pacificus* is come.
> In Bethlehem, in that fair city,
> A child was born of a maiden free,
> That shall a lord and prince be
> *A solis ortus cardine.*"

In her mind, Sarah translated the Latin—*For the King of peace is coming . . . From the rising of the sun.*

She longed for that peace as well.

After the service, they returned to Sea View. Just like the previous year, they found Mr. Gwilt and their elderly manservant, Lowen, decorating the entrance with pine boughs, holly, and ivy.

"Thank you," Sarah said. "That looks wonderful."

Once inside, they shed their outer things and continued decorating, winding greenery up the stairway banister, on the mantels, and down the center of the dining room table.

Georgiana, accompanied by Effie and Cora, went and stood at the library windows, watching for their extended family and friends to arrive.

In the adjacent drawing room, a fire blazed in the open hearth, the curtains drawn against the cold. A shallow pewter bowl sat before the fire, being warmed in preparation for a game of snapdragon. The games portion of the evening had always been Georgiana's favorite, and she saw her former enthusiasm mirrored in the eager expressions of the younger girls. But Georgie found her thoughts more focused on the guests soon to arrive. Or at least, one particular guest.

She had dressed with unusual care in one of her new dresses and kid slippers, forgoing the comfortable half boots she preferred.

She'd even asked Emily to help with her hair. Not that anyone had probably noticed. It had been so cold in the church they'd left on their coats and bonnets.

William, Claire, and Mira were the first to arrive. James and Emily greeted them. Armaan and his wife were busy at the boarding house but planned to join them for Christmas dinner and Twelfth Night.

The Hutton family arrived after a brief stop at Westmount: Viola, Major Hutton, Colin, and Mr. Hutton.

"No Miss Marriott?" Mamma asked Colin. "I do hope you extended our invitation?"

Georgiana had seen Colin greet Miss Marriott and her parents after church. Now she waited to hear his reply as well.

"I did indeed, but sadly, family obligations will keep her home tonight."

"Then perhaps she might join us for New Year's Eve or Twelfth Night instead?"

"That is very kind of you, madam. I shall ask her." In his hands, Colin carried his own Christmas decoration: the promised kissing bough, made of holly, ivy, and mistletoe.

Georgie feared her mother might frown on the use of mistletoe, but she made no complaint and suggested he hang it in one of the parlour doorways.

Meanwhile, Mr. Gwilt conscripted Jack, James, and Mr. Henshall to assist him in fashioning the Devonshire equivalent of a Yule log—a massive bundle of ash branches bound together by bands of thin green saplings.

The three men bundled up and went back outside to assist Mr. Gwilt. Georgie wanted to join them but thought the better of it, considering her thin slippers. Instead, she helped Colin by finding a nail and ribbon to hang the ball of greenery in the doorway. She then held the stepladder while he climbed up to hang it.

At her family's urging, Viola began playing "Deck the Halls" on the pianoforte while the rest of them finished decorating.

As she held the ladder, Georgiana noticed Cora helping Sarah and Jessie carry up food and drink. Mince pies, cider, gingerbread, black butter, hot rolls, and more. Soon the house was filled with the tangy aromas of wood smoke, roasted chestnuts, and mulling spices.

The men returned with the large bundle of bound branches, carried it into the drawing room, and laid it next to the hearth.

When all had gathered, Mr. Hutton senior, as the eldest present, helped place the long bundle onto the andirons. The wood soon sparked to life and distinctive orange and purple flames leapt from it.

Emily, most familiar with local customs, told them, "All unmarried women present should choose one of the bands, and whoever's burns through first means that she will be the next to marry."

Georgie said, "Cora and Mira are too young. So that leaves only me, Effie, and Sarah. Unless you want to participate, Mamma?"

"Heavens, no."

Emily urged, "Quick, you three, choose a band."

Sarah began to protest, "I don't believe in such supersti—"

Emily shushed her. "Just pick one already."

The three each did so.

As the fire consumed the bands, one after another gave way.

"Yours was first, Sarah!" Effie exclaimed. "That means ye shall be the first to marry."

Sarah's face reddened from more than the blaze of the fire, Georgie noticed, and her sister avoided Mr. Henshall's gaze.

After that, they sang carols such as "While Shepherds Watched Their Flocks by Night" and "The First Noel."

Then people rose to help themselves to the trays of savories and sweets arrayed on the sideboard in the dining room, while Mr. Gwilt handed round warm drinks.

The adjoining rooms hummed with lively conversation and laughter as people told stories, shared news, and talked of plans for Boxing Day, New Year's, and Twelfth Night.

An hour or so into the evening, Georgiana lifted the large shallow dish piled with raisins and set it at the center of a small round table. Mamma carried in a jug of brandy—the signal that the game of snapdragon was about to begin.

Those who wished to play, or were cajoled into doing so, gathered around the table as Mr. Gwilt snuffed out the nearby candles.

"Have you played this game before, Cora?" Georgie asked.

"No, though I've heard of it. Won't we burn our fingers?" Cora shot a surreptitious glance at the major's burn scars.

At that, Jack whispered something into Viola's ear and left the room.

Georgiana had not considered that he might mind the game. His burns had come from an explosion, but she supposed any reminder might be painful. She resolved not to suggest playing this game in future.

Refocusing on Cora, she said, "As long as you are quick and put the raisins in your mouth straightaway, it won't hurt."

"Cora, you need not play if you don't wish," Mamma said as she poured brandy over the raisins. "You can watch."

The girl swallowed hard. "Good idea."

The elder Mr. Hutton grumbled, "I can't believe this game has not been outlawed."

"What are we waitin' for?" Effie urged.

Georgie began the traditional chant, and the others joined in:

> "Here he comes with flaming bowl,
> Don't he mean to take his toll,
> Snip! Snap! Dragon!
>
> Take care you don't take too much,
> Be not greedy in your clutch,
> Snip! Snap! Dragon!"

"Ready?" Georgie asked.

Heads nodded and at Mamma's signal, Mr. Gwilt lit a long match in the fireplace and used it to ignite the brandy. Blue flames lit up the room.

Little Mira watched the proceedings with round eyes. Her father picked her up in his arms, saying, "How about we wait a few years before you try this game, ey, my pumpion?"

Mira nodded.

Across the fire's flickering glow, Colin said, "Show us how it's done, Miss Georgiana."

Georgie darted her hand in without hesitation, pinched a raisin, and popped it into her mouth.

"Amazing!" he exclaimed. "A regular fire-eater!"

Squeals and laughter followed as one by one the players—James, Emily, and Effie—reached in and grabbed raisins, putting them into their mouths.

Mr. Gwilt stood nearby, a basin of cold water at the ready, should anyone be burned.

Taking his turn, Colin flinched and shook his hand. "Ow!" Mr. Gwilt stepped over, and the young man dipped his fingers into the soothing water.

"Too slow," Effie teased him. She turned to her stepfather. "Your turn."

He grinned in reply and snatched out a raisin.

Sarah hung back, watching the game. No one looked her way or challenged her to play. No one expected her to take part in anything as frivolous as a game.

As a girl, she had liked snapdragon and been good at it. When had she stopped playing games, joining in? When had she become a spoilsport? She might have more responsibilities now, but that did not mean she could not enjoy herself now and again—especially during the holidays when surrounded by loved ones.

Sarah walked forward with determination and joined the other players around the table.

Georgiana's eyes widened. "Are you going to play, Sarah?"

"Why not?"

The others turned to look. She had not meant to make a spectacle of herself.

She took a deep breath, eyed a likely target, and reached in her hand. She yanked it back and reflexively stuck index finger and thumb into her mouth, raisin and all. The hot raisin sizzled on her tongue. For a moment she left the smarting fingertip in her mouth. Noticing the others regarding her in curiosity or concern, Sarah pulled it out and said, "Who's next? Oh . . . the fire is going out."

The brandy flames faded, and the game ended in a matter of moments.

Perhaps she ought to have waited a few seconds longer.

Pausing to pick up her glass of punch, Sarah smiled at no one in particular, and while the other players compared how many raisins each had eaten, Sarah slipped away.

Going belowstairs, she passed through the kitchen, where Mrs. Besley and Lowen were sitting down to a well-deserved late supper.

"Need something, Miss Sarah?" Mrs. Besley made to rise, wincing as she put weight on her gouty foot.

Sarah raised a palm. "Don't get up. Just going into the workroom for something."

She retreated into her private haven, retrieved a pitcher of water from the cold larder, and stuck her finger into it.

Proud, foolish creature . . .

Footsteps scraped over the threshold, and she looked up in chagrin to see Callum Henshall.

"Burned yourself, didn't ye, lass?"

She sighed. "Yes. I was hoping no one noticed."

"I notice everything about ye."

Pleasure at his words competed with embarrassment. "I'm all right. Just feeling foolish."

"What made ye try it?"

"I used to be good at it. Who do you think taught Georgiana? But it's been too many years. I lost my nerve for a second, and the hesitation cost me."

"Let me see."

"It's nothing."

He extended his palm.

"Oh, very well."

She placed her hand in his. He held it up and frowned at the red patch of skin at the tip of her forefinger.

"Perhaps Mrs. Besley has some liniment?"

Sarah shrugged. "Custom says to hold a minor burn near a fire, but I don't think I could stand that."

He shook his head. "Old wives' tale. A cold compress is all you need. Well, that and . . ."

"And what?"

He pursed his lips, and gently blew cool air over her hot finger. *Ahh . . .*

"Is that helping?"

Sarah's pulse raced. "Helping . . . what?"

He held her gaze and slowly pressed a feather-soft kiss to her throbbing finger.

"Y-yes," she faltered. "Helping."

Mr. Gwilt appeared in the doorway. "Oh. Uh. Pardon me. Just wanted to see if you were all right, Miss Sarah. I see you are . . . in good hands."

"I am, Mr. Gwilt. Thank you."

After the games had been played, people rose and drifted away from the drawing room to stretch their legs, refill their teacups, or select a few more dainties from the dining room.

Colin wandered out across the passage, and Georgie followed him. She found him in the quiet parlour, glancing almost forlornly toward the kissing bough.

She walked over to condole with him. "I'm sorry Miss Marriott could not join us. You might kiss me under the mistletoe instead, if you like. A sorry replacement, I know, but I do hate to see you disappointed."

"Not at all, Miss Georgie."

Even so, she leaned forward, tapping a forefinger to her cheek. He grinned and leaned down, planting a kiss there.

"There," she said. "Not so bad, I hope?"

"Quite the contrary."

Sarah came up from belowstairs and hesitated in the opposite doorway, Mr. Henshall on her heels.

He said, "Ah, someone is taking advantage of the kissing bough, I see."

Sarah looked from Georgie to Colin and back again in evident surprise but did not deliver the mild reproof Georgiana expected.

Later, after the party ended and most people had gone to their own homes or to bed, Mr. Henshall stayed to help Sarah and Mr. Gwilt tidy up the remaining plates, cups, and glasses left here and there in the public rooms.

When Mr. Gwilt carried the final tray of dishes belowstairs, Mr. Henshall lingered in the firelit parlour. He nodded to the kissing bough with a glimmer in his eyes.

"Well, Miss Sarah. What do ye say? You, me, mistletoe . . . ?"

Sarah bit her lip, feeling uncertain. Peter, as a clergyman, had not approved of the pagan tradition, so she had never been kissed beneath the mistletoe. But now . . . with this man?

How could she resist?

Pulse tripping, she walked over and joined him there. Mimicking Georgie's earlier gesture, she tipped her cheek toward him. He leaned close, but did not touch her. She turned in question, and his lips unexpectedly brushed hers. Sarah stood there, stunned, unable or unwilling to move away. He kissed her gently and she, oh so tentatively, kissed him back.

Then, pulling away slightly, she murmured near his lips, "Mr. Henshall, I . . ."

"Callum."

"Callum. I . . ."

His mouth again descended on hers, silencing further words, further thought or protest.

She had been kissed before, years ago. Peter had given her an awkward, nervous kiss upon their betrothal and one more fervent before his ship sailed. Yet nothing in her memories compared to this.

Sarah was overwhelmed with sensations: Surprise. Pleasure. Wobbly knees. She had not known this was what a kiss could feel like.

And she found she liked it, very much indeed.

TWELVE

This being Christmas Day, I read prayers and administered
the Holy Sacrament. Singers sung the Christmas
Anthem this morning and very well indeed.

—James Woodforde,
The Diary of a Country Parson

On Christmas Day, Sarah donned a pretty dress, thinking all the while of their kiss under the mistletoe.

That morning, they attended divine services once more. The vicar read prayers and administered the sacrament of the Lord's Supper. A small local choir sang a Christmas anthem, and afterward, friends and neighbors greeted one another with a chorus of "Happy Christmas."

Then they went home to put the finishing touches on a magnificent Christmas feast. This time the entire family would gather along with Mrs. Denby, Armaan and Sonali Sagar, and Mr. and Mrs. Hornbeam. They'd had to move a second smaller table into the dining room to accommodate everyone.

Sarah went belowstairs to assist with preparations. Mrs. Besley still found it difficult to stand for long but directed from the chair in the corner. Thankfully, Bibi Cordey had once again agreed to work a few additional hours a week to fill the void. Jessie, Lowen, and even Mr. Gwilt lent a hand in the kitchen as well. With everyone helping, the goose had been roasted to perfection with sage and would be served with both gravy and an apple sauce. The pudding sat on its platter, ready to be set alight just before serving.

They would begin with white soup, followed by the goose, cauliflower and broccoli with melted butter, and potato pudding. They would end with jellies and almond paste molded into fancy shapes and the plum pudding.

The day before, there had been some discussion as to who should carry in the prized Christmas pudding. Mamma, as hostess? When she demurred, Sarah had asked Mr. Gwilt if he would like to do the honors, and he had stammered and grinned like a schoolboy. "Never done the like before. I would be delighted to do so, I would."

The meal began with a prayer offered by Mr. Hornbeam and a toast led by Mr. Hutton.

When they had finished the other courses, Mr. Gwilt entered, chest puffed with pride and pleasure, carrying in the plum pudding. A sprig of holly sat on top to represent Jesus's crown of thorns, and low brandy flames burnished its surface. Everyone oohed and aahed appropriately.

Sarah wondered again what Colin Hutton had added to the pudding batter. Hopefully, traditional tokens or coins, but with him who knew?

When the flames subsided, Mr. Gwilt moved the pudding to the sideboard and began scooping portions.

Jessie served plates to each person and passed around a pitcher of brandy sauce.

"Now, take care as you eat," Sarah advised. "Colin, here, took it upon himself to slip in several tokens of his own."

"That I did," Colin admitted with a self-satisfied grin.

Tentatively, gingerly, they all began to spoon and nibble their servings of pudding.

Within moments, a few people began lifting table napkins to discreetly remove items from their mouths.

Everyone else, and especially Colin, watched with eager interest. He said, "Do tell if you've found something in yours."

Wiping a small object with her linen napkin, Georgiana was

the first to announce her find. "I have a tiny silver . . . boot?" She held it up and peered at it. "Yes, a boot."

"Ah!" Colin said, clearly savoring the moment. "That means there will be travel in your future."

"I certainly hope so," Georgie replied.

James lifted a coin. "I found a thruppence."

"That signifies wealth or good fortune."

"I have a tiny horseshoe," Mrs. Hornbeam said, holding it up.

"Ah. Good luck for you."

"I got a thimble," Effie said. "I suppose that means I shall never marry?"

"Not necessarily. It can also mean thrift."

"No, that's not it." Mr. Henshall adamantly shook his head. "Definitely not thrift."

Effie made a face at him.

"And you, Mr. Henshall?" Colin asked.

"I have a small wishbone, perhaps from a quail?"

"Indeed. And that means your dearest wish shall be granted."

Callum Henshall, seated across the table from Sarah, let his gaze rest on her, and he echoed Georgiana's words, "I certainly hope so."

A flush rose up her neck.

"Sarah? What are you hiding?" Georgie asked.

"It's . . . well, it's a bit redundant, really. I found a little ring."

"Ah!" Colin beamed. "A confirmation of last night's sapling band. You *shall* be married within the year."

The flush moved up to her face.

Eager to shift focus, Sarah turned to the newest resident of Sea View. "Anything in yours, Cora?"

The girl shook her head. "I don't mind. I'm just glad to be here with all of you."

Sarah reached over and squeezed her hand. "And we are glad you are here too."

Over the little girl's head, Mamma sent Sarah a look of gratitude.

After the early dinner, they moved into the drawing room for tea and coffee. Soon people began to disperse. The Sagars and

Hornbeams departed to their own homes with effusive thanks for the excellent meal, and Mr. Hutton senior retreated to neighboring Westmount for an after-meal snooze.

When they had gone, Mamma slipped away to her room for a nap of her own. Sarah watched her go in mild concern. It was not the first time Mamma had become fatigued recently. Sarah hoped it was just the busyness of the holidays and did not signal a decline.

Emily and James sat together by the parlour fire and soon lost themselves in the books they were reading.

Colin, Georgie, and the three younger girls—Mira, Cora, and Effie—went into the parlour as well to play a board game. Mira convinced her father and Claire to join them, while Effie conscripted Mr. Henshall. He agreed on the condition they allow Sarah to relax after all her hard work.

So Sarah found herself sitting in the drawing room in peaceful contentment with only Viola, Jack, and Mrs. Denby.

The older woman smiled from one to the next. "What a lovely day, my dears. Thank you for including me."

"Our pleasure," Sarah replied. "How are you feeling now?"

"Much better. My cough is barely a tickle now."

"I am glad to hear it."

Viola said, "You do seem somewhat better, and I'm relieved. But living where you do, where it is so damp near the river . . ." Viola shook her head. "It cannot be good for your constitution."

Sarah looked at her sister in surprise. Viola had become a bona fide champion of the poor house. What was the point of criticizing the only living arrangement available to the impoverished woman?

Mrs. Denby waved a dismissive hand. "Oh, it's not so bad. I have a roof over my head, which only rarely leaks. And while I can't deny it is drafty and damp in winter, it's rather pleasant along the river in summertime."

"Except when it floods."

"Well . . . yes."

Viola glanced at her husband, and it seemed a private message passed between them. Finding in his expression whatever reassurance she sought, Viola leaned toward Mrs. Denby and said, "Jack and I have been talking something over for quite some time now. And we are wondering if you might . . . do us a great favor."

"Of course. Anything for you! If I am able."

"I hope you don't think it presumptuous or that we are acting out of, well, charity alone. You know we are extremely fond of you, and—"

"As I am of you."

"And we are hoping . . ." Viola swallowed, and Sarah thought she had not seen her look quite so nervous since her wedding day.

Jack leaned forward as well, elbows on his knees and expression earnest. "We would like you to do us the great honor of coming to live with us at Westmount."

The woman's wrinkled mouth fell ajar, and the eyes behind her spectacles blinked fast. Sarah was almost as surprised as Mrs. Denby clearly felt.

After a moment, she closed her mouth, inhaled, and replied, "I know I have said more than once that you are like the daughter I never had, Viola, but I was certainly not hinting that you should offer any such thing."

"I know you were not. But that's just it. You have become family to us. Like a dear grandmother. And you should be living with people who care about you at this time of your life."

"I am not on death's door, for goodness' sake, despite my recent cough."

"I thank God you are not. And while we believe we could better look after you at Westmount, we want this for ourselves too."

The older woman slowly shook her head. "I don't like the thought of you having to care for me. I don't wish to become a burden to you."

"Dear Mrs. Denby. Is that not what family is for—to help bear one another's burdens? And who knows? We might have a small burden of our own one day and could use *your* help."

Now Sarah's mouth fell ajar. "How wonderful!" she exclaimed.

"One day soon?" Mrs. Denby asked eagerly, spindly brows high.

Viola placed a finger over her own lips and looked from Mrs.

Denby to Sarah. "Emily knows. But otherwise it's too early to make an official announcement, so please keep this quiet for now."

"Oh my, you are surely persuasive, my girl," Mrs. Denby said, eyes sparkling. "You know the way to my heart, do you not? The daughter I never had, and perhaps—one day—a grandchild too?" She gave them a saucy grin. "When shall I move in?"

The words *"The daughter I never had, and perhaps—one day—a grandchild too?"* were still echoing sweetly in Sarah's mind as she stepped into the hall. There she was taken aback to hear Effie's forlorn voice ask, "Would it be worse not to have a mother in your life, or to have one who didna love ye?"

The girl sat on the stairs, face in her hands.

"Oh, Effie . . ." Sarah went and sat next to her. "I thought you were playing games with the others."

"I was. But Cora started cryin', missin' her nan and her parents, who all clearly loved her, and it was enough to make me want to break my heart. Or break somethin'."

"Of course she is missing her family at Christmas. Poor girl."

"Your mam came in and is soothin' her now."

Not knowing what to say, Sarah put a tentative arm around the girl's shoulders and felt them tremble as she wept.

After a time, Effie sniffed and lifted her head almost defiantly. "I'd like to see my mam on Christmas too. I've a thing or two to say to her."

"Oh . . . ?" Sarah said uneasily.

Effie swiveled on the stair. "Will ye go to the churchyard with me?"

"I . . . Of course I would. But your . . . Mr. Henshall would be more than happy to accompany you."

"I know. But he was married to her, probably thinks she was perfect. Will ye think ill of me for not agreeing?"

"No, I won't. I'm happy to take you, Effie, although may I at least mention it to him before we go? I'd hate for him to feel we'd left him out or that I'd usurped his place."

"I don't want him to hear what I have to say to her."

"Nothing ye could say would surprise me, lass."

With a start, they both looked over to find him standing outside the parlour door. Effie appeared as guilty as Sarah felt.

"I was coming to find ye. Could see ye were upset. Didna mean to eavesdrop, but I'm glad I heard, so I can explain."

Sarah stood. "Perhaps you might prefer to sit in the library, where it's warmer and more comfortable?"

Effie rose in agreement. Sarah was about to excuse herself to let the two talk privately, but Effie took hold of her hand and did not let go.

In the library, Mr. Henshall added wood to the fire before Sarah could do so. When the three had settled into chairs near the hearth, he turned to Effie and began, "In the past, I took care in what I said about your mam. Didna want to speak ill of her or taint your view of her. In hindsight, perhaps I was too careful."

Effie stared at him, an expectant, almost fearful light in her eyes.

He sighed and went on, "The truth is, your mam suffered from a deep depression of spirits. The doctor called it hysteria. He tried and failed to treat her successfully. Due to her condition, and the abuse she had experienced, she pulled away from us both, especially during the last year or so of her life."

"But why? It wasna our fault."

"I know. Unfair as it is, I think she distanced herself because ye reminded her of Mr. McKay. And she retreated from me, because among other things, she'd had two miscarriages and didna want to risk losing another child."

"Did she? She never said."

"She refused to speak of it, and I . . . Well, ye were still so young, I wasna sure what to tell ye."

He swallowed and said, "But I want ye to hear me, Effie. Even though she didna fully love us does not mean you're not worthy of love. *You are.* Completely."

Her chin trembled. "That abusive man was my father."

"I know, love. I know. But ye are not him, nor to blame for his cruelty."

"For so long, I tried to make him—and her—love me. . . ." Effie's voice broke.

He nodded. "I know. Too well. I thought I could make her happy—that in time, she would come to love me. I failed."

Effie shook her head. "You were good to her. Good to us both. And we treated ye shabbily in return."

"It's all right."

"No, it isn't. I always thought that if I had tried harder after he died, been a better daughter . . ."

"No, lass. She was ill. It wasna your fault. Nor mine, though it took some time to realize that."

"I want to believe ye."

"Then do."

"All right." Effie rose abruptly.

He looked at her uncertainly. "All right, what?"

"You come along. The three of us. I'm ready to visit her grave."

Sarah rose and said, "I need not intrude further."

But Effie took her hand again and held fast. "You too."

They went to the hall closet and began gathering their outer things. Mr. Gwilt appeared and asked if he might be of any assistance.

Sarah said, "Please let my mother know the three of us are going for a walk."

"Will do, miss. It's cold out there. Be sure and dress warm."

Together the three walked through a quiet, late Christmas afternoon. Mr. Henshall carried a lantern, as darkness fell early in the wintertime.

When they reached the churchyard, he led the way to his wife's grave, its granite headstone topped by a Celtic cross.

Effie appeared to brace herself as she stepped forward and stood before the headstone.

She stared down at the inscription and said, "How strange to see her name like that, in stone. *Katrin McKay Henshall.* His name and yours together. *Beloved Wife and Mother.* Did ye love her?"

With a quick glance at Sarah, he nodded. "I did."

"So did I." Effie's voice quavered. "*Forever in our hearts?* Forever breaking our hearts, ye mean."

He shook his head. "She will always be a part of us, Effie. As hard as it is, we must try not to let the memories, the disappointments, continue to hurt us. It's not easy to forgive someone who should have loved ye unconditionally, who should have cared for ye and cherished ye, but I hope ye will."

Effie drew a long inhale and released a frosty breath. She faced the headstone again and said more softly, "Mam, it's me, Effie. Your daughter." She gave a rueful laugh.

"I know ye are not here. Not really. Still I had to come and face ye. I know ye didna love me . . . and that really hurts. Like a gapin' hole in my soul that won't heal. But it's Christmas and wherever ye are now, I forgive ye. I hope ye are with God, and I hope ye are at peace."

Mr. Henshall put an arm around the girl's shoulders. "Well done, lass. I don't know why God allowed her to suffer, and ye as well—fallen world, broken people. . . . I don't know. But she is at peace now, thanks to our merciful Savior."

Effie nodded, clearly reassured.

"And please never doubt ye are loved. Deeply. I love ye, and your aunt and grandfather love ye."

Sarah added gently, "And so do I." And she realized in that moment that she truly did love the girl.

Tears filled Effie's eyes, and she leaned into him, still holding Sarah's hand.

Callum held the girl close to his side, then looked up at Sarah, their gazes knitting together in understanding and so much more.

When they returned to the house, Effie seemed relieved and much happier. She went up to the attic with Georgiana, Cora, and a few others to rehearse their performance for the next day. Mr. Henshall promised to join them as soon as he could feel his fingers.

Sarah and Callum sat together before the library fire to warm up. Mr. Gwilt brought them tea, and then he too went up to the attic, having been recruited once again to take part in Georgiana and Effie's play.

After a few minutes of companionable silence, Sarah said, "You and Effie have suffered a great deal. I wonder how you manage to remain sanguine and hopeful."

He considered. Sketched a shrug. "I suppose that comes from faith, and perhaps from being raised by cheerful, loving parents."

Remembering the "charming neighbor" his sister-in-law mentioned, Sarah said, "You once told me your first marriage had left you disillusioned about the state. That you had decided to be cautious, and not hasty in forming another attachment."

He nodded. "We Scots are prone to caution, aye. After Katrin, I was reluctant to risk my heart again." He leaned forward, bridging the gap between their chairs and taking both of her hands in his. "But I'm through being cautious. Scots are known to be forthright too. So if ye think I am hesitant where you're concerned, let me make something clear. I know how I feel about ye, lass. I am only holding back out of respect for your feelings and your situation here."

Sarah swallowed and when the tension between them grew uncomfortable, she attempted to divert the conversation. "I hope I'm not giving away a secret, but Effie mentioned she doesn't like bearing her father's name and that her aunt wants her to use her own surname—Katrin's maiden name—instead."

A shadow crossed his face. "I know. Once I realized how much Effie disliked her surname, I asked her to adopt mine, to allow me to be a real father to her, in name as well as relationship. She refused."

"Perhaps she will change her mind."

"I hope so. I am a patient man. I am giving her time and biding mine, making a point not to pressure her. Though it is my dearest wish that one day she'll do me the honor of taking my name."

Sarah again became aware of the imploring way he was looking at her. The appeal shimmering in his wide green eyes.

Were they still talking about Effie . . . or about her?

THIRTEEN

Here's a day!—The Ground covered with
snow! What is to become of us?
—Jane Austen, letter to her sister

On Boxing Day, they gave Mrs. Besley, Jessie, Lowen, Mr. Gwilt, and Bibi Cordey small gifts as well as time off, as was customary the day after Christmas.

Sarah worked longer hours than usual in the kitchen to fill in for the cook and for another special reason as well.

Ever since he had joined their staff the previous year, Mr. Gwilt had taken over the majority of Sarah's onerous bookkeeping tasks—verifying invoices against orders, paying bills, summing guest tally forms, and balancing the books.

That afternoon, at Emily's urging, Sarah had approached the man belowstairs and said, "I do hate to ask, especially on what should be your day off, but would you mind taking a look at the books? I added a few entries this morning and seem to have made a mistake somewhere."

He rose eagerly. "Certainly, Miss Sarah. A pleasure to help."

Sarah would have felt more guilty, except she knew the man truly enjoyed every opportunity to use the skills he had gained in his former profession as clerk.

Once Mr. Gwilt was happily bent over the ledgers in the library, Sarah returned to her work belowstairs.

A short while later, she heard hushed voices in the kitchen, and Emily stepped into the workroom. "Ready? Good heavens. What's happened to your apron? Looks like you collided with a rainbow."

"You will understand when you see the cake."

"Well, take that off before we go up."

Sarah wiped the last of the beet juice, red cabbage, and turmeric from her hands, pulled off the apron, and followed Emily upstairs.

When they entered the library, Mr. Gwilt looked up.

"Ah, Miss Sarah. I think I've corrected the problem."

"Oh?" Sarah swallowed a guilty lump and stepped closer.

He ran a finger along a column of numbers and then turned the page. "We pay our fuel bill quarterly to attain a lower rate. But you've listed it here for this month as well, although it's not yet due until after the first of the year."

"Oh. Of course. How foolish of me."

"Not at all." He looked up with a pleasant grin. "An easy mistake to make and easily remedied."

"Thank you."

"Yes, thank you, Mr. Gwilt," Emily echoed.

When Emily had asked her to keep Mr. Gwilt busy upstairs, introducing a mistake like this one was all Sarah could think of. She had once made that exact mistake more than a year ago now. And Mr. Henshall had been the one to help her find it then.

Now Mr. Gwilt gestured toward the various piles of correspondence on the desk. "Anything else I can do while I'm here?"

"No need. Simply enjoy the rest of your Boxing Day."

"I am enjoying it, I assure you. And thank you again for the gifts. I appreciate the smart new gloves and the journal for my own jottings. Your doing, Miss Emily, I'd wager?"

"Why yes."

"Most considerate."

Emily stepped forward, and Sarah noticed her eyes shine with both eagerness and nerves.

"I have something else for you as well," she said. "Something I very much hope you will like."

"Aw, now. You've given me more than enough already, you have."

"Even so, I hope you will like this."

She handed him a folded document.

"What is this?" he asked, unfolding it.

"It's a publishing contract—for your book of Parry's adventures."

"No."

"Yes. Mr. Marsh, though bankrupt, was true to his word. His colleague is indeed interested in publishing your children's book. This is the offer—how much he is willing to pay for the copyright."

"Gracious me."

Mr. Gwilt stared at the page in wonderment for several ticks of the clock, then looked up at Emily.

"And has he offered to publish your Gothic romance as well?"

"No. No interest yet, although I have not given up. But for now, you, Mr. Gwilt, are about to become a published author. And I could not be happier."

He pressed a hand to his chest. "Be still my heart. If only dear Mrs. G were here to see this moment."

Emily squeezed his hand. "She would have been so proud of you. I know I am."

Sarah nodded. "Me too."

"Now," Emily said, "let's go belowstairs and share the good news with Mrs. Besley and Lowen."

He rose. "Very well. I don't want to boast, but they will be happy to learn of it, I know."

"And rightly so." Emily led the way down the back stairs, and he and Sarah followed.

When they reached the kitchen, Mr. Gwilt gaped around the crowded room, where staff, family, and guests alike had gathered with glasses in hand.

At Georgie's signal, they all called, "Surprise!"

On the clean worktable sat the brightly iced cake Sarah had made, and near it a brightly colored stuffed parrot—Parry, in his finely preserved plumage of red, yellow, and blue.

"Good heavens," Mr. Gwilt breathed.

Mamma handed each newcomer a glass, and Emily raised hers to do the honors. "A toast to Mr. Gwilt. Congratulations on your well-deserved publishing offer."

Everyone echoed, "To Mr. Gwilt."

While the others sipped, the small man's eyes misted over. "I am grateful, I am. You have all been so kind since Parry and I came here." He turned to Sarah. "I thank you and your entire family—for work I like, new friends, and a place to call home. And I thank Miss Emily for helping me commit my little tales to paper and seeking out a publisher. There would be no book without you. Without all of you." His lip trembled, and he raised his glass to hide his emotion.

Seeing Mr. Gwilt's unease, Georgiana announced, "Now, let's have cake!"

"Good idea," Mr. Gwilt agreed and hurried to help serve despite their protests, clearly relieved to return to his more accustomed role as helper behind the scenes.

Sarah was proud of Georgiana. Once she overcame her reticence, she had committed herself wholeheartedly to putting on another play with Effie.

They decided to perform the theatrical late on the afternoon of Boxing Day and invited their families to attend, along with any staff members who would enjoy some diversion during their time off.

They set up rows of chairs before a makeshift stage in the parlour, and at the appointed hour, family and friends filled them, including Claire, William, and Mira, as well as Lowen and Mrs. Besley, who leaned on a cane as she walked to her seat. Their maid, Jessie, was spending the day with her betrothed, Tom Cordey, but his sister Bibi had come over to watch. Jack had gone out riding with Taggart and Chown, former soldiers and friends as well as his current manservant and cook. Viola, however, joined them and played a folk song on the pianoforte as an overture to the play.

With Effie as princess, Mr. Henshall as reluctant king, and Mr. Gwilt as narrator, the amateur troupe began performing a rather silly version of "St. George and the Dragon." Even Cora had a part as a sheep, adorable in a white knitted hat with black felt ears pinned to it.

On cue, Colin entered as the dragon in a dark Oxford gown and black mask and gloves, and began mincing about, roaring and flexing his "claws."

Eyes wide, Mira nestled close to Claire's side.

The king first offered all their food and then their livestock in an attempt to appease the beast.

Colin scooped up sheep-Cora with a roar and carried her out the door, the dramatic effect lessened somewhat by Cora's giggles.

Finally the king offered his daughter's hand in marriage to any brave knight who could defeat the dragon. Enter Georgiana as St. George with wooden sword and spear-like stick, who—after a brief battle—slayed the dragon.

Colin fell in a melodramatic death swoon, while Georgie stood over him in triumph.

Mr. Henshall announced impassively, "Huzzah to St. George for ridding our realm of the fierce dragon."

After Mr. Gwilt's "And they all lived happily ever after," the actors bowed before them. The audience clapped in appreciation, for the brevity of the play, perhaps, more than the quality.

Sarah was, however, impressed that the girls had managed to recruit a few more players for their performance, which certainly added to the fun. And she was touched that they had included Cora, who now stood between Colin and Georgie, smiling brightly from one to the other.

After the play, Mira approached Cora to admire her felt ears. Cora removed the hat and placed it on Mira's head and the two giggled together.

Mira avoided Colin until he had removed his mask and cape. Then she said, "You're not so scary."

He grinned and tweaked her nose. "Only in the mornings before coffee."

Sarah went to stand beside Mr. Henshall, who looked on as Effie and Georgie talked and laughed together, accepting praise and hugs from Mamma and Emily and good-natured teasing from Bibi and Lowen.

Sarah said to him, "That was sporting of you, and I'm sure Effie appreciated it."

Perhaps hearing her name, Effie came over to join them. A teasing light in her eyes, she said, "It's a good thing you're a skilled musician."

"Are ye sayin' I'd better not give up music to become a thespian?"

"I wouldna advise it, Da'. Stick to the guitar."

She grinned at him, then turned to rejoin the others.

Did Effie realize she'd called him Da'? Had she merely referred to his role as king to her princess? Somehow Sarah did not think so.

Callum stared after Effie, then turned back to Sarah. He started to say something, cleared his throat, then said, "Now I'm very glad I agreed to take part."

The play over, Colin helped Georgie and Cora carry the various costumes and props back up to the attic. After stowing most of the things in the chest in the old schoolroom, Cora darted into her room to put her hat away. Colin lingered.

Georgie looked at him, slowly shaking her head. "You're a study in contradictions, do you know that? Often insufferable, but sometimes, like today, an absolute delight."

He bowed. "Why, thank you." His brow furrowed. "I think."

Cora returned, and the three of them went downstairs, where Mamma met them and insisted Colin join the family for an informal supper.

"Since our cook has the day off, it will be mostly leftover food from Christmas dinner, but please do stay. Sarah has baked fresh rolls."

Georgie added, "And there is plenty of cake left from Mr. Gwilt's party. If you don't mind a blue tongue."

"Sounds a feast compared to what I might find in the Westmount larder. And with Chown having his own day off, well, it will be a pleasure to stay. Thank you."

Mamma nodded. "Perhaps that explains why Viola agreed to dine with us as well."

After their informal meal, they all helped tidy up and carry dishes belowstairs, insisting Mr. Gwilt and the others not wait on them for once.

Daylight waned early in late December, and darkness was already falling when Jack came over to rejoin his wife, having returned from a day of riding and billiards with Chown and Taggart. He sat down with them and accepted a cup of after-dinner coffee. He did not, however, accept any of the red, yellow, and blue cake.

As the others talked, Colin sidled close to Georgie and whispered, "Come and see."

"See what?"

But he had already gone.

She rose and followed him out of the parlour.

When she joined him in the hall, he said, "I told you Mother Nature would come through."

"What do you mean?"

He leaned toward her and gave her a boyish smile. "It's snowing."

"No!"

"Oh yes."

He led her into the library and gestured out the windows. "See?"

Georgie blinked in wonder at the white fluff slowly falling, floating, from the sky.

"Oooh . . ." she breathed. "I almost can't believe it. It's just as I wished for. Why am I so blessed?"

"Well, you are Saint George, after all." He winked.

"Hardly a saint. But I'll take it. It's lovely."

"I agree. Now, let's not stand here gawping. Grab your cloak and let's get out there."

"In the snow?"

"Certainly, you ninnyhammer." He grinned. "We want the whole experience, do we not?"

She grinned back at him. "Indeed we do."

A few minutes later, they had dressed warmly and stepped outside. As if hearing the Sea View door open—or perhaps lying in wait—Chips appeared, tongue lolling, clearly happy to see them. He bounded through the falling snow with undisguised glee, like an excited child.

Colin said, "I wish I had a ball or something to throw to him."

She reached into her cloak pocket and withdrew a small ball. "I always keep one handy."

"Of course you do. What a girl."

She tossed Colin the ball, and he easily caught it. He reeled back and threw the ball, and Chips darted off to fetch it.

For several minutes they played with the dog, who easily found the ball despite the light covering of snow.

Then Georgie leapt onto the veranda, which ran along the house from library to dining room. The sea wind blew in at an angle, covering its floorboards with snow as well. She ran and slid across the snow-slick veranda. In a flash, Colin joined her, sliding past window after window. Soon they were embroiled in a contest to see who could slide the farthest.

Pausing to catch her breath, Georgie stilled.

"Colin, look." She pointed to the large sash windows. Lit from within by firelight and many candles, each window framed a lighted scene within.

Colin followed her example and looked from one to the next. "It's like the illuminations in the print-shop windows," he said.

"You're right," she breathed, taking in one tableau, then the next.

In one stood his brother and Viola, talking and laughing. Viola reached up and laid an affectionate hand on Jack's scarred cheek.

"What shall we call this scene?" he asked.

"Hmm. Maybe *True Love?*"

He nodded. "Or perhaps . . . *Soul Mates.*"

In the next window, Effie and Cora were sitting on the sofa, one on either side of Mamma, each holding one of Mamma's hands.

"Oh . . ." Georgiana whispered, her heart aching at the sight. "This one is sad. *Two Motherless Girls.*"

"Seems like your mother is doing her best to fill that void."

Georgie nodded. "They are lucky to have her, and so am I."

Reaching the far dining room window, they spied Emily and James, arms around each other in a fervent embrace, kissing.

"Eek. Don't look." Georgie shoved a gloved hand before his eyes.

"They shouldn't stand before windows if they don't wish to be seen."

"Probably don't realize just how visible they are, lit up like that when it's dark out here."

Forgoing the stairs, Colin hopped down from the veranda and turned back to offer Georgie a hand down. Ignoring it, Georgie hopped down herself and together they walked back around the corner of the house.

"Look there." Colin pointed to the low-to-the-ground window that let light into the kitchen belowstairs. At the big worktable sat Mrs. Besley, Lowen, and Mr. Gwilt enjoying a late supper together and a bottle of cider on their day off.

"What shall we call this one?" he asked.

"I'd call it *A Well-Deserved Rest.*"

Above this, in the east-facing library window, they saw Sarah and Mr. Henshall deep in conversation. Neither was smiling. Yet they were alone together, or so they thought. And they were talking.

"Ah, now this one is interesting," Colin said, crossing his arms. "I might call it *Will They or Won't They?*"

Georgie sighed. "I'm not sure our romance scheme has helped."

He sent her a sidelong glance. "Too early to tell."

Georgie looked from the window to the snow still twirling from the sky. "I half thought Sarah might come out here by now. She used to love snow when we were younger."

"Perhaps she has forgotten how magical it is," he said.

"Sadly, I think she has forgotten a lot of things."

In the library, Sarah turned to the window and observed, "The first real snowfall of the year. Georgie will be pleased."

"Don't ye like snow?" Mr. Henshall asked.

"I used to, very much. Snow was fairly rare in Gloucestershire. At least, rare for it to accumulate enough for sledding or sledging. So when it did snow, I lost no time going out to enjoy it. When Georgie was young, she used to look out the window and squeal in delight whenever flurries fell. I would bundle her up and take her outside, and we'd giggle and run about in it, then try to catch snowflakes on our tongues."

"That I should like to see."

She chuckled.

Voice low, he said, "We get a lot of snow in Scotland, ye know."

"Do you?"

"Aye."

Struck with a realization, Sarah felt her brow furrow. "Last year we had a great deal of snow here, and I never went out simply to enjoy it. I kept too busy worrying about and dealing with our guests—three men in the Duke of Kent's employ. But I could have. I should have."

"Three . . . single men?" he asked with a quizzical glance.

"Well, yes. One was James, the duke's private secretary, who, as you know, married our Emily. The other was the table-decker and keeper of the plate, and the third was the duke's assistant cook and pastry chef."

"A royal pastry chef . . . here? I imagine ye found him quite . . . interesting?"

"I did, yes. At first I resented his making free with what I've come to consider *my* workroom, but in the end we came to an . . . understanding."

"An understanding?" His brows shot up.

"Not that sort of understanding."

"Did he . . . suggest one?"

Sarah thought back. "I suppose he did."

"I despise him already."

She chuckled again. "Don't bother. His heart did not break when I said no. I am sure he recovered from his disappointment rather quickly."

"Are ye certain? I wouldna recover from such a disappointment quickly. If ever."

For a long moment, their gazes clicked and held.

He said, "Ye once told me you'd had one great love in your life and didna expect to have another."

"I know. I regret saying that . . . holding on to that for so long."

"Do ye? I am not surprised another man pursued ye. I dreaded the very idea yet knew it was inevitable."

Sarah took a deep breath. "Then I will confess something to you. When we arrived at your home, we were told the 'lady of the house' would be with us shortly. I thought you might have married someone else."

"Ah. And how did that make ye feel?"

"I did not like it. Then Isla told us you were seeing another woman. A neighbor, Miss Sorley? I did not like that either."

He nodded. "I did spend some time in her company, aye. Though several months ago now. I'd not seen ye in over a year and had little reason to hope. I told myself I should try to forget ye, yet I could not. Estimable as that woman is . . ." He shook his head. "She is not you."

He stepped closer and took her hands. "Sarah, I—"

Smack.

A wet, icy blob struck the windowpane and began a slow slide downward.

Smack.

A second followed.

Sarah stepped to the window, unsure whether to be relieved or disappointed by the interruption.

She peered out, past the melting blob, to the snow-covered yard beyond. Two faces grinned up at her. Georgie's and Colin's.

Mr. Henshall came and stood beside her. "Come, lass, this is your chance. Shall we go out and join them?"

Sarah hesitated, then pushed aside thoughts of cleanup and heavy decisions. For now.

She smiled at him, her heart lightening. "Yes, let's."

As Georgie had hoped, a few minutes later, the door opened and a bundled-up Sarah and Mr. Henshall came outside.

With a mock scowl at Colin, Mr. Henshall began, "All right, ye Peeping Tom . . ."

Sarah pointed at her. "And Thomasina."

"No more spying through windows, ye ken?"

"And no more throwing snow blobs at what was reasonably clear glass," Sarah added.

"We did try to make proper snowballs," Georgie defended, "but there's barely enough snow and what there is is awfully wet."

"Here. Let an old Scot try." Mr. Henshall bent low and with two gloved hands scooped a heaping fistful from the snow-covered grass. He packed the wet mass into a reasonable approximation of a snowball, and with no warning, launched it at Colin.

Slap. It struck Colin's neck.

Colin's hands shot up in self-defense. "Hey, now. Took me twenty minutes to tie this cravat." He proceeded to bend and gather a snowball of his own. "Well, two can play that game."

Sarah turned to Georgie. "Remember when I used to take you outside and we'd run about trying to catch snowflakes on our tongues?"

"I remember, but I didn't think you did."

"Of course I do."

"I am far too big for you to carry now." Georgie walked closer, the hand holding snow she had gathered behind her back.

"Perhaps so," Sarah agreed, looking up. "Yet we might still try to catch snowflakes."

"True," Georgie said. "Or I might do this instead. . . ."

Georgiana slipped the icy snow down the back of Sarah's neck.

"Aiy!" she exclaimed, reaching up to try to remove the icy intruder, to little avail.

And within seconds, the sisters were bending to scrape snow off the grass and fling it at each other amid shrieks of gleeful outrage.

All the while the men undertook their own back-and-forth battle.

Eventually, the four called a truce and made their way back inside, swatting snow off one another's backs, laughing, breathing hard, and exchanging playful barbs about who had bested whom.

As they stomped off their boots on the walkway, Colin sought Georgie's gaze. "This might be the best Christmas I've ever had."

Georgiana returned his grin. "Me too."

After the snowball fight, Sarah led the way indoors to warm up, Georgie diverting down to the kitchen to find a treat for Chips.

They returned in time to bid farewell to William and Claire, who were leaving to take a sleepy Mira home. Viola and Jack departed as well.

Cora and Mamma, meanwhile, sat reading near the parlour fire with James and Emily until Mamma complained of being overheated and moved farther back, looking rather flushed.

To avoid disturbing the readers, the snowball combatants gathered in the library instead. When Georgie returned from tossing a piece of roast beef to Chips, she joined them. Effie came in as well.

Sarah was about to go down and make tea, but Mr. Gwilt had anticipated her and carried in a tea tray with cups and biscuits for all.

"Thank you. You read my mind."

He grinned and retreated.

For several minutes, the group sat sipping tea and enjoying the crackling fire in relative quiet. Sarah was glad to find the feeling returning to her fingers and toes.

Then, since New Year's Eve was rapidly approaching, Sarah asked Mr. Henshall if there were any special foods he normally enjoyed at New Year's, or "Hogmanay" as he called it.

"Aye, several things. Venison pie, haggis, neeps and tatties, salted herrings, bannocks, black bun, shortbread . . ." He looked at her with dawning realization. "But I certainly don't expect to have those foods here."

"That's a relief, for I don't even know what most of those are." Sarah grinned. And while she made him no promises, she secretly decided to attempt some of the dishes for which she could find a recipe and the ingredients.

"How else do you celebrate?" she asked, and was pleasantly surprised when Effie did not protest.

He gathered his thoughts. "Music, sometimes dancing, raise a glass to Robert Burns, recite a few lines as well."

"Don't forget First Footing," Effie reminded him.

"Ah." He nodded and explained, "At home, we have a tradition called First Footing, meaning the first person to cross your threshold after midnight determines your fortunes for the coming year. I am not a superstitious man, but we do observe the custom."

"It's best if the first person is tall, dark, and handsome," Effie said, "as well as a prosperous bachelor. As long as he is not flat-footed—the higher the instep the better."

Mr. Henshall nodded again and continued, "He enters through the front door bearing gifts—coal, salt, cheese, shortbread, and coins, which represent warmth, good food and cheer, and prosperity for the coming year. He sets his coal on the fire and wishes the family a happy New Year. He is even permitted to kiss every woman in the house before he leaves through the back door, taking all of the previous year's troubles with him."

"I wonder who it will be," Georgie mused with a glance at Colin. "Most of the single men I can think of are fair-haired."

Colin shrugged. "I suppose that puts me out of the running."

Georgie raised her hands. "What if no one comes so late?"

"Then I suppose it shall be the dairyman in the morning," Sarah teased.

"Mr. Pym? Heaven help us."

Mr. Henshall said, "We shall just have to wait and see."

FOURTEEN

Each age has deemed the new-born year
The fittest time for festal cheer.
—Sir Walter Scott,
"Christmas in the Olden Time"

Her thoughts full of Callum Henshall, Sarah tied a clean half apron around her waist the next day and stripped the sheets from her own bed. If only it were as easy to strip away her doubts and questions.

Phrases from recent conversations with him echoed through her mind:

"I wouldna recover from such a disappointment quickly. If ever." And *"I'm through being cautious. . . . If ye think I am hesitant where you're concerned, let me make something clear. I know how I feel about ye, lass. I am only holding back out of respect. . . ."*

Sarah, however, was not through being cautious. In truth, she was struggling. Could she give up her home? Move hundreds of miles from her family? On the other hand, could she live with herself if she did not? So yes, she *was* holding back, especially now with Mrs. Besley needing more help and Emily planning to spend most of her time elsewhere. Would it not be wrong of her to leave? For even though Viola lived next door—close enough to help Mamma if need be—her sister would soon have her hands full with a newborn.

Mr. Henshall had made it clear during his first stay with them that he was needed in Scotland. He had a man of business and tenants to keep the estate going for a month or two, but he could not stay away much longer. He had responsibilities at home, just as she had at Sea View. Even if his cousin was to inherit instead of a son, he was duty bound to be a good steward, to manage the land well and keep Whinstone Hall in good order.

A secret part of her would love to be the woman to provide Callum with a longed-for son and heir. Though of course there was no guarantee they would have any children, and even a daughter could not inherit due to the dictates of the entail.

Would it be worth it to give up her family, to risk the success and security of Sea View for a husband and potential children of her own—children who would rarely see their grandmother and aunts in Devonshire? Was it selfish of her to even consider the desires of her heart above what was best for her mother and sisters?

As Sarah spread clean sheets over her bed, her thoughts continued to swing like a pendulum—toward him, and away again. With each practical argument against the match her emotions swung away. Then she recalled the appeal in his sea-green eyes when he said, *"It is my dearest wish that one day she'll do me the honor of taking my name,"* and her emotions swung toward him once more.

Oh, Lord, what would you have me do?

Bed made, Sarah gathered up the sheets and took them out to the laundry basket in the passage. Jessie came up the stairs humming a Christmas carol. The maid was carrying two folded towels under one arm, and in her hand, the bin they used to collect rubbish from the guest rooms.

"Ah, Jessie. I've barely seen you to ask. Did you enjoy your day off with Tom?"

"Yes, miss." The young woman's eyes sparkled. "And I wanted to tell you. Tom thought we should save up for a nice place of our own first. But I don't want to wait. As long as we're together,

I'll be happy. So we're to marry in February, as soon as the banns can be read."

Sarah congratulated Jessie even as her spirits sank. She knew it was unlikely Jessie would continue working at Sea View once married, or at least once a baby came along. Another factor to consider . . .

Mrs. Besley limped to the bottom of the stairs with the aid of her cane. "Soup pot boiled over. Lowen stoked the fire too hot again. I could use Jessie's help in cleaning it up."

Sarah took the towels from the young woman. "You go on. I will do that."

"Those are for Scots Pine." Jessie handed over the bin as well, then hurried downstairs to help.

Sarah's heart gave a small twist at the name of the room . . . and the thought of its occupant.

Sarah carried the freshly laundered towels and bin to the door of Scots Pine. She had last seen Mr. Henshall in the parlour with a newspaper, while Georgie and Effie played draughts nearby. She was quite certain the bedchamber was empty yet knocked anyway.

When no one answered, she let herself in.

Inside, she found the bed neatly made. She laid the towels on the washstand and bent to pick up the room's small rubbish bin, preparing to dump it into the larger one. When Jessie left, who would take on her duties?

Footsteps sounded behind her. Startled, she turned and found Mr. Henshall just over the threshold, no doubt surprised to find her in his room.

"What are ye doin', lass?"

Embarrassment flared. "I only came in to bring fresh towels and empty the bin. Jessie would have done it, but she was needed belowstairs."

He made no reply. For a moment longer he stood there, then he advanced into the room, the door swinging partway shut behind him.

He took the bin from her and set it on the floor. "You, my Jo, should be mistress of your own home. Not emptyin' bins." He held out both hands. "Give me that apron and I'll do it myself."

"What? Don't be silly," Sarah said, feeling incredulous until she recognized the teasing glint in his eyes.

"Why not?" He grinned and lunged for it, catching the half apron's ruffled hem.

She chuckled and leapt back. In a rare streak of mischief, she threw one of the towels at him.

Catching it, he said, "Ah, a weapon. Excellent." He unfurled the towel, twisted it into a rope, and snapped at her skirts with it.

She squealed, then began twisting the other towel, intent on revenge.

"Oh no you don't." He playfully grasped her around the waist, pulling at the bow that held the apron.

It fell to the floor.

She stilled, suddenly conscious of his nearness, the fresh scent of shaving soap, his strong arms around her.

Looking up, she found his face close to hers. Her breath caught, and her heart pounded.

For a moment both of his hands remained at her waist. Then he lifted one and cupped her cheek. His grin faded, his playful expression transforming into something far more serious. Even tense.

"Sarah . . ." he whispered, voice hoarse.

"Y-yes?"

His intense gaze moved to her lips, and the air between them thickened. "I have been wanting to kiss you again ever since I stole that kiss under the mistletoe. . . ."

He slowly lowered his head. She leaned toward him, ignoring the warnings flashing in her mind.

When his mouth was a mere breath from hers, he paused, and instead of kissing her, he groaned and rested his forehead against hers. "Yet I should not. Not here and now." He dropped his hands. "Oh, lass, when will ye put me out of my misery?"

The door to the next room banged open, and Sarah started, nerves leaping. She stepped back as Effie's and Georgiana's voices reached them from the adjoining room.

What was she doing? Flirting with a man in his bedchamber— a man who had been hurt by a woman before? Heaven help her.

Regret flooding her, Sarah ducked her head. "I should go."

He stopped her with a gentle hand and lifted her chin. "You have done nothing wrong, Sarah. I started this. I want very badly to kiss ye, but I will wait for a more appropriate time and place. I pray ye won't make me wait much longer."

She wanted to reassure him, but the reply caught in her throat. "Excuse me." Grabbing her apron, Sarah scuttled from the room. Were she his wife, she would have every right to be there with him. But she was not.

Longing to talk to Claire and ask her advice, Sarah dressed warmly and walked over to the boarding house.

When she crossed the marketplace, she saw Claire at Broadbridge's front door, showing out an older woman with a leather case in hand.

"Thank you, Mrs. Jones. We are most grateful."

The older woman nodded, said something Sarah couldn't hear, and walked away in the opposite direction.

Seeing her approach, her sister waved and waited for her. When she drew closer, Claire said, "What a night! Mary had her baby. A boy. That was the midwife just leaving."

"How is Mary?"

"Exhausted, of course, but otherwise she seems perfectly well."

"Thank God."

"Yes. A healthy birth is always a relief to be sure. We have engaged a monthly nurse, who is up there with her now. Do come in out of the cold."

Sarah wiped her feet on the rug and entered the front hall.

"Any word from her intended?"

"Unfortunately, no. William has written again to inquire about the ship's whereabouts. I pray no harm befalls that young man—or I should say, that young father."

"I shall pray as well."

"For now, mother and child are both sleeping peacefully, so please come to our rooms for a chat."

"Where are Mira and William?"

"He is playing with her up in the attic so I could have some time to myself. I did not get much sleep last night."

"Oh, then I will go and let you rest. . . ."

"Nonsense. I'd much rather talk with you." Claire led the way upstairs to the sitting room of their apartment.

Once they both were seated, she said, "Now. Tell me how you are."

"If I'm honest, I don't know how I am. Torn, I suppose you could say. Would it be selfish of me to put my desire for love and marriage above what is best for Mamma and the rest of the family?"

"Selfish?" Claire repeated. "I think you might be idealizing the wedded state. William and I are very happy together, yet marriage is not all romance and kisses. It is also a serious responsibility. As is becoming a stepmother, I've learned. Both are challenging and important callings. And in your case, taking on a girl in her teens?" Claire raised her light eyebrows high. "You will find it far more demanding than any of your tasks at Sea View, I'm sure— though a joy too."

"I had not thought of it that way."

"Sarah, we all want you to be fulfilled and happy. None of us would ask you to give up something—or someone—you love. But . . . do you love him?"

Did she?

"How does one know? I certainly admire him, respect him, trust him. I find him attractive, kind, considerate, and patient. Talented and honorable . . ."

Claire's eyes shone, and a soft smile tilted her lips. "I think you have your answer."

"Even if I do love him, there is more to life than attraction or affection. There is duty and responsibility, and self-sacrifice."

As she had many times over their lives, Claire placed a hand over her eyes and slowly shook her head. "Sarah, Sarah, Sarah . . . Don't make this more complicated than it needs to be."

"Too late," Sarah said, and they both chuckled.

Then Sarah met her sister's gaze. "Are you trying to get rid of me?"

"No, my dear. I would really miss you, but I want what's best for you."

"Thank you. It's been difficult to think it through clearly, especially now with Mrs. Besley laid low, and Jessie soon to wed. And Mamma hasn't seemed herself since our return. I pray she's not relapsing after doing so well these last several months."

"I am sorry to hear it and will visit her as soon as I can. But, Sarah, there will always be something."

Sarah groaned. "I know. That's what I'm afraid of."

New Year's Eve would fall on a Sunday that year, so they all joined forces to give the house a thorough cleaning on Friday and Saturday instead. "Redding up the house," as Mr. Henshall called it, was another pre-Hogmanay tradition. They would also eat or discard any remaining perishable food to start the year fresh.

Emily was needed at the printer's again, so she was excused from her share of the cleaning. Sarah was relieved when Cora, and even the Henshalls, insisted on taking part.

Mamma began by sweeping the carpet in the library-office with a brush, but when Sarah found her leaning against a bookcase, fanning herself, Sarah suggested she sit at the desk and sort through old newspapers and magazines instead, which would be less taxing.

"Sorry," Mamma said as she sat heavily in the chair. "Not feeling my best today."

After finishing the carpet there, Sarah went into the drawing room to sweep that carpet as well. Then she held the ladder for Mr. Henshall as he dusted the candle chandeliers and frames of paintings high on the walls while Effie dusted the furniture.

Eventually, Emily returned from the printer's and brought the post with her. She handed a letter to Effie.

Effie accepted it with some surprise. Glancing at the handwriting, she said, "It's from Aunt Isla."

Feather duster forgotten, Effie plopped down on the sofa, opened it, and read quickly. "Well, that's good news."

Mr. Henshall descended the ladder. "What does she say?"

"It seems she and Granda' are getting on well after their former rift, and he continues in improved health."

"That is good news," Mr. Henshall said, studying Effie's profile with interest and perhaps concern.

"Aye, to be reconciled with your father after such enmity. I'm glad for her. She also says . . ."

Effie broke off and darted a glance at her stepfather from beneath her lashes.

"Says what?" he asked.

"Ach, ye know Aunt Isla. Just some other fanciful ideas." Effie refolded the letter and rose, tucking it into her apron pocket. "Now, we had better get back to reddin' up this place before the New Year."

She retrieved the discarded feather duster and purposefully left the room.

Sarah and Mr. Henshall shared a raised-brow look. Effie eager to clean the house? Just what else had been in that letter?

Now that his sister-in-law had left her role as housekeeper, Sarah assumed Mr. Henshall would engage a more capable woman to take her place. Sarah was tempted to recommend some qualities to look for but held her tongue. It was not her place. She was not mistress of his house. Though daily she found herself wishing more and more that she was. Was Claire right? Would it not be selfish to give up her responsibilities at Sea View for a place in his life, one with its own demands and challenges?

She returned to her tasks. She had not planned to pry into Effie's letter from her aunt—that was not her place either—but when she took the carpet brush upstairs, she found Effie sitting on her unmade bed, rereading the letter.

She looked up and seemed pleased to see her. "Sarah, may I tell ye somethin'?"

"Certainly. If you'd like."

Effie leaned forward and pulled her dressing gown off the room's single chair. Then Sarah sat, facing her.

"Aunt Isla has asked me to come and live with her and Granda' in Perth."

Sarah's stomach dropped, but she endeavored to keep her expression and tone neutral. "Did she?"

Effie nodded. "She said it would only be right as she and Granda' are my kin. And that my . . . Mr. Henshall could visit whenever he wished."

"I see." Sarah hesitated, then said, "Though when we called at Whinstone Hall, I believe your aunt mentioned Perth is rather far away."

"Aye. Half a day or more by horse and carriage."

"And how do you feel about the idea?" Sarah asked.

Effie shrugged. "I love my aunt, of course. My granda' can be fearsome, but he's usually kind to me, though a bit crotchety, if that's not mean to say. And I'm sure she's right that I'd be a more cheerful companion for her than he is."

Again Sarah hesitated, not sure how to respond and not wanting to say the wrong thing.

Finally, she said, "And you did not mention this to your stepfather, because . . . ?"

"It would hurt his feelings. And I wanted to think it through first."

Effie chewed her lip, then asked, "Do ye think I am . . . obligated to live with them? They are my blood relations, after all. My mother's sister and father."

Sarah said, "Mr. Henshall is your family too. Your mother's husband, and more than that, he has been a loving father to you from what I've observed."

"He has," Effie agreed. "Though annoyin' at times, wanting me to go to school and such."

"That's because he cares for you, wants you to have the best possible future."

"I know. And I'd rather have an annoyin' da' than a cruel one, that's for certain. He's nothing like my first father, thank the Lord."

"I think you should talk to him about this. But to answer your question, no, I don't think you're obligated to leave your home to go and live with them. It seems Mr. Henshall is perfectly willing to take you to Perth on occasion, and perhaps visits will become even more frequent now that your aunt lives there as well."

Effie slowly nodded, taking this in.

Afraid of the answer, Sarah asked, "What do you want to do, Effie?"

The girl drew a deep breath followed by a long exhale. "I want to stay home. With my annoyin' step-da'."

Sarah smiled, reached over, and patted Effie's knee. "Then that, dear heart, is what you should do."

Later, after Effie had gone to bed that night, Mr. Henshall stopped to speak to Sarah in the library.

He said, "Effie told me about Isla's invitation and what you said about it."

"I hope I did not speak out of turn."

"Not at all, and I agree with your advice. A woman should not feel duty bound to live with her family." Humble humor shone in his eyes. "Instead, she should follow her heart."

FIFTEEN

"A guid New-year to ane and a',
And mony may ye see,
And during a' the years to come,
Oh happy may ye be.
  —Traditional Scottish ballad

After church and a light meal the next day, Sarah resumed her preparations for that night's New Year's Eve party. She certainly hoped Georgiana was enjoying all the holiday celebrations they were hosting for her benefit. Sarah trusted she had fulfilled her promise to make this year's Christmastide far more festive than the last. After all the food, candles, and other supplies to feed their guests and light the rooms during evening parties, they would certainly need to economize in the New Year to make up for their extravagance now.

For Sarah's part, she was growing exhausted. Had all the effort, long hours, and expense been worth it? She doubted it.

Late that afternoon, Mamma came into the workroom and found her arranging sweets and savories on silver trays.

"Sarah, go and change! We are dressing formally tonight, remember?"

"Just a few more minutes . . ."

Mamma untied her apron and tugged it free, which did *not* have the same effect as when Mr. Henshall had done so.

"Now, my girl. I will finish this."

Sarah looked up from her work at last. Her mother stood there in an elegant long-sleeved gown of fawn silk with lilac and green stripes.

"Mamma, you look lovely."

"Thank you. Now it's your turn. Go on."

Sarah studied her a moment longer. "How are you feeling?"

"Impatient with a dawdling daughter at the moment, but otherwise fine."

"Very well. I'm going."

Sarah went up to change into a dress of blue silk taffeta printed with silvery ornaments. It had the newer low-fitted waist, and the celestial blue color flattered her complexion and brought out the blue of her eyes—or so the modiste had assured her.

Emily came in to help with her fastenings and to add some curls around her face with the hot iron.

"A lot of fuss," Sarah murmured, "when I shall be busy serving most of the night."

"No, you shan't. You shall be enjoying the company of your family and guests. Come now, put a smile on that pretty face of yours."

Again Sarah wondered if all the extra effort was worth it.

She went downstairs and, with a sigh, picked up a fallen hair pin from the floor. Georgiana's, she guessed. Hearing footsteps on the stairs behind her, she straightened, turned . . .

And froze.

Callum Henshall slowly descended . . . wearing a kilt.

Sarah stared, unable to do otherwise, cataloging every inch of his person, from his black buckled shoes, tall stockings tied around strong calf muscles, bare knees peeking out, to the belted tartan kilt in a subdued blue, green, and black pattern, over which an ornamental . . . something . . . hung on a chain. He looked like the man she knew yet startlingly different too. Dangerously new and not quite the civilized gentleman he'd seemed before.

The foreign garments stood in sharp contrast to those of his upper body—a traditional waistcoat, neckcloth, and tailored coat.

For a moment the strange image of a merman came to mind: gentleman above, wild Scot below.

Sarah's mouth went dry.

He paused on the stairs, studying her, and when she remained silent, he continued his descent.

His gaze traced her face, her hair, her gown. "Ye look beautiful."

"You are . . . do too."

His eyes shone. "I can see I've surprised ye. But a Scot must wear his kilt for Hogmanay."

"Of course. I . . . I don't mind at all."

In fact, Sarah decided then and there that her puny efforts for this holiday had been very much worth it indeed.

Effie came down next wearing a green dress with a tartan scarf over one shoulder.

Georgiana descended after her in a new gown of figured mulberry satin with a square neck and a single, plain flounce at the hem. She had rejected the modiste's suggestions of festooned flounces, beribboned sleeves, and a ruffled bodice, even though Mamma favored them. She would feel foolish, she'd insisted, as though wearing a costume meant for some fine la-di-dah lady and not herself. Mamma had finally relented. Although rather simple, the dress suited Georgie, and she looked feminine and pretty in it.

Emily followed, beautiful as usual in a rose-colored gown, James handsome in dark evening attire at her side.

Finally, Cora came down, dressed in a frock that was both charming and familiar—a yellow dress with pink flowers embroidered at the hem and a wide pink ribbon at the waist. There had not been time to order anything new for her, so she wore a favorite dress that Mamma had saved, one that had been passed down through her daughters. She planned to have a new dress made for Cora after the busyness of the holidays had passed.

Soon their other guests arrived. Claire and William first, followed by the four Huttons: Jack, Viola, Colin, and Mr. Hutton senior. Mira had remained at the boarding house with Armaan and Sonali, but all three would join them on Twelfth Night.

Everyone was well dressed and in good spirits, greeting one another and commenting on the cold weather as they shed outdoor garments, which Mr. Gwilt whisked away.

They soon sat down together at a table crowded with serving vessels mounded high with an appealing variety of foods, including traditional English dishes as well as some of the fare Mr. Henshall had suggested for Hogmanay.

Sarah had given Mrs. Besley a recipe for haggis, but the cook had turned up her nose at the idea of preparing anything involving a sheep's lungs, stomach, or ox bung. The butcher refused as well.

They did manage to make venison pie, thanks to a gifted roast from Sir Thomas Acland, James's employer, who kept deer on his estate. They also prepared a side dish of neeps and tatties, made of potatoes and "swede," also known as Swedish turnip or rutabaga. And they easily acquired salted herrings from local fisherman Mr. Cordey.

Sarah herself made shortbread, the round oatcakes called bannocks, and black bun—a pastry-covered fruitcake.

Mr. Henshall was clearly impressed and shook his head in astonishment. "Ach, I could close my eyes and be at home in Kirkcaldy."

"Aye, except without the haggis," Effie said, "for which I am grateful."

"I considered making it myself," Sarah admitted, "but I decided an inexperienced Englishwoman should probably not attempt Scotland's national dish. At least, not without tutelage."

Effie nodded. "Very wise."

"No matter," Mr. Henshall said, looking at her earnestly. "I am most grateful for the kind efforts you've made on our behalf."

Pleasure at his words and fond gaze warmed Sarah's cheeks, and she hoped her blush was not obvious to the others. Daring a glance around the table, she noticed her sisters share meaningful looks. They knew her too well.

After dinner they all moved into the larger drawing room for tea, coffee, and more conversation. Georgiana tried to instigate a game of charades to no avail, although she did convince James,

Emily, and Colin to sit down with her to a game of whist. Nearby, Effie and Cora played a game of spillikins. When the games ended, the players rejoined the others in the drawing room.

By popular request, Viola played the pianoforte for a time. Then she asked Mr. Henshall and Effie to play and sing for them. He retrieved his guitar and Effie stood beside him, their Scots accents strong as they sang:

> "The year is wearin' to the wane,
> An' day is fadin' west awa'
> . . . Now let us tak' a kind farewell,
> Good night an' joy be wi' you all. . . ."

As the two sang, Sarah's gaze returned often to the handsome Scotsman in his kilt. She found herself growing pleasantly accustomed to this version of Callum Henshall.

After the song, Georgie applauded along with the others. Colin came and stood beside her. She had thought he might bring Eliza Marriott but was pleased he had not. He'd said earlier he would ask her, so she must have turned down his invitation once again.

In a low voice, he said, "Remember our scheme to foster romance between Sarah and her Scotsman?"

"Yes?"

He winked at her, then addressed Mr. Henshall in a louder voice. "I think this evening calls for a Robert Burns tribute. Won't you recite a poem for us? And I know just the one—'The Red, Red Rose.'"

Mr. Henshall hesitated, then countered, "How about 'To a Mouse'? Or 'Address to a Haggis'?"

"No. And it's too early in the evening for 'Auld Lang Syne.'"

"Very well then, lad. A Scot never turns down an opportunity to honor the great Rabbie Burns, Scotland's favorite son."

He set aside his guitar and returned to stand before them. For a long moment he stood silent, and Georgie feared he might not recall the words. But after collecting his thoughts, he began.

"O my Luve is like a red, red rose
That's newly sprung in June;
O my Luve is like the melody
That's sweetly played in tune.

So fair art thou, my bonnie lass,
So deep in luve am I;
And I will luve thee still, my dear,
Till a' the seas gang dry . . ."

Georgie cast a surreptitious look at her sister and was chagrined to see tears in her eyes. Had Colin's scheme had the opposite effect of the one he'd intended?

". . . And fare thee weel, my only luve!
And fare thee weel awhile!
And I will come again, my luve,
Though it were ten thousand mile."

When he'd finished, Sarah joined in the applause, then abruptly excused herself to replenish the trays of black bun and shortbread, although they were already quite full.

After that, people rose and refilled their teacups or moved chairs to speak with someone new. Georgie ate a piece of black bun, and then talked to Claire for a time, asking after Mira, who would be in bed by now with Sonali and Armaan watching over her.

She then played a game of dominoes with Cora, until Mamma noticed the girl yawn for the third time in as many minutes and put her to bed in her own room.

Georgiana soon grew restless. She wanted to play another game of whist or perhaps charades. She looked around for Colin, hoping he would second the notion and help her rouse enough players from among the well-fed, relaxed crowd. Where had he gone? Up to the water closet? She waited a few minutes, but the only person to descend was his father.

"Mr. Hutton, do you know where Colin is?"

"I believe he left, oh, some twenty minutes ago."

Her stomach sank. "He left? Did he say why?"

"I thought he mumbled something about running to Westmount for something. Though he should have been back by now, if that was the case. Perhaps he's gone to Temple Cottage. That pretty Miss Marriott invited him to join their small celebration there. I did not think he intended to go, but I suppose he might have changed his mind."

Disappointment coursed through her like ice water. Had Colin merely fulfilled his obligation at Sea View and then left as soon as he could to go where he really wished to spend New Year's Eve? Most likely. Georgie's shoulders slumped.

She returned to the drawing room and sat heavily in an armchair, her interest in games dissipating. Her enjoyment of the evening too.

As midnight approached, those remaining rearranged their chairs in a large circle.

When the hands of the clock approached the hour, Mamma, as the head of the family, went to the door and opened it wide to usher out the old year and bring in the new. In the distance the church bells pealed, ringing in the New Year. When the last stroke of midnight died away, she shut the door quietly and returned to the others. Yet she had barely crossed the threshold when someone knocked on the door.

Effie looked up eagerly. "I wonder who that is? Who will be our first footer?" She rose and dashed into the hall to find out, and curious, Georgie followed.

Effie herself opened the door before Mr. Gwilt could do so.

There was indeed a tall, well-dressed, and prosperous-looking young man on their doorstep.

She could tell nothing about the shape of his foot, but what showed of his hair from beneath a fashionable beaver hat was decidedly dark. In fact, his forehead bore a dark streak as well.

Georgie burst out laughing. Colin Hutton stood there, his hair blackened with soot or lampblack or some such.

Hands on her hips, she proclaimed, "Colin Hutton, you are incorrigible."

Effie narrowed her eyes at him. "I don't think he counts."

"I was not in the house at midnight," Colin defended. "And I come well supplied." He lifted the sack slung over his shoulder.

Sarah stepped out from the drawing room doorway. "Who is it?"

Georgie went along with Colin's guise. After all, she had wanted to play charades.

"It's our first footer—and he comes bearing gifts!"

Sarah's lips parted, but before she could object, Georgie ushered him past her into the drawing room, where the others responded with laughter and good-natured groans, while his father shook his head and gave an exasperated sigh.

"Good evening. Your first footer has arrived," Colin said, adjusting the coarsely woven sack.

His brother Jack muttered, "Are you supposed to be Father Christmas or a chimney sweep?"

"Come in, young sir," Mamma said, going along with the farce. "You are very welcome."

"Let us see your feet," Effie insisted. "If he is flat-footed as well as fair, the entire next year will be ruined."

"There is nothing wrong with my feet." Colin sniffed as though affronted.

"Let's take his word for it," Mr. Henshall interceded on the young man's behalf. "At least he does not come empty-handed."

"True." Colin reached into the bag. "First, a coin for our generous hostess." With a bow, he handed a gold sovereign to Mamma. "May this family always know prosperity."

"Hear, hear."

"And for you, sir, a wee dram." He handed a small flask to Mr. Henshall. "To celebrate a special occasion in the coming year. I hope."

"Good choice, lad."

"And sweets for the sweet." He gave Effie a piece of shortbread—shortbread that looked suspiciously like the batch Sarah had made.

"And salt for you, Miss Sarah." He handed her a small paper packet. "For flavor, since you are responsible for most of the flavorful foods we have enjoyed tonight."

Sarah accepted it with a little smile. "I'd rather have a pound of sugar."

He turned to Georgie and held up a lump of coal. "For warmth in the coming year."

Georgie took it and tossed it onto the fire.

"Sadly, no cheese." Colin sighed. "The cheesemonger was closed."

"Then how about a toast?" Mr. Henshall offered him a glass.

"Good idea." Colin accepted it. "To Sea View and all gathered here—" he raised his glass and, in an imitation of Mr. Henshall's accent said—"a *guid* New Year."

They all raised their glasses, repeated the words, and then sipped their tea or punch or whatever drink was at hand.

Colin emptied his in a single swallow, then set down his glass. "Now there is something else I must do."

"Escort last year's troubles out the back door?" Effie asked.

"Trying to get rid of me already? No, I recall Mr. Henshall saying the first footer might claim a kiss from all the ladies in the house?"

"Careful," Jack warned, a protective arm around his wife.

Colin hesitated, making a show of tugging on his collar as though suddenly too tight. "Then perhaps only the unmarried ladies. For my own safety."

To ward off actual kissing, Sarah offered her hand. Colin raised it gallantly to his lips. Mamma followed suit.

Effie was next and presented her cheek for a kiss. He obliged her with a peck.

Then Effie looked back at her. "Your turn, Georgie."

It had been one thing for him to kiss her cheek alone under the mistletoe, but with all these people watching? Georgiana huffed to cover her unease. "How silly! Oh, very well. Get it over with." She held out her hand as Sarah had done. Instead he leaned in close and pressed a warm kiss to her cheek. A cheek that now blazed with embarrassment.

He smiled into her eyes as he slowly pulled back, then turned to the others.

"*Now* I shall usher last year's troubles out the back door. And with that, I bid you all good night."

He bowed and slipped out of the room, heading, Georgie guessed, for the back stairs and the rear kitchen door below.

Was he hurrying off to play the role of first footer at another house? One with other females to kiss—slightly older, far prettier young ladies? Probably.

"Look, Georgie," Effie enthused, pointing out the window. "You got your wish. It's snowing again!"

Georgie walked to the window that overlooked the veranda and the outside world beyond. Feathery white snowflakes fell lazily from the sky, clinging to tree branches and glazing the ground.

It was beautiful, yet she felt oddly deflated. What was wrong with her?

Yes, she had got her wish. It had snowed not once but twice. Then why did some tender shoot of longing yet remain? Like a hunger pang, but one that originated in her heart instead of her stomach.

At Effie's pronouncement, Sarah and a few others rose and joined them at the windows to enjoy the sight of fresh new snow christening the fresh New Year.

It really is lovely, Sarah thought, glad that her first thought was not, for once, about the practicalities: having to sweep the outside stairs and walk or needing to clean up all the wet footprints that would soon muddy the hall.

"Now, if ye will indulge me," Mr. Henshall said, "let us join hands and sing 'Auld Lang Syne,' which means 'old long since.' We have sung it on Hogmanay in Scotland for generations, and I gather it is now sung here as well."

Those standing at the windows walked toward the middle of the room, and those sitting stood to join the circle, clasping hands.

Sarah found herself holding one of Effie's hands and one of Callum Henshall's. Her hand felt warm and secure in his sure grip.

"The song reminds us not to forget days gone by or old friends," he said. Then to Effie he added, "We'll sing the more English version, aye?"

She nodded. Then in his rich, lilting voice, he began to sing and the rest of them joined in:

"Should auld acquaintance be forgot, And never brought to mind?
Should auld acquaintance be forgot, And days o' lang syne?

"For auld lang syne, my dear, For auld lang syne,
We'll take a cup o' kindness yet, For auld lang syne."

After a few more verses, he looked at Effie and prompted, "The next verse as we sing at home?" His stepdaughter nodded, and the two sang together:

"And here's a hand, my trusty fiere! And gie's a hand o' thine!
And we'll tak a right guid willy waught, For auld lang syne.

"For auld lang syne, my jo, For auld lang syne,
We'll tak a cup o' kindness yet, For auld lang syne."

Sarah's ears caught on the phrase *my jo*.

On the last chorus, the jocularity faded from Mr. Henshall's expression, and his fair eyes took on a nostalgic light. He looked somberly into the distance, his voice slowing and deepening as he sang the familiar words with true feeling.

"We'll take a cup o' kindness yet, For auld lang syne."

After the final note, a few moments of silence reigned. Then around the circle, people began to separate. Sarah gave Effie's hand a final squeeze before releasing her, then turned to Mr. Henshall. She made to slide her hand from his, but for a moment longer he held fast, gaze boring into hers.

She pressed her lips together and then echoed, "A guid New Year to you."

He slowly nodded. "I hope it shall be."

The others went into the hall to gather coats and hats, or to bid farewell to those departing. Sarah lingered with Mr. Henshall.

She mustered her courage and asked, "I heard the words 'my jo' in the Scots version you and Effie sang. What does it mean?"

"Comes from the word *joy*," he explained. "It's an endearment that means sweetheart or darling or dear."

"Oh." She swallowed. "You may not have realized but . . . you've called me that a few times now, so I wondered."

"It may have slipped out only a few times, but it's how I often think of ye." He reached out and stroked her cheek. "My bonnie lass. My jo."

Sarah's skin tingled, and her heart did as well.

He studied her. "Do ye mind?"

"No. I rather like it."

"I'm glad."

He took her hand again, raised it to his lips, and pressed a warm kiss to the back of it. "Good night, Sarah."

"Good night." And she carried the warmth of it all the way up to her room.

SIXTEEN

Distance sometimes endears friendship,
and absence sweetens it.
—James Howell, *Familiar Letters*

Georgiana's family had decided in advance to exchange small gifts on New Year's Day instead of on St. Nicholas Day, as they had last year, or on Twelfth Night, which would be busy enough with the planned party—and because they were not giving gifts to everyone who would be in attendance.

They did, however, invite Mr. Henshall and Effie to join them for their modest time of gift giving over tea and leftover pastries. Of course, they had assured them there was no expectation of gifts being exchanged between the two families.

Given time off for New Year's, James spent the day with them as well. William, Colin, Jack, and Mr. Hutton, however, had been invited to Salcombe Hill for a day's shooting with local magistrate and landowner George Cornish.

When they realized Cora and Mira would be joining them, they selected a few small gifts for the girls as well. For athletic Cora there was a new Chinese diabolo to juggle. For Mira, a tiny knitted muffler and hat for her doll.

Much as last year, Mamma and the sisters exchanged primarily handmade gifts. Sarah had made fragrant lavender water and rose lip salve in the workroom belowstairs. Claire had painted lovely designs on small decorative boxes for each of them. Viola had netted coin purses for her sisters and a fine needlepoint fire screen for Mamma.

In turn, Mamma gave them a shared subscription to a ladies' magazine and beaded bracelets.

Emily, now being paid for her editing and proofreading work, bought a new history book for her husband and a small volume of Robert Burns poetry for Sarah, explaining, "I have lately become aware of your growing interest in all things Scottish."

Georgiana noticed Sarah blush.

Emily had also purchased new sheet music for Viola. And for Mamma, quality writing paper, hot pressed for a fine, smooth surface and printed with her initials.

She'd bought a pretty hair comb and a new sketch pad for Claire. And, finally, a slender book on fencing for Georgiana.

"Emily, it's too much!" Mamma objected.

"Not at all. You've had to suffer my neglect and homemade cards for the last few years. It is my pleasure to give nice gifts for once."

James handed Emily a gift. "And for you, a new novel."

Emily unwrapped a finely bound leather book. She opened it, and her brow puckered in confusion. "The pages are blank."

"That's because you have not written it yet."

With a soft smile, she reached over and touched his cheek. "Thank you for your confidence and encouragement."

Georgie's gifts would pale by comparison, she knew, but at least she'd managed to buy something. Last year, she had given her mother and sisters handwritten certificates good for one service from her, like walks with her mother and chores for her sisters. This year, she'd wanted to do something different. Her options were limited without money, so she'd returned to the lime tree alone and cut down the rest of the mistletoe. This she took to the man who sold winter evergreens door-to-door in his holly cart for people to use in decorating their own houses on Christmas Eve. He couldn't give her much money, but it was enough for a trip to the confectioner's. There she'd bought small packets of pralines and chocolate drops studded with white sugar beads called nonpareils.

Now she handed the packets around. "It's not much, I'm afraid. Though a little better than last year, I hope."

"My dear, you need not remonstrate with yourself," Mamma said. "Your certificates were much appreciated."

"Especially by me," Emily said. "Mine was good for one turn cleaning the water closet."

Sarah opened her packet. "Mm. These look delicious. Thank you."

"Yes, thank you, Georgiana," Viola said. "We shall enjoy them, I know."

Claire added, "Though I, for one, may have to wait until I am not so full."

Sarah watched in anticipation as Mr. Henshall gave Effie the pretty parcel she had helped him wrap, which contained the dancing slippers he had purchased and she had embroidered with a Scottish thistle each.

"Dancing slippers," he explained.

"I know. They're lovely! Thank ye."

"Sarah did the embroidery."

"They're perfect. Thank ye both. If only I had somewhere to wear them."

"I understand we are to have dancing at the Twelfth Night party," he said. "Might ye not put them to use then?"

"Indeed I shall."

Sarah handed her another small parcel. "Just something I made. A reticule with matching embroidery."

She opened it. "I love it. Thank ye."

In turn, Effie gave her stepfather a pair of riding gloves, as gloves were a traditional gift for the New Year.

He thanked her kindly, and looked at Sarah, opened his mouth, but then seemed to think the better of whatever he'd been about to say. Just as well, Sarah thought, with so many prying eyes and interested ears surrounding them.

After the gift giving had concluded, people dispersed, most to take the gifts to their own rooms.

Sarah tidied up the various wrappings and a few remaining plates and teacups, then carried them downstairs.

Mr. Henshall met her in the workroom.

There, he handed her a small tissue-wrapped box. "A little something for ye, Sarah."

Sarah's stomach dropped. She had nothing for him. Men and women did not exchange gifts unless they were married, engaged, or related by blood. "But I . . . You shouldn't have."

"Just open it," he gently insisted. "It's from Effie and me both."

Not a ring, then, she thought, relieved and disappointed in turns.

Noticing her reticence, he said, "It's not a ring, if that's what has ye worried."

"I would not presume . . ."

"No?"

"I don't know what to think." Discomfited by his watchful gaze, Sarah unwrapped the small box. Inside lay the simple gold cross necklace she had admired at the jeweler's shop.

Surprise and guilt flared. "I never meant you should buy it for me!"

"Of course not. I know that. It was my pleasure. A small token of our appreciation and affection, Effie's and mine."

"I am astonished nonetheless. Thank you. It is lovely, but I . . . should not accept it."

"Why not?"

"Because here in England, unrelated men and women do not exchange gifts unless they are married or engaged."

"Have I not been trying to bring that about?" He huffed a sigh. "Am I just another man, Sarah? I thought I was more to ye."

"Yes. I . . . I am very fond of you . . . and Effie," she faltered, setting the box on the worktable.

"You must know there is a question I want to ask ye," he said. "Yet how can I, when ye keep putting me off?"

Agitated, Sarah picked up a teacup and saucer she had left on the table earlier that morning.

"You would rather redd up than answer me." Irritation tightened his voice. "Am I wasting my time here? If ye have decided against me, just tell me and have done."

"I've been too busy to decide anything."

"You're not building the pyramids, Sarah. You've had time to think while baking and organizing and whatnot."

"Uh . . . !" she sputtered. "This is not a simple decision."

"And will ye be making it any time soon? I've tried to be patient, lass. God knows I have, but—" He grimaced and ran a hand over his face.

The teacup rattled against the saucer.

"Put the dashed thing down, Sarah, and look at me." He took the cup from her, set it down, and then firmly braced her shoulders. "I've given ye time. Tried not to pressure you, but this suspense. This . . . wavering . . . is maddening."

"Of course I'm wavering. You're asking me to give up my home and move hundreds of miles away from my family."

"Yes, I am. Or I would be—were I not sure to be rejected." The muscles in his face and neck tensed.

She had never seen him look so frustrated. Her fault. Dread curdled the dregs of tea in her stomach.

He released her and raked his fingers through his hair. "I had better take my leave of you, before I say something I'll regret."

Sarah stood there after he left, feeling sick and remorseful.

Then, leaving the dirty cup where it was, she went back upstairs.

Viola and Claire had remained in the parlour after the gift giving and now sat at the pianoforte together, the two musical sisters playing a duet.

In a haze of self-reproach, Sarah wandered into the parlour and joined them there.

Under other circumstances she would have been cheered by the sight of Claire and Viola sitting together, laughing and playing.

The two finished their duet with a flourish, and then Claire rose and sat in an armchair near Sarah.

"You go on, Vi. I can't keep up with you."

Viola began playing something soft and sweet without looking at the keys or music, as though barely aware of what she played.

Claire glanced at Sarah and then looked again, concern creasing her lovely face. "What is it? What's happened? You look upset."

"I am. Mr. Henshall and I have just had a . . ." *A what? An argument, row, altercation?* "A discussion."

"Oh?" Viola stopped playing and came over to sit with them. "About what?"

Sarah told her sisters about the gift, her reaction, and his frustrated response.

"Have you decided against him?" Vi asked.

Sarah blinked, not ready for a second inquisition so soon. "I have not decided anything. If things were different, I might have, but I don't think Mamma is ready for me to leave . . . permanently."

"Mamma . . . or you?"

Sarah picked up a stray piece of string on the arm of the chair, left from one of the parcels. Claire reached out and laid a hand over hers, stilling her movements.

She said gently, "It seems to me you have been living in near-constant motion the last few years while I was gone, endlessly striving just to keep your head above water. But those trying days are over."

"Are they?"

"They could be. That's up to you."

When Claire lifted her hand, Sarah began toying with the string. "He has not come out and asked me to marry him, by the way."

"Oh, come, Sarah," Claire gently chided. "Don't be daft. Traveling all this way to spend Christmas with you? I think he has made his intentions perfectly clear."

Yes, Sarah knew that he had.

And she had reacted poorly. And ruined everything.

The next day, Georgiana and Effie had just finished a game of draughts when Colin came by. She heard the door open and Mr. Gwilt welcome him and offer to take his coat.

Leaving Effie to reset the pieces for another match, Georgie went to greet Colin in the hall. "How was the shooting party yesterday?"

"It was all right. Our host served a hearty meal with excellent roast partridge at midday."

"I was not asking about the food. I was asking about the shooting."

"Do you mean if I bagged any birds, that sort of thing?"

"That is generally the point."

"Not for me. I like being out-of-doors. The good company. Jocularity among fellows. And I like the dogs. That Cornish fellow has the smartest dogs, and so well-mannered. Springer spaniels, pointers, cocker spaniels . . . I'd like to have a dog one day. Would you?"

"So you did not bag any birds."

"Nah. My father did. And Jack is a crack shot, of course. Hammond has less experience than I, but even he managed one pheasant."

"Were you disappointed?"

He shook his head. "Not keen on shooting birds."

"You don't mind eating them, I notice."

"True. The sauce they served with the partridge . . . delicious!"

"Perhaps your brother might give you shooting lessons."

Colin shrugged. "It was not that I shot and missed. I did not even shoot. Except once. Thought I spied another clump of mistletoe high in a tree. Wanted to test our theory that shooting would be the best way to bring it down."

"And was it?"

He gave her a self-effacing grin. "I ended up with a tatty old bird's nest on my head, so we shall never know."

Georgie laughed. "Well, shooting isn't the only sport. And you are quite good at cricket."

"Thank you. That reminds me. Brought you a gift." He dug in his coat pocket and pulled out a Duke six-seam cricket ball.

Georgie stared at it. "That's your last one. . . ."

"No one more deserving. Oh, and while I may not be a great shot, I am a capital dancer. When I was at school, my father offered to pay for a tutor in either fencing or dancing. You can guess which I picked."

"Too bad," Georgie replied. "I like fencing. James has given me lessons, which I enjoyed far more than I ever liked school lessons. Detested sitting indoors for hours on end."

"You're not alone there," Effie said, coming out into the hall to join them. "I was so relieved when the last governess left. My step-da' wants me to have more schooling, but I'd rather play music or ride."

Colin nodded. "I can relate. I liked sports and history, but otherwise, I was not a great student." He raised a pointer finger. "But you should see me dance a quadrille. Then you'd be impressed."

"Perhaps we shall. We are to have dancing on Twelfth Night. You will attend our party, I trust?"

"Would not miss it."

"Will Miss Marriott be joining us?"

He shrugged again. "I asked her. Your mother said I might. But she has not come the other times I've invited her, and I'm beginning to take the hint."

Georgie wanted to say she was sorry, but she could not, at least not honestly.

"It's all right," he added. "She's not the girl for me—that's all. So you two will have to take pity and dance with me."

Effie's brow creased with worry. "I dance at home in Scotland, but I fear the dances here are different." She sent Georgiana an imploring look.

"Don't ask me," Georgie said. "I attempted to dance at a few evening parties at Finderlay but never formally learned. I was rather young when my sisters took lessons from a dancing master."

Colin pressed a hand to his chest, mouth agape. "What? Two fair ladies who don't know how to dance? Unthinkable. It shall be my pleasure to teach you."

Since their argument the previous day, Sarah had seen Mr. Henshall only once in passing, heading out somewhere in his greatcoat. He had not joined them for dinner. Nor had she seen him this morning at breakfast.

The scene in the workroom kept running through Sarah's

mind. She regretted her words more and more by the minute. Remorse and guilt mounted and churned within until she couldn't sit still at the desk nor turn her hand to anything productive. She wanted—no, needed—to apologize.

Sarah went looking for the man but could not find him. Instead, she sought out her mother and found her in her room with Cora, the two stitching companionably together.

"Mamma, have you seen Mr. Henshall today?"

"No, my dear."

"What about Effie?"

"Hmm. Now you mention it, I have not seen her either. Then again, I've hardly seen anyone. When I went to breakfast, Emily was just leaving. I did not think to ask where James was. Gone to Killerton for the day, I assume. And of course with Georgiana one never knows. Likely off on one of her rambles."

"Or at the school," Cora added shyly.

Mamma patted her hand. "Good point, Cora."

"Did Mr. Henshall say anything to you about leaving? I thought they planned to stay at least through Epiphany."

Mamma frowned. "Leaving? No, my dear. Why should they leave now? Did you two quarrel?"

"Well yes, I suppose we did."

She had certainly not responded to his gift or his attentions the way he had hoped. Had he assumed the worst? He had definitely grown tired of her wavering. Had he given up on her? Decided she was not worth the trouble?

Mamma said, "Surely he would not just leave, not without saying good-bye."

"I am sure you're right, Mamma," Sarah replied, although worry continued to gnaw at her insides.

Her mother studied her. "I have said it before, my dear, but if you do decide to marry and move away, I will miss you terribly—we all will. But I would not prevent or begrudge your happiness for all the world."

"Even with Mrs. Besley ailing, Emily spending less time here, and Jessie soon to marry?"

"Yes. Even so."

Sarah managed a weak smile and turned to go, yet she very much feared she had lost her chance to marry or move anywhere.

She went next to the hall closet. His hat and greatcoat were gone. She walked through the parlour and saw that his books were gone as well. She told herself she was panicking for nothing. Her mother was right. Callum Henshall would not leave without saying goodbye. Then where *had* he gone? To find alternate lodging? Or what?

Sarah's stomach knotted. Here she'd had the admiration and attention of a good man—a man she liked. Respected. Found attractive. Someone who made her laugh and feel special. A man who had not once but twice pursued her, and she had discouraged him both times.

Oh, Sarah, what have you done? Who cared about a party if he left, her chance at happiness with him?

Mr. Gwilt hurried by, silver polish and cloths in hand.

"Mr. Gwilt, have you seen Mr. Henshall today?"

"Yes, miss. Saw him leave this morning, I did."

Her heart plummeted. "Leave . . . for good?"

"Oh, no. I did not mean that. Just for the day, I gather. Off on some errand."

Relief. "Did he say where he was going?"

"No, miss. All I know is Major Hutton came for him in his carriage."

"Really? He said nothing to me. I wonder where they were going. Well, don't let me keep you."

"Right you are. Giving all the silver an extra polishing before Twelfth Night, I am."

"Thank you."

Sarah still had much to do to prepare for the upcoming Twelfth Night party as well, but she was too agitated to settle down to work. First she would walk over to Westmount and ask Viola where the men had gone.

She found Viola in the Westmount sitting room, knitting something near the fireplace. She glimpsed light green yarn before Viola tucked it away into her work bag.

"Oh, Sarah. It's you. I suppose I don't have to hide this as you already know."

Viola made to rise, but Sarah said, "Don't get up on my account. What is that you're making?"

"A little blanket."

They spoke about the coming baby for a few minutes, and then Sarah asked the question uppermost in her mind.

"I understand Jack and Mr. Henshall have gone off somewhere together. Do you know where?"

"Exeter."

"Exeter? Why?"

Viola shook her head. "Jack did not explain. Said it was not his secret to tell. All he said was they were going to Exeter and would be gone for most of the day. Did you ask Emily? James went with them."

"Did he indeed?" Curious and curiouser. "No, I did not ask her. I have not seen her yet today."

"I think she is correcting proofs for Mr. Wallis."

"That's right. She did mention her plans last night, but I forgot. I shall ask her when she returns."

Viola tilted her head to one side. "What is it, Sarah? Do you mind Mr. Henshall spending time with Jack and James? You don't seem best pleased."

"No, it is not that. I . . . just didn't know where he'd gone or if he . . . intended to return."

"Ah. And you don't wish for him to leave, I take it?"

"No. At least not while we are on uneasy terms. I wish now I had not been so slow to make up my mind."

"Well, you have had a lot on that keen mind of yours lately, what with the holidays and all."

"Yes, but I fear that was merely my excuse for putting him off. And now he has given up on me."

"I doubt that, Sarah."

Sarah heaved a sigh and rose. "Well. We shall see."

When Sarah returned to Sea View, she found Georgie and Effie in the parlour, Effie demonstrating the high-stepping and leaping moves of a Highland fling.

Sarah was illogically relieved to see her.

"Where were you girls earlier?" she asked them. "No one seemed to know where you'd gone."

"We were up in the schoolroom," Georgie said. "Colin gave us a dancing lesson. And he has offered to give us all another lesson before the party."

"Has he? That is an excellent idea. I promised you dancing but had not thought about either a dancing master or a caller. I am glad he has offered to help you."

"Don't forget my step-da'," Effie added. "Man needs all the dancin' help he can get."

Shortly before the dinner hour, the Huttons' carriage stopped at the end of their drive. Sarah hurried to the library window, hand to her chest. The carriage door opened, and James stepped out. A moment later, Callum Henshall alighted, and Sarah exhaled in relief.

James and Callum waved farewell to Jack, who was still inside the vehicle. And then Taggart urged the horses to continue on to Westmount.

The two men started for the house, and Sarah pulled back, not wanting to be caught spying.

She walked to the library door and peeked out into the hall as James and Callum Henshall entered, Mr. Gwilt taking their coats and hats. She tried to gauge their moods. They spoke amicably but quietly, and Mr. Henshall patted his pocket and said something Sarah couldn't hear.

James replied, "Don't worry. Mum's the word."

Sarah wanted to hurry over and express her relief at Callum's return. And ask what business had taken them to Exeter. But she resisted the impulse to ambush him the moment he returned. Nor did she want to bare her heart in front of James.

The two men started upstairs to their respective rooms, probably to wash and change before dinner. She would wait, although perhaps not patiently.

Sarah forced herself to follow suit, going to her room to change into a prettier frock and repin her hair.

Emily often stopped by before dinner to see if she needed any help, but apparently her work for Mr. Wallis had her running late. Sarah was struggling to reach behind herself for the last few buttons when someone tentatively knocked.

"Yes?" Sarah called.

Cora entered and, seeing what she was doing, offered, "I can do that. I often helped my nan."

"Thank you, my dear." Sarah turned back around. Wondering what had brought the girl to her door, she asked, "Did you need me for something?"

"No, miss. Emily just arrived home and still must wash and change. I said I would come in her place."

"That was considerate of you."

As Cora's little fingers made quick work of the task, Sarah asked, "And how are things going, Cora? I know we can't expect you to be happy, at least not so soon after losing your grandmother, but I hope you are content here."

"Yes, miss. Everyone is very kind. Especially your mamma."

"I am glad to hear it. I know she enjoys having you here. And you are good for her," Sarah added, realizing it was the truth. Having a young girl under her roof again had given Mamma new purpose.

"All done," Cora said.

"I appreciate your help. And while you're here, may I brush your hair?"

"Is it untidy?" The little hand flew to her wayward curls in distress.

"Not at all," Sarah soothed. "Your curls are charming. I only wanted to return the favor."

"Oh. Then, yes, thank you."

"And please call me Sarah, all right?"

"All right, Miss Sarah."

A short while later, Cora left to go up to the attic to see if Georgiana needed any help, and Sarah went downstairs alone.

She found Mr. Henshall dressed for dinner and waiting in the parlour. He rose when she entered.

Pulse pounding in her ears, Sarah began as casually as she could, "You were gone a long time today. May I ask where you went?"

"I had some business in Exeter. Took longer than expected, but we managed to get what we went for."

"And that was . . . ?"

He hesitated. "I wish I could tell ye. But I fear you're not ready to hear it."

Contrition burned like a hot coal in her chest. She was eager to make things right between them, or at least, as right as she could. "I am so glad you are back. Back safely, I mean. I regret how I reacted to your gift. I spoke hastily and unkindly. I also know I've disappointed you. Being so slow to . . . respond. I hope you will forgive me."

He stepped near and stroked gentle fingers over her cheek. She barely resisted the urge to lean close. To invite a kiss.

"I forgive ye, lass, and I am sorry too. I know ye have a lot on your shoulders. I should have been more understanding. More patient. I will leave ye in peace until after the party. But when it's over, I hope ye will be ready to discuss the future. Our future."

Sarah nodded. "I will. And thank you."

Georgie, Effie, and Cora flew down the stairs and into the parlour like a flock of vociferous birds, chattering all the while.

Sarah gave Callum a final smile, then turned toward the dining room, relieved to be reconciled and grateful for the welcome reprieve.

SEVENTEEN

Just at this time these shops are filled with large plum-
cakes, which are crusted over with sugar, and ornamented
in every possible way . . . for the festival of the kings.
—Robert Southey, *Mr. Rowlandson's England*

Sarah thought back to the few Twelfth Night parties she had attended. They had hosted only one at Finderlay that she recalled, and what an evening it was. Could she manage anything half as grand?

Twelfth Night concluded the Twelve Days of Christmas and was followed by the Feast of the Epiphany, which marked the arrival of the wise men in Bethlehem to see the Christ child.

In preparation for the final celebration of the season, Sarah set out to prepare a Twelfth Night cake big enough to serve a houseful of guests.

She assembled the ingredients and began. First she weighed out several pounds of flour and scooped it into a large basin. Making a cavity in the flour, she filled it with some warm milk mixed with yeast. Then she added sugar, chopped butter, eggs, cream, brandy, cinnamon, nutmeg, and mace. The recipe instructed her to beat the batter with the hands until stiff. A lengthy effort she did not relish. She was about to reach in and begin the arduous task when Mr. Henshall entered the workroom.

"Came to see if ye needed any help down here."

She smiled at him. "I could do, yes. Excellent timing."

He walked around the worktable and stood beside her. As always, she was instantly aware of his nearness, the warmth and strength of his broad shoulder close to hers.

"What's it to be?"

"A Twelfth Night cake. My first. Although I made a bridal cake for Claire that was somewhat similar."

"What can I do?"

"We need to mix the batter by hand until it is as stiff as a hasty pudding." She hesitated, then said, "You helped me make my very first cake, the summer you were here. Remember?"

"Aye."

She still remembered him standing close, his superior strength easily accomplishing the task in a fraction of the time it would have taken her.

"That was only a simple pound cake," she said. "I hope I have improved since then."

"Ye have indeed, and I've tasted the proof daily."

He removed his coat and rolled up his sleeves before washing and drying his hands. "I'm happy to help. I am not much good in the kitchen, but I can stir with the best of them."

"And I greatly appreciate your willingness."

He reached into the basin and began mixing with his strong hands. She thought again of his long-ago quip about cooks having muscular arms. His certainly were. As he kneaded the mixture, the muscles of his forearms rippled beneath skin covered with fine golden hairs. She resisted the urge to touch them, just as she had that first time.

Forcing her attention elsewhere, Sarah busied herself by measuring out the fruit and dredging it in flour.

In short order, the batter was well combined and thick.

"Keep going while I add the fruit," Sarah said and gradually added the floured currants, candied orange, and lemon peel. Finally, she dropped in a dried pea and a bean.

When all was incorporated, he helped her transfer the stiff batter into a papered and buttered pan and then washed his hands again.

When she began to heft the pan, he said, "Allow me. That must weigh two stone at least." He carried it to the oven for her, carefully placing it inside.

She said, "That reminds me of what you said the first time you helped me stir something, about cooks having arms like caber tossers."

"As I recall, I excepted you from that description." After shutting the oven door, he walked back and stood before her. He encircled her wrists with his hands and slowly slid them up and over her arms, all the way to her shoulders.

She shivered with pleasure.

"As I said then, yours are slender and feminine." His hands slid lower once more, as if testing the firmness of her muscles.

"Although on closer inspection, uncommonly strong for a gentlewoman." He smiled into her eyes. Still lightly clasping her arms, he lowered his gaze to her mouth.

"I want to kiss ye, lass."

In response, she unconsciously pulled her lower lip between her teeth, before her mouth parted to reply. No response came.

When she did not object or pull away, he slowly leaned down, bringing his face close to hers. Her pulse leapt in anticipation. His nose lightly brushed hers as he angled his head, and then his lips touched hers. Again pleasure ran through her. How could one mere touch light a wick within her, body and soul? First one gentle kiss, then another. Kisses that expressed desire but also love and devotion. Oh yes, this was the man for her. . . .

She tentatively responded, returning the sweet pressure, the sweet caress, with her own. Then he broke the kiss and wrapped his arms around her, holding her tenderly close.

Mrs. Besley hobbled in and drew up short upon finding the two of them locked in an embrace. Sarah pulled away.

"Sorry," the cook said. "Came for the cream, but I can return later."

"No need. I shall fetch it for you. Mr. Henshall was just helping me with the cake."

"So I see."

Sarah hurried into the larder, pausing long enough to draw a deep breath, and hoping the cooler air would extinguish the heat in her cheeks.

When she stepped back out, she adopted an unconcerned air, although she doubted either of them were convinced.

"Here you are." She handed over the jug of cream, and when the woman left wearing a barely concealed smile, Sarah turned to Mr. Henshall. "Thank you for your help. Nothing more to do now until after it bakes and cools."

"How long will that take?"

"Maybe two hours in the oven. I shall have to add another paper to the top once it's colored to keep it from scorching. Then another few hours to cool."

"What do we do in the meantime?" he asked, and the low timbre of his voice and the warm way he looked at her made her pulse leap anew.

Sarah swallowed. "I . . . suppose I shall do the washing up."

He gave her a lopsided grin. "Ach, well. Not my first choice, but I can help with that too."

Since they were planning to dance in the larger drawing room during the party, they went ahead and moved the pianoforte from the parlour into that room for their group dancing lesson. Jack came over to help, and together he, Mr. Henshall, James, and Mr. Gwilt moved the heavy instrument from one room to the next. Georgiana had offered to help, but her mother snapped at her, "You need not always play the Amazon, young lady."

Georgie reared her head back, stung, and was only slightly mollified when Sarah caught her eye and mouthed the word *Sorry*.

Viola had come over with Jack, ready to play for them. Once the piano had been moved, James departed for Killerton, and Jack to attend a horse auction with his father. Emily was already an accomplished dancer but joined them to watch and turn the sheet music for Viola.

The prospective students gathered for the lesson: Georgie, Effie,

Mr. Henshall, and Sarah, although Sarah said she might not be able to stay long as she still had much to do in preparation for the Twelfth Night party two days hence.

While they waited for Colin to arrive, they moved the furniture from the middle of the room to the walls and rolled up the Turkish carpet.

Their teacher was late. How were they to proceed without him?

A few minutes later, a knock sounded. Mr. Gwilt opened the door to their tardy tutor. Colin entered in a fur-trimmed greatcoat, but he did not enter alone. A second man accompanied him. Mr. Gwilt took their coats, hats, and gloves, and Colin led his guest across the hall to join them.

"Pray forgive my tardiness," Colin said. "Had a capital idea, but as often happens, it came a bit late."

He turned to the young man beside him, who was, Georgiana knew, the same age as she was.

"This, as you may know, is Hubert Cornish. Met him at Salcombe Hill when his father hosted the shooting party. Home from Oxford for Christmas. Asked him to come as we need another gentleman to even our numbers."

Hubert nodded and bowed. "Happy to oblige."

Georgiana suppressed a groan. Her sisters were better acquainted with Hubert's older sister, Charlotte, the magistrate's proud daughter, but they were only slightly acquainted with her brother, as he had been away at school. Georgiana, however, had encountered Hubert several times during her walks when he'd been home between terms. He was always so terribly polite to her—formal and flattering. It was awful. And the way he looked at her made her want to look behind herself. Surely he must have been gazing so admiringly at someone else.

And he was looking at her that way now.

She acknowledged him with a dry "Hubert."

He bowed. "Miss Georgiana. What a delight to see you again. And who is your fair friend? I do not believe I have had that pleasure."

"This is Miss Effie . . . em, McKay?"

She noticed Effie wince at the surname. "Effie will do, if ye don't mind."

"A pleasure, miss," Hubert said with another bow. "Do I detect a Scottish accent?"

"Indeed, ye do. We've come a long way to be here."

"In that case, let us delay no longer. After all, we are here to dance."

The other introductions quickly dispensed with, Colin rubbed his hands together and said, "Let's begin. My dear sister-in-law, Viola, and I have devised a simple program. We shall start with an easy country dance."

"Easy sounds like a good idea," Georgiana said.

Colin nodded and turned to Emily. "Viola mentioned you are partial to the Duke of Kent's Waltz, in honor of your former royal neighbor, so we have included it."

"Excellent."

Mr. Henshall, however, did not look as pleased.

Colin held up his hands. "Now, Mr. Henshall, I see your scowl, but never fear, I shall not subject young Effie to a dance of dubious repute. Despite its name, this is an innocent country dance in three-quarter time, and not the German partner waltz known to raise eyebrows."

"Good lad."

They partnered off: Sarah with Mr. Henshall, and Hubert with Effie, which left Georgie with Colin.

"Let's walk through it. First we form a star with another couple. Yes, yes, good. Next join hands with your partner, and step forward and back in a balance step—like this." He demonstrated.

A strange sensation passed through Georgie when Colin held her hand. Goodness. What was wrong with her? She hoped no one had noticed her odd reaction.

"And now move down the line and back up again. Excellent. Shall we try it with music?"

They did so. On the first attempt, young Mr. Cornish bumped hard into Georgiana.

"The other way, Hubert."

"My deepest apologies, Miss Summers."

After a few more false starts and steps, they managed to follow the simple pattern.

Once they had mastered that country dance, Georgie said, "What about a quadrille, Colin? You mentioned we would be impressed to see you dance a quadrille. I do hope you plan to include one."

"You read my mind, Miss Georgiana. Next, we shall try a very simple quadrille. It is danced in groups of four couples." He regarded the three couples gathered, then turned to Emily. "We need another couple, if you would oblige and . . . Ah! Mr. Gwilt. Just in time."

The small Welshman hesitated just over the threshold, tea tray in hand. "I've never done the like, I haven't. But if I'm needed, I shall certainly try." He set down the tray and joined them.

The dance began with bows and curtsies, followed by a series of advancing and retreating steps, turns, and changing places with the person opposite. Mr. Gwilt followed along, mastering the steps far more quickly than Georgie did.

The pattern was again a simple one, although Colin added his own flourishes and skipping steps.

Mr. Henshall teased, "I would be more impressed to see ye dance a reel in true Caledonian style, or better yet, a Highland fling."

Effie shook her head. "He'd need a kilt."

Mr. Henshall grinned. "Then perhaps I shall have to dance it myself."

"Oh no!" Effie moaned. "Ye promised. Never again!"

"Ye may have wished to ban me, but I made no such promise, lass."

"We have no bagpipe or piper," she reminded him, almost desperately.

He gave a heavy faux sigh. "True. Then, I suppose we shall all have to forgo that pleasure for the present." Over the girl's head, he winked at Sarah.

"Never fear, Mr. Henshall," Colin said. "We have not forgotten you. Viola and I plan to include a Scotch reel, very popular at English balls and even at Almack's."

"Excellent."

"Let's attempt it now, shall we?"

Colin demonstrated the basic steps, with optional flourishes like a hop step, a cross step, taps, and stamps. Mr. Gwilt followed along once more, proving to be remarkably adept.

Colin said, "This is an opportunity for men in particular to show off their fancy footwork."

"Why only the men?" Georgie asked.

Sarah spoke up. "Because ladies—at least, English ladies—are taught to dance with decorum, with no capering about or kicking up their heels."

Effie's lip curled. "Sounds borin'."

"Thankfully ours is to be a private ball," Georgie said. "So we can do as we like."

"Exactly." Colin grinned. "So caper to your heart's content."

When the lesson ended and Hubert Cornish had taken his leave, Georgiana praised their instructor. "Well done, Colin. Thank you."

"That is kind of you to say."

"I know you mentioned you were not a great student, but you could be an excellent teacher."

"Me, a dancing master? My father would die of an apoplexy." Suddenly Colin's entire face withered like a prune. "Sorry. What a thoughtless thing to say when your own father . . ."

"Never mind. I know what you meant. And I was not thinking of a dancing master specifically. You might teach any number of things. You said you liked history."

"True, though I doubt I could teach Latin, Euclid, or Homer."

"Perhaps not. But students at, say, the Sidmouth School would not require such lofty classical education. They need to learn to read, write, and cipher, and perhaps some world history and sport."

"That I might be able to manage, were there a need."

"There is. The Sidmouth School does good work for poor children. But Mr. Ward will retire eventually. And, at present, there is no academy for young gentlemen here, so that might be another opportunity."

"Do you think so? As a younger son, I know I should have some profession, yet I can't seem to settle on anything. Well, thank you, Miss Georgiana. You have given me much to think about and some needed confidence as well." He looked at her more closely. "And what is it you'd like to do?"

"Me?" For a moment Georgiana stood there, mouth agape. "Do you know, you are the first person to ask me that."

"Am I? My father has been asking me that for years. Drilling me, more like."

"He has high expectations of you. That's not all bad. No one expects anything of me. Except perhaps to marry one day. Shudder."

"Would marriage be so bad?"

"As a formality? It seems so to me. Though to be fair, my sisters who've wed seem sickeningly happy."

"My brother too. What else, though? If it were only up to you?"

"I wish. If only I were independently wealthy."

"Let's say you were."

"Hmm . . . I suppose if money were no object, I should like to travel. I have only ever been here and May Hill. I also dearly love visiting the children at the charity school. So I suppose, after I'd traveled, I would like to help children like them, like Cora, somehow. And I would have my own dog. Not just adopt the town stray."

He nodded. "Those seem modest, attainable goals."

"To you, maybe."

"Georgiana Summers, I have absolutely no doubt that with God's help, you can do anything you set your mind to."

Georgie smiled. "And now you're giving me confidence. We are quite a pair, are we not? Um. Platonically speaking, of course."

He hesitated only a fraction of a second. "Of course."

"Speaking of the school, shall we go there again?" she asked.

"Why not? I could kick something."

"What?"

"A ball, I mean."

"Oh. In that case, let's go."

They donned their outdoor attire and set out for the school. As they walked up Fore Street, they came upon Miss Marriott, her lovely face framed by the fur-lined hood of her cloak, a parcel in hand.

"Ah, Mr. Hutton, a pleasure to see you again. And you, Georgiana."

Colin bowed. "Miss Marriott."

"What a fortuitous meeting," she said. "My father was saying only this morning how much he enjoyed your last visit. I am sure he would be pleased to see you again. I am on my way home now with some queen cakes from the bakery to have with our tea. Would you care to join us?"

"Very kind of you. But Miss Summers and I are on our way to the Sidmouth School. We hope to read to the students and join them for games in the yard. You might accompany us, if you like. The more readers the merrier, and all that."

"Oh, I don't think so. My parents are expecting me. Are you sure you can't come for tea? You could easily visit the school another day."

Georgie steeled herself for his agreement. For him to abandon their outing as he had before.

She said in an undertone, "Colin, if you want to accept, then—"

"Not at all. I am eager to return to the school with you." He turned back to the young woman with a smile. "Though I appreciate the invitation, Miss Marriott. Perhaps another time?"

She lifted her chin, and her eyes turned frosty. "Perhaps."

His smile did not waver. "Thank you again, and please do greet your parents for me." He tipped his hat and gestured for Georgie to walk on.

When they were out of earshot, Georgie said, "You could have gone with her. You need not feel obligated to go with me if you don't wish to."

"But I do wish to." He gave her a teasing grin. "Now, come on—no more dallying. Young minds and feet await!"

Sarah iced the Twelfth Night cake with layers of first almond, then sugar icing. She could not rival the intricate sugar work decorations of a pastry shop, but she did manage to cut out festive shapes—crowns and stars—from almond paste to adorn the top and sides of the cake.

Early during the party, the cake would be cut and served to guests. The person who found the bean became the Bean King. And the woman who found a dried pea would be the Queen of Twelfth Night. The king and queen reigned for the evening, no matter their normal status in society.

As she worked, Sarah thought again of Mr. Bernardi, the duke's pastry chef who had stayed with them last winter. He had recently written to let her know he had taken her advice and was now *chef de maison* of a small hotel in Mayfair that served French and Italian cuisine. *I invite you to visit and enjoy a meal gratis should you ever find yourself in London.* She had no plans to travel to London, but she was pleased for the man.

While Sarah decorated the cake, her sisters were busy with other preparations for the party. Emily had bought a large sheet of paper from the stationer's and cut it into slips. She and Claire worked together, Emily writing Twelfth Night character names and introductions on the slips, and Claire illustrating them with funny little drawings.

Since guests would not learn which character they were to be until after they arrived, Georgiana and Effie spent time digging through trunks in the attic storage room and visiting the second-hand shop to compile a selection of costumes. They also made crowns of felt adorned with gold ribbon and paste gems.

Who, they wondered aloud, would be this year's king and queen?

After dinner that evening, Sarah returned to the workroom to prepare jellies and pastries for the party and to put the final touches on the Twelfth Night cake. The party was only two nights away now. Mr. Henshall's words echoed in her mind once more, *"I will leave ye in peace until after the party. But when it's over, I hope ye will be ready to discuss . . . our future."* And she would be ready.

Late that night, most likely after the others had gone to bed, Sarah finished her tasks. When she finally ascended the stairs, quiet strumming caught her ear along with a low, familiar voice. She changed course and, instead of continuing up to her bedchamber, diverted to the parlour.

She paused outside its open door. Callum Henshall sat alone by the light of a dying fire, softly strumming in experimental fashion: stopping and starting again, trying different chords, singing a few words, pausing, and then singing them again in modified form.

As she listened to him pottering about with a new song, her heart burned within her and her throat tightened painfully.

> "My darling one, my jo,
> Will we ever meet again?
> For I shall long for you always,
> My would-be love and friend.
>
> I will pray for you, my jo,
> Whate'er happens, wherever I go.
> But I leave my heart right here.
> It does me no good anywhere . . ."

Stepping into the room, Sarah blurted, "Don't."

He froze and then stood. "Don't what?"

"Don't leave your heart here."

He uttered a humorless laugh. "I'm afraid it's not a choice. It's the truth. You have my heart."

"Then take me with you."

For a moment he stared at her, then he sighed and set down his guitar. "Sarah, don't."

"Don't what?" It was her turn to give a rueful laugh.

"It's only a rough little song. I'm still tinkering. It will get better, but—"

"I don't think I could stand it if it got any better."

He shook his head. "I don't want you to make an impetuous decision because of our argument and certainly not because of an insipid ditty sung by firelight. I told you I would wait for an answer."

"But I am not—"

"*And,*" he persisted, "I don't want you to regret tomorrow anything you say tonight. My feelings will not change. Even so, I don't think I can bear to get my hopes up again and then . . . No. I would feel better if you said the same thing by the cold light of morning. Until then, let us make no promises we may not keep."

"I won't—"

"Shh." He pressed a gentle finger to her lips. "Tomorrow will be soon enough. Tell me then."

"I doubt I shall sleep."

"I know I shall not. But still. Tomorrow."

"Very well, then. Until tomorrow."

On the way up to her bedchamber, she saw Mamma coming out of the water closet. Impulsively, Sarah hurried over and threw her arms around her mother's warm frame.

"Sarah, what is it?"

"I am in love."

"Well, I could have told you that. Does this mean you have given him an answer?"

"Not yet. Though I will tomorrow." With another squeeze and a smile, Sarah floated to her room.

EIGHTEEN

"... it was settled that they should be married as soon
as the Writings could be completed. Mary was very
eager for a Special Licence and Mr. Watts talked of
Banns. A common Licence was at last agreed on."

—Jane Austen, *Juvenilia*, "The Three Sisters"

Sarah awoke the next morning from a honeyed dream. She
and Callum, hand in hand, climbing a heather-strewn hill
together.

"Miss? Miss!"

"Hmm?"

Sarah opened her eyes with a start.

Cora stood there, shaking her shoulder. "Sorry to wake you.
It's your mum."

"What is it?"

"Heard her and Bibi talking. Her sheets are damp through.
Bibi fears it's a fever."

"Oh no." Sarah sat up, instantly alert.

"Mrs. Summers said not to trouble you, but I'm that worried.
I knew you'd want to know."

"You were right to tell me."

Sarah scrambled out of bed. She remembered her mother had
felt noticeably warm when she'd embraced her last night.

"I told Emily too," Cora said. "She is in with her now. Mr. Thomson has gone for the doctor."

"Good. Good. Would you mind helping me dress?"

"'Course not."

With the doctor coming, Sarah thought it best to change out of her nightclothes. After a little prompting, the girl was able to lace her stays, albeit rather loosely, and do up the fastenings of her frock.

When she was dressed, they left the room together. Cora said she would try to wake Georgiana, who was notoriously difficult to rouse. Meanwhile Sarah hurried downstairs to Mamma's room.

She passed Mr. Henshall in the hall. For one second his countenance lit up, then whatever he saw in Sarah's face doused that light.

She said, "I can't talk now. Mamma has a fever, apparently. I must go to her."

"Of course. May I do something? Fetch a doctor?"

"James has already gone."

"Ah."

And in his expression she saw dejection and grim resignation.

When she knocked and let herself into her room, Mamma still lay in bed.

She looked up with a frown. "I told Bibi not to trouble you."

"Cora heard you and Bibi talking and was worried. I am glad she told me. What is it, do you think? Cora mentioned a fever?"

"She woke up burning hot and soaked with perspiration," Emily said. "Nightdress. Sheets. Bibi has gone for fresh bedclothes."

"I am sure it is nothing," Mamma said. "Or nothing serious."

"You mentioned recently you've not been feeling your best."

"Perhaps I was a little . . . off, but I am feeling better already."

"Mamma, if it's a fever, then that settles things. I will stay . . . at least for now."

"Sarah, no."

"But, Mamma—"

"No," Mamma insisted, sitting up with surprising strength. "You will not postpone your life on my account any longer."

"But if I am needed here . . . ?"

"Sarah Jane Summers. Do you hold my life in your hands, or does God?"

Sarah recoiled as though struck. "Well, of course God does, but—"

"Do you number my days—know the future—or does He?"

Emily sent Sarah a sympathetic look.

"He does," she replied. "Although if you are ill, I will need—want—to look after you, after things here."

"But I don't want you to do that. I want you to go. Live your life. Accept the love this good man is offering."

"Mamma, I . . ."

"Am I alone? Helpless?" She gestured toward Emily. "Do I not have other daughters, sons-in-law, and friends? Not to mention competent and kind retainers?"

"Yes, but should something happen . . ."

"Something will happen. That's a certainty in this fallen world. Difficult things. Someone you love will disappoint you. Or fall ill. Or even, someday, die. And not living your own life will not stop any of it. My days, my health, my life are in God's hands. And I raised you to believe that as well."

"I know. I . . . do."

"Do you? Sometimes I wonder." Mamma paused and moderated her tone. "I know your intentions are good and pure. But, my dear Sarah, you are not in control, as much as you or I might wish you were."

Emily defended, "Her heart is in the right place."

"Is it?" Mamma asked.

Sarah thought of the words Callum had sung, about leaving his heart with her. Perhaps her heart had *not* been in the right place.

Chagrined, Sarah hung her head. Then a different sensation washed over her, and she breathed it in and released a long sigh—released much more as well. Her hands, which had been fisted, opened and relaxed.

Bibi knocked and poked her head in. "Dr. Clarke is here, ma'am."

"Good. Show him in."

"Shall we stay with you?" Sarah asked.

"No, my dear. Not this time, thank you."

Leaving the room, Sarah saw Callum sitting on a bench in the hall, elbows on his knees, head bowed in an attitude of prayer. He rose when she came out. Sarah strode up to him, took his face in her hands, and gave him a firm, decisive kiss. "My feelings and wishes have not changed, but they may need to be postponed a bit, depending on what the doctor says."

"I understand."

"Now, please excuse me. I feel the need to keep busy to distract myself from worry."

"I understand that too." He gave her hand a reassuring squeeze, and then Sarah hurried away.

A mere thirty minutes later, Sarah was busy belowstairs, helping sort and put away an order from the greengrocer for Mrs. Besley, when Bibi came down and mentioned seeing the doctor go.

Sarah excused herself and hurried back upstairs. Perhaps having seen the doctor leave, Emily and Georgiana came out of the office and caught up with her, and the three sisters entered Mamma's room together.

"Well? What did he say?" Sarah asked. "Did he give you something for the fever?"

"I have no fever."

"What? Emily said you were burning up. And your bedclothes were damp through this morning."

"All true. Yet I am not ill but apparently perfectly normal."

"Then how did he explain your symptoms?"

"I am simply in my climacteric period."

Georgie's face wrinkled. "What's that?"

"I'm going through the change of life."

"Oooh."

"I never thought I'd be happy to receive confirmation that I am getting old, but in this case, I am relieved. For your sakes as well as mine."

"But you've been overheated. And perspiring profusely."

"Also," Georgie added, "I hate to mention it, unusually snappish."

"Yes, sorry. All part of it, evidently. Dr. Clarke was rather surprised I have only recently begun experiencing these symptoms. He said many women begin sooner. His theory is that the late onset of my, well, cycles, and my years of inactivity as an invalid may have delayed the inevitable change."

"Goodness," Emily said. "Is there nothing he can do or prescribe for your relief?"

"He said some physicians prescribe bleeding to lower the pulse and heat. But after what Prince Edward went through last year . . ." She shook her head. "No, I could not bear the thought. So besides a gentle laxative, he prescribed only less meat, less tea and coffee in the evenings, and less wine, which I scarcely ever take anyway. Oh, and less heating exercise."

"How long will this *climacteric period* last?"

"He estimates several months to several years."

Georgie shuddered. "Horrors."

"As unpleasant as that sounds," Sarah said, "I am excessively relieved you are not ill."

"We all are," Emily agreed.

"Yes, I thank God," Mamma said with a sigh. "Although I may have to ask Him one day why He deemed this unpleasant business necessary. One would think pain in childbirth was enough." She grinned, and her daughters chuckled.

Then Mamma looked at Sarah and added, "I am sorry I was a bit harsh with you earlier."

"I understand. It seems that a loving parent sometimes uses 'unpleasant' things for our good." Sarah smiled, bent to kiss her mother's forehead, and turned to go.

Sarah lost no time in finding Callum to tell him the good news. She drew up short, however, when she found him in the parlour, frowning down at a piece of correspondence.

He looked up and rose when she entered. "How is your mother?"

"She is well," Sarah said, not daring to explain the particulars. "Nothing to worry about, according to Dr. Clarke."

"I am relieved to hear it."

"You don't look relieved. What is it?"

"A letter from my man of business."

"Bad news?"

"I'm afraid so. A violent storm struck Fife, and Kirkcaldy was hard hit: strong winds, high seas, widespread flooding. Much of the town is flooded and some of our estate as well. The storm damaged sections of the roof, and water is getting into the oldest part of the house. He is doing what he can, but I need to go home as soon as may be to help with the cleanup and repair efforts."

"Oh no. I am so sorry."

He nodded. "As I mentioned, Effie's aunt Isla has left. Despite her flaws, she had directed the household staff, and in her absence, there is a lack of leadership about how best to manage the extra work."

"Sounds like you shall need help."

Again he nodded, expression troubled as he gazed into his own thoughts.

Sarah tapped her chin. "If only you knew someone who was good at managing staff, and organizing, and getting things done. . . ."

"True." For a moment he continued to stare into the vague distance, his mind clearly elsewhere. Then his gaze snapped to hers, pleasure brightening his face.

A second later, his expression sobered. "I don't want a housekeeper, Sarah. I want a wife. A helpmeet, yes, but more than that. A cherished partner, true love, and lover."

At his words, her heart seemed to swell almost painfully in her chest. She nodded. "I want that too."

He stepped forward, bracketed her shoulders in both hands, and gave her a swift, hard kiss.

"Does that mean you'll marry me?"

"It does."

He kissed her again.

Then aloud, Sarah realized, "You will need to leave straightaway."

"I can remain one, maybe two days at most. He has engaged a few local men to do a makeshift patch job of the roof, which should hold until I can assess the damage and decide how best to proceed. Besides, Effie would hate to miss the Twelfth Night party."

"What will we do? You and I, I mean. I can't travel with you. Even if Effie might suffice as a chaperone for the journey itself, to live in your house as an unmarried woman . . . ?"

"I know."

"Calling the banns will take more time than you have."

"Were you hoping for a long engagement?"

"No."

"Good." He raised her chin with his fingers. "Because now you've finally agreed to marry me, I'll not risk leavin' without ye again."

"But . . ."

He softly stroked his thumb over her lower lip, and she instantly stilled.

"Will ye trust me, lass?"

"I will."

"Then get ready to say those same two little words again soon. Give me an hour or so, and I'll see what I can do. All right? Do not worry. I'll be back as soon as I can."

"Are you going to Exeter again?"

"No. Although I'm glad I already did."

He gave her a final sweet kiss and left on his errand.

After about an hour, Sarah began to pace. What was he doing? What did he hope to accomplish? To avoid the three weeks' delay needed to call the banns, they'd probably have to acquire a special license, which would require a lengthy trip to London, connections to the archbishop he did not have, and more money than he could spare—especially with costly repairs awaiting him in Scotland. She prayed he would not suggest eloping. Not after Claire's disastrous attempt. She did not wish to break her mother's heart all over again.

From the library window, she saw him return on foot. Yet when he entered the house, he came not to find her, but to speak to her mother. A short while later, the two of them joined her in the library.

He took her hand. "Sarah, my jo. Will ye marry me . . . tomorrow?"

"What? I mean yes, I will marry you. But how can we possibly marry tomorrow?"

"With the help of your vicar, Mr. Jenkins, and two of your brothers-in-law, I have acquired a common license from the bishop of this diocese."

"Common license?"

He nodded.

Mamma explained, "It's sometimes called a standard license here, or a bishop's license."

"That's what you were doing in Exeter?" she asked him.

"Aye. It was presumptuous, I know, but I wanted to be prepared. It was either that or convince ye to marry once we crossed the border. Considering your sister's regrettable experience, I didna want to suggest it. I also knew you'd want to be surrounded by your family if and when we wed. With this license, we can marry in the parish church tomorrow morning or the next. I went to talk to Mr. Jenkins just now. He was not home, but I tracked him down and he has agreed."

"Has he?" Sarah said, suddenly breathless.

"Aye. All that's left is for ye to agree too. So I repeat my question. Will ye marry me and make me the happiest of men?"

Excitement bubbled through her. "I will."

He smiled and his sea-green eyes shone.

"Thank God," Mamma murmured. "Though the day after might be better. We have the Twelfth Night party tomorrow."

His warm gaze remained on Sarah. "That suits me, if it suits my bride?"

"It does indeed."

"Good. Then I have something for you." From an inner pocket he retrieved a small velvet pouch. He tipped the contents onto his palm and held it out to her.

Another gift? She resolved to react more favorably this time. "What is it?"

"A Luckenbooth brooch. A traditional Scottish token of betrothal. It symbolizes love and loyalty."

The gold brooch was in the shape of two entwined hearts with a crown above.

"It's lovely!"

She pinned it to her bodice, and they both looked down at it with satisfaction.

Mamma, however, clapped her hands. "Now, let's get busy. We have much to do."

There was no time for a new gown or written invitations. Instead, they sent Georgiana to spread the word to friends and family alike. This was a task she eagerly undertook, donning warm clothes and setting out on a house-to-house mission.

"Be sure to tell Fran," Mamma called after her. "Or is that too far to go on foot?"

"Not at all," Georgie assured them. "It's an easy walk for me."

Mamma lamented the fact that there was not even time to plan and prepare sufficient food for a proper wedding breakfast.

Sarah responded easily, "No matter. Many of the people who would have attended a formal wedding breakfast will be at the party tomorrow night. The party can serve as a wedding celebration too. There is sure to be plenty of food left over for a simple meal after the ceremony."

Mamma looked at her in surprise. "I am proud of you and your pluck, my dear. You are right to focus on the main thing: that you be married before God and family. The other details are far less important."

Soon, Sarah was receiving well-wishes and embraces from her sisters and brothers-in-law. Georgie, Emily, and James were the first to congratulate her. Viola and Jack came over a few minutes later—Westmount likely having been Georgie's first stop in her role as messenger.

Seeing Effie come down the stairs, Sarah opened her arms, and the girl sailed into them, accepting and returning Sarah's embrace. "I am happy for the both of ye, and for me! I am glad ye are joining our little family. You'll make us more of a family, a better family, I know."

"Thank you, dear heart."

Effie then turned to Mr. Henshall and accepted his embrace as well. She said, "And if the offer still stands, Da', I'd like to take your last name when Sarah does."

Tears misted his eyes. "That would make me very happy, lass. A double blessing, indeed."

Later that day, Claire came over to offer Sarah her heartiest congratulations.

"I'm delighted for you both. And I'm especially glad William and I have decided to keep the Edinburgh house. He says he can decipher codes for the foreign office and write his diplomatic memoir from anywhere. We plan to live there at least a few months a year and find a cottage near Sidmouth for the remainder."

"That is excellent news!" Sarah exclaimed, squeezing her hands.

Sarah considered, then said, "I wonder . . . Everything is so new, we've not yet had time to propose the idea, but since Georgiana has a strong desire to travel, and Effie would surely appreciate her company on the long journey, Callum and I were thinking of asking her to accompany the three of us. Like I accompanied you and William on your wedding trip."

"Ah! And when William and I come up to visit, we could bring her back with us."

"Yes, if that might be agreeable to you both."

"I don't see why not, but I will ask William and let you know if he foresees any problems."

"Thank you. I think it would make Callum feel more assured of Effie's safety. This way, the two girls could share a room at the inns we stop at along the way, while he and I . . ." Sarah stopped, face burning.

Claire failed to hide her smile. "I understand perfectly. What has Mamma said?"

"I wanted to talk it over with you first so have not yet broached the subject. But I shall."

Georgiana was still out spreading the news when Sarah went and spoke to her mother in the parlour, where she sat with Emily. Sarah expected Mamma to be reluctant to agree but her reaction surprised Sarah.

"Perhaps that would be a good idea. Give her some distance from Colin Hutton. I like the young man a great deal—don't mistake me—but he's too old for her."

"I am not defending or encouraging their friendship," Sarah replied, "but I feel it only fair to point out that their age difference is less than Viola and Jack's. Or yours and Papa's."

Emily spoke up. "And far less than Marianne Dashwood and Colonel Brandon's in *Sense and Sensibility*."

"That's different! They are fictional. And Viola was already one and twenty when she met the major."

"And how old were you when you met Papa?"

Mamma lifted her chin. "Well . . . seventeen was older back then."

Sarah grinned. "If you say so."

After a thorough discussion of the merits and drawbacks of the plan, Mamma agreed, saying, "As long as she's back by summer, when things get busy here. And as long as Claire and William can deliver her home again, then, yes. I cannot deny her the experience. She's been longing to travel for some time."

"Are you sure you won't be too lonely without her?"

"I will miss you all, of course. Yet children flying from the nest is an expected part of life. Cora is young, but she is already a great help to me and excellent company as well. And Viola and Jack are right next door, and Emily and James will be here a few days a week. That's more time with adult children than many mothers enjoy."

"You are very good, Mamma. Very selfless."

"Selfless? Not a whit." She winked. "I've been hoping to get you married off for years."

After gaining Mr. Hammond's and Mamma's approval, Sarah then asked Georgiana if she had any interest in traveling with them to Scotland.

Georgie's eyes widened into blue saucers. "Really? Could I? Yes, please!"

"You would be with us for a few months. Claire and William plan to come up in March or April, and they could bring you back to Sidmouth with them later in the spring."

Georgiana hesitated. "That's a long time to be away from home. What has Mamma said?"

"She said you may go, as long as you're back in time to help with the busy summer months. She also said Cora is a great help and excellent company."

"Did she? I am glad."

Sarah nodded. "Cora has been good for Mamma. And we have you to thank for befriending Cora in the first place."

Georgie shrugged. "Emily went to the school before I did. But she can't kick a ball to save her life. That's why I became better acquainted with Cora."

"And we are all exceedingly glad you did."

Sitting at her dressing table that night, Sarah unpinned and brushed her dark hair, taking notice of her blue eyes in the mirror. Peter had often said she had fine eyes. . . .

She supposed it was only natural to find herself thinking of her first love at such a time. She had grieved his loss for more than three years, saying she'd had one great love in her life and did not expect to have another.

All that had changed. Thinking of Peter now no longer brought feelings of sadness and loss. She was ready to move on.

Sarah did not have much to remember him by. A rough sketch Claire had attempted years ago. The last letter he'd sent to her before going to sea. And memories of his gentle, serious nature.

She knew he probably couldn't hear her, yet even so she said, "Dear Peter. I hope you don't mind. I don't think you would, being as practical as you were. But I am finally going to marry someone else. His name is Callum, and I think you would like him. I certainly do. In fact, I love him more than I ever imagined loving anyone ever again. . . ."

Her imagined conversation with Peter changed into a real conversation with someone who definitely heard her. "Thank you, God, for healing my broken heart and for this second chance with Callum Henshall."

NINETEEN

CHRISTMAS goes out in fine style with Twelfth Night.
It is a finish worthy of the time. Twelfth Night is . . .
brilliant with innumerable planets of twelfthcakes.
—Charles Knight, *Leigh Hunt's London Journal*

Sarah had originally planned the Twelfth Night party to please Georgiana. Now she looked forward to it for reasons of her own. It would be her last night as a single woman. All her family and many friends would be there, and she would enjoy the company of the man she loved—dance with him too.

As the guests began to arrive, they were welcomed with glasses of spiced cider or punch and urged to partake from an appealing array of dishes spread on the long sideboard: smoked salmon, roast ham and beef, jellies, mince pies, and more.

Guests filled their own plates, and when everyone had seated themselves in the dining room or drawing room, Mr. Gwilt went around offering tea and coffee.

The Twelfth Night cake sat at one end of the sideboard, and received, to Sarah's satisfaction, appreciative glances and eager comments from those who beheld it.

Soon Sea View's public rooms were warm with firelight, candlelight, and good company. The pleasant hum of friendly conversation punctuated by laughter and teasing warmed Sarah's heart all the more.

When she judged the time right, she began cutting slices of cake and Mr. Gwilt handed them around. When all the guests had been served, she insisted their servants take slices as well, in old Twelfth Night tradition.

Mr. Gwilt was still busy offering refills of tea and coffee, so Sarah set a piece aside for him, while Jessie carried down slices to Mrs. Besley, Lowen, and Bibi Cordey, who had come over to help in the kitchen for the special night.

"Chew carefully now," Sarah warned. "And do let us know if you find the bean or pea."

"Looks delicious," Mrs. Denby said, taking a big bite. She chewed for a moment, then her face puckered. She gingerly worked something to her lips and extracted it with pincer fingers. "A pea."

Georgiana clapped. "How perfect! You are the Queen of Twelfth Night, Mrs. Denby!"

"Am I indeed? I have never been a queen before."

"It suits you."

Sarah took a tentative bite and paused to consider her work: good texture, moist, spicy, flavorful. A delicious cake, though she said it herself. She watched the others as they chewed, wondering who would find the bean, hoping it had not cooked too soft to be noticed, and hoping it landed in a man's piece, if at all possible.

Her gaze landed on Mr. Gwilt, standing in the background near the rear door, chewing thoughtfully. His usually pleasant expression creased into a frown.

Becoming aware of her scrutiny, he looked up and said, "I'm afraid I have stumbled upon the piece with the bean. I do apologize, I do. Please appoint another man."

Emily spoke up. "Not a bit of it, Mr. Gwilt. If you found the bean, then Bean King you are! On Twelfth Night, everything is topsy-turvy. It's only right that a dear humble soul should be raised to such lofty distinction. So enjoy every moment." She grinned. "You only have till midnight, after all."

"If you are sure. And if Miss Sarah and Mrs. Summers do not

object. . . . Again, I am happy to give over to one of the gentlemen, I am."

"No need, Mr. Gwilt," Sarah said. "But if you will help me pass the bonnet and hat?"

"Certainly."

Colin Hutton rose in playful protest. "Nay, nay! The king must be served, not do the serving. I shall pass the hat to the gents. And Miss Georgiana, perhaps you might pass the bonnet to the ladies?"

She grinned. "With pleasure."

Colin handed the top hat to each gentleman in turn while Georgiana went around to the ladies with the bonnet. One by one the guests picked a folded slip and read with amusement or mutterings.

When Major Hutton unfolded his, Viola leaned over and read it. "And here you bemoaned having to act. No need, Major Matchless."

"And what is your role tonight?" he asked.

Viola looked at her slip. "Lady Racket."

"That's rather more out of character."

"I agree. Sounds like fun." Viola turned to her twin. "What did you get, Em?"

"Mine is Miss Romance." She read, "Miss Romance to accept for her partner proposes, One who'll print in his press ev'ry work she composes."

Viola laughed. "That's perfect!" She turned to Georgiana and teased, "Are you sure you did not assign these parts?"

"I did not!" Georgie insisted. "It's the hand of fate at work— that's all."

"If you say so."

When everyone had their assigned parts, Georgie clapped her hands to gain their attention. "Now it's time to choose your costumes. Ladies first, if you please."

She rolled Mrs. Denby's wheeled chair into the library. There, while the other ladies helped themselves to masks and props, Georgie and Effie spread a cape around Mrs. Denby's shoulders and placed a felt crown on her head.

They had not assigned formal roles to the youngest attendees, but they dressed little Mira as a cupid with wings and a toy bow and arrow. And for Cora, they had fashioned butterfly wings and pinned bobbing antennae to her curls. Both looked charming. Effie, meanwhile, reenacted her role as princess from the play.

Sarah was the last to come in, her expression wavering between incredulity and amusement.

"I drew Miss Busy, although I imagine you planned that."

"I did not!" Georgie replied. "I would have given you something more out of character."

Seeing an apron and feather duster on the desktop, Sarah pointed. "I suppose those are mine?"

Georgie glanced to the doorway, then said, "Actually, change of plans. You are no longer Miss Busy, but rather Miss Busy Bride-to-Be."

Mamma entered with a long white veil and a wreath of fine white and blue silk flowers. These were stunningly beautiful items—not mere props.

She said, "I know there is not time for a new dress, but we thought you might wear this tomorrow. It will look well with the blue gown you wore as Claire's bridesmaid."

"It's lovely," Sarah breathed. "But how did you . . . ?"

"We ladies put our heads together for something special for you. I purchased this veil from a local lace maker, and Fran created the wreath."

Tears shone in Sarah's eyes. "Thank you. It's perfect."

When all the ladies were costumed, Georgie returned to the drawing room and summoned the men.

Serious Major Hutton groaned, but his wife gave him a playful jab to the side and urged him not to be a curmudgeon.

In the library, Georgie handed the major a sash and faux medal and one of James's practice foils. He took one look at them, grimaced, and walked out again empty-handed.

Colin shook his head. "Viola is right. He is a curmudgeon. Good thing it does not run in the family."

"Yes," Georgiana agreed. "I am glad you are game for any diversion. Which character are you to be?"

"Sir Tim Spruce."

Georgiana burst out laughing.

"What is so funny?"

She took his slip from him and read it. "Spruce and fly I'll always be. For I'm a Buck of high degree."

"So?" he challenged.

"So you are perfect as you are."

Colin grinned. "Well, if you say so, who am I to disagree?"

Mr. Henshall turned out to be Giles Diligent, a perfect match for the former Miss Busy turned Bride-to-Be. They handed him a straw hat and a pitchfork.

Finally, each guest was outfitted for their role.

Except Georgiana.

Colin asked her, "And what about you? Which character did you pick?"

In all the busyness, she'd barely glanced at her slip. She looked at it now. "I am Miss Gadabout." She read, "Yes, all I like is gadding about. To the play or a ball, the park or a rout. And what if I get a push or a squeeze? A crowd so delightful can never displease."

She expected him to laugh, but he did not. Instead he said, "I know you like to play ball and walk, but the rest of it?" He shook his head. "It's not how I see you."

She wanted to ask how he did see her, but did not dare. "It's only a game," she reminded him—and herself as well.

Wearing the veil, Sarah returned to the drawing room with the others, everyone ready to recite their parts. The major was nowhere to be seen.

Mr. Gwilt had to be cajoled to enter in his long cape and felt crown, a toy scepter in his hand. The kindly, humble man looked supremely uncomfortable.

The others encouraged him. Emily said, "You look perfect, Mr. Gwilt, I mean, Your Majesty. Now, it is your place to begin the proceedings."

His Adam's apple rose and fell on a hard swallow. Then, rising to the occasion, he straightened and read, "Fate decrees me your

King: grave and glad, wise and fools, must consent, for this night, to submit to my rules."

Emily clapped. "Well done."

Taking her cue, Mrs. Denby adjusted her spectacles and read, "I am your Queen and tonight shall reign, as the Queen of the cheerful, happy refrain."

She tittered, and the others laughed in response.

One by one, the guests read their introductions, some like Armaan and Sonali self-consciously, while others, like Colin, read theirs with comic, theatrical air.

"You're next, Sarah."

Too happy to be truly offended, Sarah rose and began to read, "Yes, Busy I am from morning till night. For Betty my maid can never do right—"

"Oh!" Emily interrupted, taking the slip from her and handing her another. "Read this one instead."

Sarah looked at it and read, "Happy am I, Miss Bride-to-Be. For my true love and I are soon to mar-ry."

Emily gave her a sheepish grin. "Sorry. It's the best I could do on short notice."

Mr. Henshall stepped up beside Sarah, took her hand, and said, "By any name, Sarah, you're my heart's desire." He glanced at the slip in his other hand and crumpled it into a ball. "I drew Giles Diligent. The verse is nonsense, but my devotion is true. I shall love ye diligently all the days of my life." He kissed her cheek.

"Awww!" Georgie exclaimed.

"Hear, hear." Colin applauded, and Sarah noticed the two share triumphant, conspirators' smiles.

William Hammond raised his glass. "A toast to the bride and groom to be!"

They all toasted the couple.

As the toast ended, Major Jack Hutton returned in full dress uniform. Real medals. Real sword. And a masculine, commanding presence that drew all eyes.

Viola rose, hand to her bosom. "Good heavens. Is it any wonder I fell in love with you?"

In reply, he slid an arm around her waist, pulled her close to his side, and kissed her.

Well, Sarah thought. *If that is what marriage is like, then, yes, please.*

After that, the guests did their best to remain in character throughout the rest of the evening. In fact, Mira, as Cupid, kept flitting around the room despite her father's insistence that she stop and finish her cake.

The youngest among them played a game of Hunt the Slipper and then bobbed for apples. Mira, Cora, Effie, Georgie, Colin, and even Mr. Gwilt joined in the fun, while the others opted not to dunk their faces and end up wet.

When the games concluded, Colin rose and said, "Come, dear sister-in-law, won't you favor us with some music?"

Viola, ever shy of solo attention, replied, "If Mr. Henshall shall accompany me."

He rose and bowed. "My pleasure."

Callum accompanied Viola on his guitar for a few songs, and Effie sang one as well.

Then, it was time for dancing.

Soon, they were all dancing as rehearsed. A country dance, the Duke of Kent's Waltz, a quadrille, and a reel. Mr. Gwilt, still embodying his role as king for the evening, stepped and hopped and clapped with zeal and confidence. He was a pleasure to watch.

Sarah recalled attending an evening party with Claire and William a few months ago at the Killerton estate. She had observed the other couples dancing, feeling wistful and out of place and wondering if she would ever have a chance to dance with Callum Henshall. Now here she was, dancing with him and about to marry him on the morrow.

He had once told her he was not much of a dancer—an opinion Effie shared—but Sarah thought he danced well, or at least as well as she did and with even more enthusiasm. And despite her earlier admonitions to dance with decorum, that night even Sarah kicked up her heels with the best of them.

After dancing with her and then Effie, Callum took Sarah's hand and led her from the loud, crowded drawing room across the passage into the cooler, quieter parlour.

"Good idea," Sarah said. "I could use a rest."

"Not exactly what I had in mind . . ." He tipped his head to the side, indicating the kissing bough still hanging in the parlour doorway.

He led her to stand beneath it, wrapped his arms around her, and drew her close.

"One more kiss beneath the mistletoe, my jo?"

She smiled sweetly up at him. "Or two."

He smiled back, his pupils seeming to grow larger and darker as he gazed at her. Then he lowered his head and pressed his lips to hers. He kissed her tenderly, and Sarah reached up and twined her hands behind his neck, kissing him back with all the love and adoration she felt.

Happy Christmas, indeed.

Georgiana bid farewell to the Sagars and Hammonds, who were the first to leave, Mira asleep in her father's arms. Then Jack and Viola departed, wanting to take a sleepy Mrs. Denby home as well. Mr. Hutton went with them.

By eleven, all the outside guests besides Colin had departed.

Traditionally, decorations had to be taken down by midnight to avoid bad luck in the coming year. Georgiana's family didn't hold to such superstitions, but it was a good way to get the house restored to pre-Christmas order in a hurry.

The family and servants worked together to take down all the decorations before the clock struck twelve, although Mamma insisted Sarah be excused to get a good night's sleep and finish her packing. Georgie half expected Sarah to insist on working till the last, but she agreed. And with a kiss to Mamma's cheek, she started dreamily up the stairs, the veil still on her head, trailing behind her as she went.

Mamma said Georgie could be excused as well, since she would be traveling with them, but she was too excited to sleep. She remained with the others in their fine evening clothes, pulling down greenery from the mantels and stairway and unwinding it from the porch columns.

Mr. Henshall and Mr. Gwilt built a bonfire outside, and Colin, Georgiana, and Effie carried out all the pine, holly, and ivy, tossed the branches onto the fire, and watched them flame to life.

Eventually, Effie took her stepfather's arm and led him back to the house, saying, "Come on, old man. Need your beauty sleep. Big day tomorrow." Mr. Gwilt followed.

Colin and Georgiana lingered. After a few minutes of companionable silence, punctuated by the snapping fire, Colin said, "Well, we did it, did we not? Sparked romance between your sister and her Scot."

She looked at him with fond amusement. "We get all the credit, do we?"

"We certainly helped them along. Mistletoe, dancing, poetry . . . Perhaps instead of a teacher I should take up matchmaking. What say you?"

Georgiana shook her head and looked heavenward. As her gaze swept the clear, starlit sky the flippant retort on her tongue evaporated. "Look how beautiful . . ."

She glanced over and found him watching her. "I am looking."

Georgiana shook her head once more.

For a few minutes longer she remained outside, enjoying the warmth of the fire, talking and laughing with Colin over the events of the evening. But soon weariness settled over her like a soft, cozy blanket.

Their Sea View Christmas had come to an end.

TWENTY

Soon after the breakfast the bride and bridegroom departed. They had a long day's journey before them.
　　—Caroline Austen (Jane Austen's niece), letter

The next morning, Sarah rose eagerly. She washed and
dressed in the pretty blue gown that had been made for
her when she stood as Claire's bridesmaid last autumn.
Since attendants were usually unmarried younger sisters or friends,
Sarah had asked Georgie and Effie to be her bridesmaids.

Fran, former lady's maid and longtime friend, came to Sea View
to curl and arrange Sarah's hair as she had for all the Summers
sisters upon their wedding days.

"Four married. One to go," Fran said, grinning at Georgiana. She
insisted on curling and arranging Georgiana's and Effie's hair as well.

When everyone was dressed and ready, Mamma took Sarah's
hands and smiled at her. "You look beautiful and happy, my dear,
and that makes me happy."

Sarah smiled in return, pleasure and satisfaction flowing
through her.

Then they all went downstairs and began donning warm cloaks.
Mr. Gwilt assisted Sarah with hers and said in a low, confidential voice, "You're as pretty as Mrs. G on our wedding day. Now
don't you worry, Miss Sarah. We will take good care of Sea View

and your mamma. You go and enjoy married life. All right? You deserve every happiness."

Sarah's heart hitched. "Thank you, Mr. Gwilt."

The ladies would be taken to church in the Huttons' carriage while the gentlemen walked. The bridegroom had left earlier to confer with the vicar and make sure all was in order.

The women went outside and climbed into the carriage, which waited on the drive, festooned with greenery and ribbons.

A few minutes later, when they arrived at the parish church and entered, Mr. Henshall was already standing near the altar, looking handsome in a dark coat and tartan kilt. Sarah could hardly believe she was about to marry her handsome, talented Scotsman.

She recalled the mixed feelings she had experienced during Claire's wedding, wondering if anyone would ever vow to comfort, honor, and keep her. For she too had longed to be held. Loved. Cherished.

And now she knew she was. Had been all along.

Sarah had expected a small turnout due to the last-minute nature of the wedding and the cold weather. But she was heartened to see many friends in attendance. So much to be thankful for.

When her extended family and friends had filled the foremost pews, the Reverend Mr. Jenkins stood ready to read the service, and in place of a father, dear Mr. Hornbeam gave her away.

Callum's gaze remained fixed on her as Sarah joined him at the altar, admiration and profound joy evident in his expression.

The vicar began, "Dearly beloved, we are gathered together here in the sight of God to join together this man and this woman in holy matrimony; signifying unto us the mystical union that is betwixt Christ and His church."

Sarah did her best to focus and hear each word over her rapidly beating heart. She wanted to commit every moment to memory.

The vicar continued, "First, it was ordained for the procreation of children, to be brought up in the fear and nurture of the Lord."

Would she and Callum have children? Perhaps the son that would ensure his entailed estate remained in the immediate family? Sarah sincerely hoped so.

"Callum Henshall, wilt thou have this woman to thy wedded

wife, to live together after God's ordinance in the holy estate of matrimony? Wilt thou love her, comfort her, honor, and keep her in sickness and in health; and forsaking all others, keep thee only unto her, so long as ye both shall live?"

Without hesitation Callum replied, "I will."

The clergyman turned to her and asked her a variation of the same questions.

Blinking back tears, Sarah nodded. "I will."

Then they repeated their vows, and Callum placed a simple gold ring on her finger.

"With this ring I thee wed, with my body I thee worship. . . ."

Sarah's skin tingled to hear him say those words in his rich, accented voice. She looked forward to her wedding night with equal parts eagerness and trepidation.

The vicar prayed over them, blessed them, and pronounced them man and wife.

Sarah felt blessed indeed.

After the ceremony and the writing of the marriage lines into the parish register, the new Mr. and Mrs. Henshall departed the church hand in hand.

Georgiana looked at Effie, and the two shared satisfied smiles.

They returned to Sea View for an informal wedding breakfast, mostly consisting of the copious amounts of food left over from the previous night's party.

The new-wed couple with their attendants, Effie and Georgiana, remained only long enough to eat a few bites and to accept the well-wishes of friends and the embraces of family. Mamma held Sarah tight before letting her go.

Then they gathered their baggage in the hall, which Mr. Gwilt carried out to the post chaise Mr. Henshall had hired to transport his bride to her new home.

Everyone bundled up and followed them outside to the chaise to see them off.

Claire said, "We will join you in the spring, remember. And we will bring you back with us then, Georgiana."

A teary Mamma added, "Take care, my dears."

Their other family members waved and shouted final farewells.

Georgie opened the chaise window, and Colin came to stand near it. He said, "I am glad you are getting to travel, but I will miss you."

"Will you? Well, when I return, you shan't recognize me. I shall be so much more mature and refined."

"I hope not. Don't ever change, Georgiana Summers. I like you just the way you are."

Georgie swallowed and feigned more confidence than she felt. "I should hope so!"

Mr. Henshall shut the door. "Time to go."

Colin lingered at the window. "No falling in love with a Scot now, hear? I expect you back here by summer, if not before."

She gave him a saucy grin. "No promises."

The horses began to move. Over the rumble of hooves and tack, he called, "Wait! No promises about coming back or about falling in love with a Scot?"

"Neither one!" She grinned and waved, first to him, then to her assembled family and friends: Claire, William, Mira. Emily and James. Viola, Jack, and Mrs. Denby. Mamma and Cora. Mr. and Mrs. Hornbeam. Mr. Gwilt, Mrs. Besley, Lowen, Jessie, and Bibi. All the people she loved and who loved her. She would miss them, but she was glad to be embarking on an adventure. To be traveling somewhere new and experiencing new things. And despite teasing Colin, she had every intention of coming back. And when she returned, she would be older, more well-traveled, and more experienced. A woman of the world. Then, look out, Sidmouth. And look out, Colin Hutton.

As the hired post chaise traveled north, Sarah shared a smile with her new husband and settled back against the cushions. She recalled the last time she had set off on the long journey to Scotland. How agitated she had been, how sure that Sea View and Mamma would suffer in her absence. She had been unable to give up her desire for control—to try to manage everything and everyone—for the desire of her heart. Unable to rest in the knowledge that God held her family in His hands.

On that last trip she had felt the cord that bound her to Sea View and to her family stretch tighter and tighter until it threatened to snap and tear a hole in her chest. Now she felt happy and hopeful.

Of course her attachment to her family would remain strong, yet it no longer tethered her. Those bonds would easily survive the distance and the time apart.

In the coach now, Sarah silently thanked God yet again for this second chance with the man she loved, and who loved her back quite *diligently.*

Upon their departure, Emily had thrust a thick envelope into her hands, and now Sarah opened it. Inside she found a cover letter that introduced the other pages. She read:

Dear Sarah,

I have decided to set aside, at least for now, my Gothic novel of mystery and horror, better suited to Ann Radcliffe, no doubt. Instead, I have returned to my former novel about sisters. I hope you will approve of the opening pages. If nothing else, perhaps it will give you something to read to pass the time.

With love,
Emily

Sarah turned to the next page and began to read.

Sarah Summers carefully lifted the family heirloom, a warm mantle of nostalgia settling over her. The porcelain plate rimmed in gold had been painted with a colorful image of three sisters in Chinese robes, clustered close as a fourth read to them. Papa had given it to their mother long ago.

Sarah ran a gentle finger over the figures, a lump forming in her throat. . . .

As Sarah read on, that same lump formed in her throat once again. She continued reading with a wavering smile and a gratified heart.

Georgie asked, "What is it?"

"The opening pages of Emily's new novel," Sarah replied. "About sisters. About us."

"Us? Good heavens, whoever would want to read that?"

Epilogue

JULY 1821

Sarah Henshall left the bedchamber she shared with her Scotsman, humming a jaunty tune. She wore a flattering deep blue riding habit of her own, one she'd had made soon after arriving in Kirkcaldy. Tailored specifically for her, it fit her perfectly, as did her new life.

As she went downstairs, she saw the new housemaid polishing the gilt-framed mirror in the hall. "Well done, Betty. Everything looks tidy."

Indeed it did. They had completed the repairs and cleanup after the winter storm in good time. Sarah looked around the ground-floor rooms and felt a sense of satisfaction, knowing her efforts and leadership had been useful as well as appreciated.

Passing the open study door, she glimpsed Effie inside, having a lesson with her music tutor. The girl had finally agreed to more schooling. Not to going away to school, which none of them wanted, but Callum and Sarah had offered to provide a local music tutor and dancing master if Effie cooperated with a new governess who would instruct her in history, literature, and mathematics. In between, she seemed to enjoy spending time with Sarah and her stepfather and was even, on rare occasion, seen reading a book.

Sarah left the house and walked across the gravel drive toward the stables. There stood Callum, leading a chestnut horse, talking in friendly tones with the groom adjusting a sidesaddle on the sweet brown Thoroughbred Sarah enjoyed riding.

After helping her onto the sidesaddle, Callum effortlessly mounted his own horse, and then closed the distance between them, leaning near for a warm, lingering kiss.

They set out for a ride together, as they often did, around the estate and through the nearby woods and fields. Sometimes Effie joined them, as her lessons allowed.

It was summertime in Scotland, and Sarah relished every warm, sunny hour, which reminded her of balmy days in Devonshire. The countryside around them was carpeted in purple heather, red haw-thorn berries festooned the hedgerows, and birdsong sweetened the air. As they rode along the trail, they occasionally disturbed a roe deer or startled grouse into flight. Otherwise, all was peaceful.

Claire and William had traveled to Scotland as promised that spring. They had all enjoyed a nice long visit, spending time in Edinburgh together as well as at Whinstone Hall.

During their stay, Claire had confided the good news that their former maid, Mary, had finally married her surgeon's mate, who had safely arrived in Sidmouth in February, when their child was about two months old. Mary's new husband had already found employment as an assistant to one of the surgeons in town, and the new family now lived in small lodgings of their own.

When William and Claire left to return to Sidmouth, Georgiana went with them. She had been ready to return to Devonshire, but Sarah and Effie were sorry to see her go.

Since leaving Sea View, Sarah had corresponded regularly with her mother and sisters, and by all accounts, everyone was doing well. Cora continued to be a help and encouragement to their mother and a joy to everyone who met her. And Sea View was thriving with a promising number of guests writing to request rooms for the summer.

Viola was due to have her child any day, and Sarah eagerly awaited news of the birth, praying faithfully that both mother and child would be healthy and happy.

As she and Callum rode on, Sarah crossed a narrow stone bridge ahead of him and halted her horse on the other side. Waiting for her husband to rejoin her, Sarah reflected on the pleasure she used to take in riding as a girl, and now, after the difficult years in between, she could look back over all she had lost and gained and learned, and better appreciate the freedom to enjoy the pastime with the man she loved.

In fact, she embraced all the aspects of this fresh season of life with immense gratitude. Yes, she remained busy, meeting with and directing the new housekeeper and cook, as well as getting to know her neighbors and being of service to the poor and elderly in their midst. Yet she also took time to relish her role as wife and stepmother, as well as mistress of Whinstone Hall.

Returning from their ride some time later, Sarah saw Effie near the stables, finished with her lessons and playing with a new litter of kittens—ginger tabbies, of course.

Effie greeted them as they neared. "Good ride, Da'?"

He stilled as he always did whenever she called him that. He smiled fondly at her in reply. "Aye."

She turned next to Sarah. "Good ride, Mrs. Henshall?"

"Yes, thank you, Miss Henshall."

Effie had taken his surname. Their surname. They were a family now, in both name and affection.

Sarah sometimes missed her sisters, and Effie missed Georgiana, but both took comfort in the fact that they would visit again. Mamma had hinted that she might come too, especially if and when Sarah and Callum had a child of their own, a blessing they both hoped for.

In the meantime, they had each other, a beautiful home, and a life of love, service, and diligent devotion ahead of them.

Author's Note

Thank you for returning with me to the south coast of England (and Scotland!) for the final ON DEVONSHIRE SHORES book. I hope you enjoyed it, and I hope you enjoyed this small taste of a Regency-era Christmastide. If you'd like to learn more about old English Christmas traditions, I invite you to refer to the sources quoted in the chapter epigraphs.

A few notes:

Sir Robert and Henrietta Liston departed Constantinople in July 1820, though they returned to Scotland a few months after the time period of this novel. I included them because of Henrietta's connection to Sidmouth (her brother being buried there). Publisher Mr. Wallis, George and Hubert Cornish, and Miss Eliza Marriott are also historical figures, but they appear in the novel in fictionalized form. As I mentioned in the previous book, *The Seaside Homecoming*, Miss Marriott's shells are now a rare and valuable conchology collection that you can view online.

Once again I am deeply thankful to Nigel Hyman, Sidmouth resident, author, and former museum curator, who reviewed the manuscript for me. He also kindly contacted Professor Brian Golding, Exeter Met Office, for help with local weather history when I wanted to make sure it was realistic for it to snow in Sidmouth in 1820. (Yes!)

As always, I appreciate the helpful input I received from first reader and treasured friend Cari Weber, as well as Anna Shay, who is as delightful as she is insightful and creative.

Warm gratitude also goes to author-friends Michelle Griep and Erica Vetsch, my agent, Wendy Lawton, my editors, Karen Schurrer, Rochelle Gloege, and Hannah Ahlfield, as well as my entire team at Bethany House Publishers.

Finally, thank you again for reading my books. I appreciate each and every one of you! For more information about me and my other novels, please follow me on Facebook or Instagram, and sign up for my email list via my website, JulieKlassen.com.

Read on for an excerpt from

AN IVY HILL
CHRISTMAS

December 1822
London

Walking past a linen draper's, Richard Brockwell surveyed his reflection in the shop windows with approval. He cut a fine figure, although he said it himself. Inside, he glimpsed a pretty debutante he had been introduced to at some ball or other. She had flirted with him, and they had danced once, but he had not asked her again nor called on her afterward. Nor did he stop to renew their acquaintance now. She was too young and too . . . eligible.

He walked on. A stern-looking older woman stood outside the humble chapel on the corner. In hopes of avoiding her, he crossed the cobbled street. Too late. Her voice gripped his neck like a mother cat grasping the scruff of her wayward offspring.

"You, sir! Will you make a donation to our most worthy charity?" Dodging a passing hackney coach, she strode across the street to accost him.

Richard turned and pasted on a smile. His upbringing, while not without its faults, had taught him to feign politeness with ease.

Reaching him, she went on with her appeal, "I am Miss Arbuthnot, directress of the St. George Orphan Refuge. We rescue orphans from the retreats of villainy and teach them skills like printing, bookbinding, and twine spinning to enable them to obtain an honest living." She held out a basket. "Our institution is supported by voluntary contributions."

Voluntary or coerced? Richard wondered. He warmly replied, "My dear madam, how I look forward to you or one of your comrades addressing me almost every time I pass this way. Your

231

. . . stamina is breathtaking. You rival an athlete in a Greek pentathlon."

Her eyes narrowed, but he persisted with his most charming smile. "I applaud your philanthropic spirit. Truly. And like you, I give all I can spare to my charity of choice. My favorite coffeehouse and bookshop have first claim on my heart—and my purse."

With a pert bow, he turned and walked on, leaving her sputtering and him quite satisfied with himself.

Richard was, he knew, a selfish creature. A person could not change his nature, his very heart, could he? He thought not.

Reaching the coffeehouse, he tipped his hat to the beggar outside and entered the beloved establishment, the aromas of coffee, pipe tobacco, newsprint, and books rushing up to greet him. Seeing his bespectacled editor bent over a newspaper at their usual table, Richard walked over to join him.

"Murray. Good to see you, old boy."

David Murray raised his dark curly head and stood to shake Richard's hand. "How are you, Brockwell?"

"According to the papers, I am a handsome rake bent on seducing all the widows of Mayfair." He smirked at the exaggeration and sat down. At one time, he probably deserved his roguish reputation, but no longer.

"Better than my lot," Murray grumbled. "According to this morning's edition, I am about to be taken to court on charges of libel again and am on the verge of bankruptcy."

Richard grinned at his friend, only two years his senior. "Ah well, we each have our crosses to bear. Perhaps this will help." He extracted several sheets of paper from his leather portfolio. "Here is the article you asked for. I shall have to mail you the next piece from Wiltshire."

The man's bushy eyebrows rose over his spectacles. "Thought you planned to stay in Town and work through Christmas."

"I did, but my mother is insisting I come home this year. I dread it, but she is not taking no for an answer."

"Christmas surrounded by doting loved ones?" Murray said dryly. "Horrors."

His editor had no family, Richard knew. An idea struck him. The distraction of an unexpected houseguest might come in handy. "Why don't you come with me? That is, if you can bear the thought of Christmas in the country?"

"When do you leave?"

"On the nineteenth."

The man hesitated. "You go on, but I trust you will submit a new piece of scathing satire by the tenth of next month, as usual? Or will the comforts of Christmas in the country addle your brains and make you soft?"

"Never. But perhaps you had better come along to make sure I keep my wits about me."

He did not tell his friend that he was also working on a second novel. The first had already been rejected by two publishers. In fact, Thomas Cadell, of the eminent London publishing firm Cadell & Davies, sent only a curt *Declined by Return of Post*. Richard was still awaiting a reply from a third and fourth firm. Unfortunately Murray did not publish books, preferring to focus on his magazine.

"Would your family not mind a houseguest?" Murray asked.

"Not at all. They always invite guests at Christmas."

"May I have a day or two to think about it?"

"Of course. Just let me know when you decide."

Richard himself spent as little time at Brockwell Court as possible, preferring to live in the family's London townhouse, away from his mother's matchmaking schemes and the guilt of knowing he had disappointed her yet again. For all intents and purposes, he was the master of the fine London residence with its small, efficient staff.

He gladly left the responsibilities of the country estate to his older brother, dutiful Sir Timothy. And why not? He was heir after all, and not him.

Richard had no desire to travel to rural Wiltshire, attend church services and parties, politely greet people he barely remembered, and listen to his widowed mother's doleful sighs. The dowager Lady Brockwell had always been somber and reserved, though perhaps now that Timothy and his pretty wife had their first child, she would cheer up and leave off pressuring him to marry.

And Richard *would* enjoy spending time with his younger sister, Justina. Hosting her for a London season had been a real pleasure. In Justina's eyes, he could do no wrong, and he had relished her youthful adoration and easy laughter at his jokes. Shepherding her through the season had also funneled more money into their London accounts, which he had not minded at all. Money that was sadly long gone.

Thankfully, his mother had always been persuadable where money was concerned and would write to the bankers to advance more funds whenever he asked.

Until now.

Now she was taking a hard line, insisting there would be no more bank drafts, at least until he came home for Christmas.

That evening, Richard sat down to a dinner of roast beef and potatoes. He eyed his half glass of claret with displeasure, then raised it toward Pickering.

"That's the last of it, sir," replied his aging valet who also waited at table. "And there's no money for more."

Richard sighed and shifted his focus outside.

The evening had turned dark, and a storm descended, matching his mood. Rain pelted the French doors while branches of a nearby shrub, propelled by the wind, lashed its panes.

Lightning flashed, illuminating a pair of eyes beyond the glass. Curious, Richard rose and looked closer. A bedraggled dog sat outside the door. Noticing Richard, the pathetic creature rose on short hind legs and placed its paws on the glass. Eyes large and pleading, he looked longingly at Richard's snug room and warm fire—or perhaps simply at his plate of roast beef.

Another flash of lightning. And in that flash, Richard saw himself as a boy, standing all alone at a cottage window, staring at a scene of comfort—an outsider looking in, wanting to belong. To be loved and accepted.

"Ignore it, sir," Pickering said dully, "and it will go away."

Richard rose and went to the door. "Let's feed it something at least."

The elderly man shook his head. "I am not going out in that. Besides, if you feed a stray, you'll never get rid of it."

Well Richard knew. But rare pity stirred in his heart. He unlatched and opened the door, then cajoled the skittish dog inside with a soothing voice and piece of beef.

Pickering shook his head. "Mrs. Tompkins won't like it. She's struggling to make do with a sparse larder as it is."

He knew Pickering was right, but he did it anyway.

Julie Klassen loves all things Jane—*Jane Eyre* and Jane Austen. Her books have sold over 1.5 million copies, and she is a three-time recipient of the Christy Award for Historical Romance. *The Secret of Pembrooke Park* was honored with the Minnesota Book Award for Genre Fiction. Julie has also won the Midwest Book Award and Christian Retailing's BEST Award and has been a finalist in the RITA and Carol Awards. A graduate of the University of Illinois, Julie worked in publishing for sixteen years and now writes full-time. Julie and her husband have two sons and live in St. Paul, Minnesota. For more information, you can follow her on Facebook or visit JulieKlassen.com.

You Are Invited!

Join like-minded fans in the **Inspirational Regency Readers** group on Facebook.

From book news from popular Regency authors like Kristi Ann Hunter, Michelle Griep, Erica Vetsch, Julie Klassen, and many others, to games and giveaways, to discussions of favorite Regency reads and adaptations new and old, to places we long to travel, you will find plenty of fun and friendship within this growing community.

Free and easy to join, simply search for "Inspirational Regency Readers" on Facebook.

We look forward to seeing you there!

 BETHANY HOUSE

Sign Up for Julie's Newsletter

Keep up to date with Julie's latest news on book releases and events by signing up for her email list at the link below.

JulieKlassen.com

FOLLOW JULIE ON SOCIAL MEDIA

Author Julie Klassen   @Julie.K.Klassen